Recipes &
Wooden
Spoons

Tales from Grace Chapel Inn®

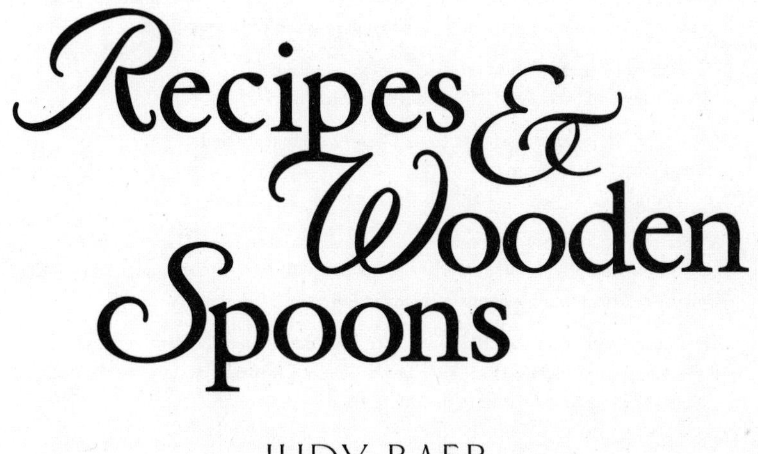

JUDY BAER

New York, New York

Recipes & Wooden Spoons

ISBN-13: 978-0-8249-4701-9
ISBN-10: 0-8249-4701-0

Published by Guideposts
16 East 34th Street, New York, New York 10016
www.guidepostsbooks.com

Distributed by Ideals Publications, a Guideposts company
535 Metroplex Drive, Suite 250, Nashville, Tennessee 37211

ACKNOWLEDGMENTS
All Scripture quotations, unless otherwise noted, are taken from The Holy Bible, New International Version. Copyright © 1973, 1978, 1984 International Bible Society. Used by permission of Zondervan Bible Publishers.

Scripture quotations marked (RSV) are taken from the Revised Standard Version of the Bible. Copyright © 1946, 1952, 1971 by Division of Christian Education of the National Council of Churches of Christ in the U.S.A. Used by permission.

The characters and events in this book are fictional, and any resemblance to actual persons or events is coincidental.

Library of Congress Cataloging-in-Publication Data

Baer, Judy.
Recipes & wooden spoons / Judy Baer.
p. cm. — (Tales from Grace Chapel Inn)
ISBN 0-8249-4701-0
1. Sisters—Fiction. 2. Mothers and daughters—Fiction. 3. Cookery—Fiction. 4. Bed and breakfast accommodations—Fiction. 5. Pennsylvania—Fiction. I. Title: Recipes and wooden spoons. II. Title. III. Series.
PS3552.A33R43 2006
813'.54—dc22

2006005586

Cover illustration by Deborah Chabrian
Designed by Marisa Jackson

Printed and bound in the United States of America

10 9 8 7 6 5 4

GRACE CHAPEL INN
A place where one can be
refreshed and encouraged,
a place of hope and healing,
a place where God is at home.

Chapter One

They had all been avoiding the basement.

Now, Jane decided, it was time to face the inevitable. Even her sister Alice, who had lived in the big Victorian with their father, the Reverend Daniel Howard, had made only brief visits to the stone cellar over the past twenty years. Who knew what might be nesting in the rafters by now?

Jane pulled a white flour-sack dishcloth out of a drawer and bent over at the waist to gather her hair into a casual knot. She wrapped the fabric around her neck and hair and secured it in the front like a bath towel. When she was an impressionable eight or nine, her oldest sister Louise had spun an elaborate tale about bats swooping down from rafters, eaves and trees and getting tangled in one's hair. The towel wrap was just in case.

Cobwebs were little better than bats, Jane decided as she descended the steep and narrow wooden steps into the stone cavern. Midway down, she ran into a feathery mass. She paused to wipe the web from her face and blow strands from her lips. She turned around. Gripping the handrails resolutely and closing her eyes, Jane extended her toe and cautiously felt her way down the remainder of the steps backward.

The trek took her back in time to her childhood, when she had ventured into the basement with the vain, childish hope that it would give up some secrets about Madeleine Howard, the mother she had never known. Back then, quarts and quarts of canned peaches, pears and thick ruby jams had lined shelves near the stairs. Jane remembered staring at them, speculating about the woman who had canned them. The meticulous rows of shiny gold peaches, reptilian green dill pickles and pale, creamy pears had fascinated her. She made up stories about her mother, closing her eyes and pretending that she could see her in the kitchen working, pouring boiling water over peaches and then plunging them into ice water to encourage the fuzzy skin to fall away from the glowing fruit. Finally, Ethel, her father's sister, had discovered Jane's "morbid" pastime and removed all the ten-year-old preserved foods that Daniel had not been able to part with. Another piece of Jane's mother had disappeared.

Jane's flashlight, hooked by a clip to the pocket of her jeans, bumped rhythmically against her hip, bringing her back to the present. How could a forty-year-old memory still resonate so strongly with her? She had not expected this when she agreed to help her sisters turn their childhood home into a bed and breakfast, the Grace Chapel Inn.

It was more of a job than she had first imagined. Managing the food and the kitchen was easy enough, but she was also responsible for overseeing the inn and keeping it running like a finely tuned machine. There were also more pleasures involved than she had expected. Guests from varied walks of life flowed through the inn's doors. Their appreciation of her cooking and of the beautiful setting was most satisfying, and having free rein in the kitchen with the opportunity to try as many new recipes as she desired was a source of delight.

At the base of the stairs, Jane unclipped the flashlight from her jeans and turned it on. The bare bulb hanging above her head was too feeble to pierce the darkness, but the flashlight caused shapes to emerge from the gloom. A peeling cupboard here, a set of rickety shelves there, an old kettle and a workbench that was last used when Noah built the Ark gradually came into focus.

As her eyes adjusted to the shadows, Jane could make out an old cast-iron stove, an assortment of mismatched antique chairs, a bed frame, several egg crates and, if her memory served her correctly, a milk separator left over from the turn of the century, when many local families owned their own cows. There were copper kettles hanging from the ceiling along with a beekeeper's netted mask, an old wooden sled and part of a slatted wooden cask. There were dark brown bottles, old crocks and rusted saws propped along the wall. All, no doubt, were remnants from the home's previous owners, Jane's grandparents, who had died within months of each other and left the house to Jane's mother Madeleine and her husband, the beloved young pastor of Grace Chapel.

"This place is filthy!" Jane sent the beam of the flashlight into every corner. It wouldn't have surprised her if she exposed a nest of baby mice or something even more unpleasant. With hands on her slender hips and with eyes narrowed, she scowled at the dust and debris. Only recently had Grace Chapel Inn become busy enough to warrant more storage for bulk cleaning supplies. She had banished those from the kitchen to reclaim the extra pantry space for food items. Neither Alice nor Louise had volunteered to scope out the basement's potential for storage. Since Jane *was* the officially designated innkeeper and chef, a title she inherited because both her sisters had outside occupations, the job was left to her.

It made Jane shudder to think of someone tumbling down those steep stairs. What might happen to someone who wandered uninvited into the inn? Even in a place as idyllic as Acorn Hill, Pennsylvania, unlocked houses were sometimes too much of a temptation for would-be vandals and the terminally curious. Alice and her father had not locked the doors in years, and everyone in town knew it.

Not that robbery or breaking and entering were common problems. Just the opposite was true. Acorn Hill residents had, however, taken to locking their cars and homes during the month of August to prevent well-meaning local gardeners from leaving mountains of zucchini, tomatoes or apples in the backseat of cars or on kitchen tables.

Despite the sweet, low-keyed pace of the community, the inducement of finally making peace with her much older sisters, and the growing longing to learn more about the mother who had died when Jane was born, it had not been a simple decision for her to return to Pennsylvania.

With the exception of her nursing school years, Alice had lived in Acorn Hill all her life and spent much of it tending to their father in the big old house. She loved the idea of turning their former home into a charming bed and breakfast in this small, sleepy village.

Louise, since the death of her husband Eliot, had been looking for something other than her music and occasional visits from her daughter Cynthia to fill her life. The circumstances that brought Jane here were entirely different from those of her sisters. But she couldn't think about her home in San Francisco or the man who had disappointed her there. What she needed now was to keep busy.

She made her way around the cavernous basement in a clockwise circle, examining the castoffs of two generations. Every paint bucket ever used at the house was still sitting in ordered rows, marked with cryptic messages. *PLR, ptd '48-gr*, which, if her translation was correct, meant "Parlor, painted in 1948-green." Feeling a bit like an archaeologist, Jane plucked the paint can from the shelf and gave it a shake. Dry as a bone, as were all the others, no doubt. Making a mental note to learn how best to recycle old paint cans, she moved on to a more interesting display. Mason jars filled with old coins; metal toys, including a circus monkey who, when wound with the key fixed in his back, clapped real tin cymbals; and a stack of cracked and broken dishes. Jane added "coin and toy appraisal" to her to-do list.

When she pulled on the broken handle of a drawer beneath her grandfather's workbench, she barely avoided having the entire thing fall onto the floor at her feet. Bracing the drawer with her hip, she shoved it back into place, but not before examining the collection of rusty pliers, screwdrivers and boxes of nails. There was an entire shelf of bundled magazines, cardboard tubes—the kind that might protect art posters—and dozens of egg cartons.

Then she noticed a relatively new, hard plastic storage

cabinet, the kind Fred Humbert sold in his hardware store to people who could not clean out a garage or basement but were willing to spend money to make it look as though they had. When had that arrived? And who had wrestled it down these stairs? She opened the door and got at least a partial answer.

The Great Depression had made Daniel Howard a cautious, waste-not, want-not kind of man. Even in his later life, he obviously could not part with stacks of yogurt cups and plastic cottage cheese containers that were stored on one shelf and a wobbly pile of aluminum TV-dinner trays on another. As she wrenched open an inside drawer, a collection of plastic grocery bags bloomed out. Neatly broken down and folded cardboard boxes and jars of nails, bolts and screws sat alongside chipped jelly glasses filled with pens and pencils engraved with the names and logos of local businesses. Stacks of notepads advertising everything from the Time for Tea shop downtown to the latest in pharmaceuticals were neatly bound with large rubber bands. A ball of string, a jar of paper clips and old *Reader's Digests* filled other shelves.

She paused to imagine her elderly father inching his way down that precipitous staircase to stockpile these things and felt tears forming in her eyes. "Be a good steward of the earth, Jane," he had told her one particularly harsh winter as together they hung globs of suet on a post outside the kitchen window. "God created birds too, you know. In a cold winter like this, when they can't find food for themselves, it's up to us to help them." She had never since left a bird unfed if it passed through her yard, much to Justin's consternation over the mess it created. Though she had not inherited her father's pack-rat tendencies, she did fully embrace his idea of stewardship for the earth.

To this day, it was his voice in her head that made her feed strays and take them to the no-kill animal shelter, pick up other people's trash as she walked in the park, and buy earth-friendly cleaning supplies.

She had been a handful for Daniel sometimes. Alice and Louise had been so focused as girls—Alice on helping anyone in sight and Louise on her music—that she must have been a shock to her gentle, kindly father. What is more, without a mother, Jane had depended mightily on her father to guide her. It was he who held her when she wept over a betrayal by a friend at school, a bad grade or a lost boyfriend.

And she had reciprocated by immersing herself in Daniel's beloved Psalms. Never had a day gone by that Daniel had not applied a verse or two to whatever was happening in her life. Even when she was a restless teenager, his wisdom had somehow gotten her through.

"He heals the brokenhearted, and binds up their wounds" (Psalm 147:3). How many times had she come to him crying over the years? And how many times had he put his arm around her and said those comforting words? Her shoulders sagged. And here she was again, having strayed from the passion for her faith that Daniel had instilled in her, guiltily trying to rekindle it only now that she and Justin had parted.

Shaking off the thought that took her down a path she did not want to travel, she spoke heavenward, knowing that was exactly where Daniel Howard was. "At least I'm not a pack-rat like you, Father. I wonder if Alice knew you were still hiking up and down these stairs."

Still as limber as a girl at fifty, Jane crouched to peer into the deep recesses of the chest. Suspiciously she dug around in the back of the cabinet looking for any food items Daniel might have put there. To her relief there were no canned goods, only a few empty fruit jars, some mismatched mangled and tarnished silver spoons and another ball of twine.

Done with the cabinet, she let her gaze fall on a dry sink in the corner where clay pots and a rusty hand spade sat. Leaning against the wall was an assortment of yard tools—rakes, hoes and a shovel. The handles had cracked and split over the years, but spots worn smooth by the hands that had once held them still remained. The area beneath the sink was covered by a gathered fabric skirt. Jane experienced a little thrill of excitement, sure that it was her mother who had fashioned the bright spot in the otherwise colorless basement. How vivid the yearnings to know her mother became here!

Jane moved to explore the sink. In her jeans and long-sleeved T-shirt, she, at first glance, could have been mistaken for a teenager. Athletic, she had run daily and enjoyed resistance training and weight lifting during her workouts at the gym near her home in San Francisco. Always aware of style and willing to spend time and money in consignment stores searching for "just the right thing," she had built a wardrobe that was remarkably elegant, practical and attractively unconventional—just the way she liked it.

She lifted the cloth and found more clay pots and a small carton, not much bigger than a large briefcase.

"Not much here . . ." Shielding her nose and mouth from dust with one hand and reaching deep under the sink with the other, she pulled out the carton and wiped the grimy bundle with the back of her arm.

She carefully laid back the top. Inside was a box made of thick cardboard, embossed with a leaflike pattern, and a thick manila envelope pale with age.

Her muscles complained as she crouched near the floor, and the dim light provided little help for reading what was written on the envelope. This was as good as any excuse to leave this dankness for a while. Jane picked up the two parcels and went up to the kitchen with them.

The room gleamed brighter than a brand-new penny, the floors and counters waxed to a high shine. It was still an old kitchen. They saved as much of its nineteenth-century look as they could while still installing professional ovens and cooktops and state-of-the-art appliances. On a rack hung her pots and pans, collected, prized and seasoned with love.

Sighing, she shook the contents of the big envelope onto the table. There were yellowed newspaper clippings of recipes and how-to articles, one of which Jane picked up and began to read aloud. "Ways to control bed bugs. Go to a drugstore for ingredients: two ounces corrosive sublimate, one ounce camphor gum, one pint turpentine, one pint alcohol. Brush mixture on portions that bugs use."

"Very helpful." She grimaced. "I hope it worked." She moved to the cupboard and poured herself the last of the coffee from the carafe. Her sisters had nearly had simultaneous strokes when they heard the price of the professional coffee maker she insisted on buying. She had not even told them how much she paid for a pound of imported coffee or that she insisted on grinding it herself until Louise had tasted it and fallen in love with the rich, dark brew. Alice, a tea drinker, had to take their word that the coffee was worth the cost. Their most recent guests had consumed an entire pot before they checked out in the morning.

Humming, she added cream to her coffee and returned to the stack of papers on the table. She tucked the clippings back into the envelope and turned her attention to the box.

Inside, wrapped in a dishtowel so thin and old that it resembled tissue paper, was a dark blue, leather-bound book.

She gently lifted the book from the box and opened the cover. In the upper right corner of the first page, well-formed script proclaimed, "Property of Madeleine Howard ~ Recipes." Below was the inscription: "Congratulations on your upcoming marriage. May you have many happy moments cooking for that new husband of yours. Gracie." *A shower gift perhaps?*

The pages were yellowed with age but surprisingly well preserved. There was a mere trace of the odor of old paper. It was thick and heavy, printed with recipes and embellished with notations in her mother's own hand. Jane's hands tightened around the book as it suddenly pulsed with the life of the person she had never known, her own mother.

The sad part of Jane's otherwise happy childhood had been the absence of a mother to help her grow up. Madeleine had died an hour after Jane's birth of what now would likely be diagnosed as an intracranial hemorrhage, a result of severe eclampsia. Today, she might have been saved by an early Caesarean section. More poignant was that Jane, even after all these years, still blamed herself for Madeleine's death. Neither her father nor her sisters had even once suggested that she was responsible for her mother's demise but Jane believed it nonetheless. She had always felt that, somehow, her mother had traded her own life for Jane's.

Jane was in high school when she heard the full story of her mother's death. Unfortunately, it had come from an angry girl named Shirley Taylor who had found the swiftest way she could to be vindictive over a boy whose last name Jane couldn't even remember.

She cradled the book to her chest for a moment, imagining her mother from the many pictures she had seen—a woman with a brilliant smile and long brown hair gathered into a helter-skelter twist, a woman who was known community-wide for the bread and the caramel rolls that she baked for anyone who was suffering. From what Jane had gathered, the only thing more endearing than Madeleine's sweetness was the generosity of her heart. A yellowed newspaper clipping slipped from the book and drifted to the floor. She crouched to pick it up. It was her grandmother's obituary.

> Sarah Pitman Berry, born November 2, 1887, to Franklin and Gracia Pitman, wife of Matthias Berry and mother to Madeleine Berry Howard, died peacefully in her sleep on . . . .

Fascinated, Jane might have balanced there for a very long time, rocking on her toes and clutching the book, if a furry missile had not collided with her backside and nearly bowled her to the floor.

"Wendell! You scared me half to death!" she exclaimed,

standing and picking up her father's beloved but persnickety cat. She scratched him behind one perked ear before letting him loose again.

She sat down at the kitchen table and turned to the next page of the recipe book, giving a squeak of pleasure.

Not only was the book filled with recipes, every page was graced with Madeleine's own handwriting. Next to a recipe for a luncheon salad with lemon gelatin, grated cabbage and shrimp, her mother had written,

> *Ladies' Aid women loved this. I served it with party buns and completed with a Strawberry Surprise (see page 174 for recipe).*

When she got to the bottom of the recipe, Jane burst out laughing. In tiny print bracketed in parentheses, her mother had added *(Recipe a dreadful waste of canned shrimp).*

Much to Jane's delight, the entire book was embellished with running commentary, opinions about the recipes and the people to whom they had been served and comic doodles, mostly of chubby men in billowing pastry hats. In the margin of the pecan pie recipe, Madeleine had written, *So tempting it must be a sin.* There were hand-drawn stars around a sweet roll recipe and a big *Ick* beside the recipe for borscht. On the inside back cover was a hand-drawn heart with the words boasting, *Daniel and Madeleine, 1935, In Love Forever.*

Jane did not even know tears were streaming down her face until Wendell jumped into her lap and put a soft paw on her cheek. She put the book on the table and squeezed the cat until he squirmed.

"Oh, Wendell," she whispered, overcome, "this is what I've been looking for as long as I can remember, a window into my mother's life."

"What is going on in here?"

Jane looked up to see Louise standing tall and imperious in the kitchen doorway. "Louie, just wait until you see what I've found."

Louise flinched but said nothing. Jane was the only one in her family who called Louise by that or any other nickname. It had driven proper Louise, always the dignified older sister, wild when they were youngsters. That, of course, had spurred Jane on even more. Now the nickname was simply one more quirk Louise had to put up with from her lively sister.

"It's mother's recipe book."

Louise opened the wire-rimmed glasses that hung from a chain around her neck to peer at the book. "Oh yes. I remember this. Mother used it all the time. Where did you find it?"

"*All* the time?" she asked, her heart was racing.

"Yes. It was her favorite. It has a recipe for 'Toad in a Hole.' I used to make it for you after Mother died. Do you remember? It was a poached egg sitting in a hole torn in a piece of toast. You also loved it fried. That was the first thing she taught me to cook. I must have been all of six or seven years old." Louise smiled. "How nice that you found it, since you are the professional chef in the family."

"Mother taught you to cook." Jane's voice was a whisper. "But she wasn't able to teach me."

Louise put a hand on her arm. "Perhaps not, but she gave you her talent just the same. What you didn't get in lessons, I believe must have been transferred to you with her DNA. Mother was a marvelous cook—and you are too. You two are so much alike."

"So we *are* alike?" Jane ventured. "Really?"

"You undoubtedly inherited your artistic talent from her. Our birthday cakes were true works of art. When Alice was five and I was eight, Father took us to ride the carousel at the fair in Potterston. Alice was so enamored with the whole idea that for her next birthday, Mother made her cake a miniature carousel with colorful horses prancing around the sides. Father said it was too pretty to eat."

Then the wistful look on Louise's face grew slightly disapproving. "Mother was also impulsive and unpredictable. That was *so* disconcerting for Father." The implication was that Jane was genetically impulsive and unpredictable too.

Jane, however, liked the idea. "What was so perplexing to him?"

"Her spur-of-the-moment ideas. She would decide that we *had* to have a picnic one day or perhaps go into the attic and play 'dress up' with the clothes in Grandmother Berry's trunks. Sometimes we would have elaborate tea parties with our dolls. Mother would make tiny sandwiches and cookies and we would sit on the floor holding teacups with our pinkies in the air. She would always call Father to come join us." Louise looked Jane over with affection, but also with a touch of dismay. "When I look at you, I remember those times with Mother."

Warmth surged through Jane. *Like Mother*.

Louise glanced at her watch. "All this talk of food reminds me that it is time for a break. Shall we walk to the Coffee Shop to see if there is any blackberry pie?"

Jane could have spent the rest of the day asking Louise questions about those tea parties and picnics her mother invented for her daughters, but she knew from experience that she would get no more from Louise right now. Her sister had to be in the mood to reminisce, and there was no hint of that in her demeanor today. Louise lived her life as though she were running a business. There was little time for tomfoolery.

Although she hated to leave the book, it had been a long morning already though it was barely ten o'clock. Another cup of java and a dose of sugar would hit the spot. "What is Alice doing?"

Louise rolled her eyes. "Reading. The Philadelphia newspaper came. She's looking for news of the city zoo."

"Mark Graves?" Jane's brows lifted in inquiry. Graves had been Alice's college sweetheart and, although she seldom mentioned him, she still kept abreast of his activities as director of the zoo in Philadelphia. "It's been a years since Alice was in nursing school. That's a long time to carry a torch. Living alone in Acorn Hill all these years . . . she must be lonely."

She had never spent much time thinking about Alice's love life. For as long as Jane could remember, Alice and Louise had been her surrogate mothers, and that had never tallied with the idea of Alice's having a boyfriend.

"She never says much," Louise said, "but when the paper comes, she is the first to read it."

"We won't get the house ready for tonight's guests that way." Then Jane added mischievously, "Maybe she's reading the Personals."

"And you are no better, sitting there reading recipes and spoiling Wendell."

"Leave Wendell alone. He's a good companion. More dependable than my former husband."

"I always liked Justin," Louise commented carefully. She took a lace handkerchief out of the pocket of her cotton skirt and began to clean her glasses.

"I did too," Jane said sadly. "You'll have to excuse me,

Louise. I tend to joke about things when I don't want to deal with them. I still love Justin, or at least the Justin that used to be. I still wonder if I could have done more to save our marriage—if I should have seen what was happening. It was such a high for me to have my work recognized that I didn't stop to think about his ego or that my success might make him feel overshadowed. I blame myself for not being more sensitive to that, but truly if things had been reversed, I would have been happy for him. I guess Justin had issues I just didn't know about."

"Yes, we are all such complicated creatures," Louise said with a sigh. "We bring history to our relationships that our partners do not recognize or cannot understand. Apparently, for Justin two famous chefs in the same kitchen were simply one too many."

Jane nodded, tears forming in her eyes.

Louise gently patted her arm. "Let's go, little sister," she said. "I will call Alice. I think a dose of the Coffee Shop's blackberry pie would do us a world of good."

They gathered on the front porch and then walked three abreast on the wide brick sidewalks that crisscrossed Acorn Hill. Summer was in full, radiant bloom, from grass the color of emeralds to vibrant red and pink geraniums punctuated with spike, vinca vine and asparagus fern in the planters that lined Main Street, while begonias and petunias rioted out of freshly painted window boxes.

Sometimes Jane thought the village was too pretty to be true—like a scene imagined by an artist. Grace Chapel was a prime example. Its spire poked heavenward from the bell tower, and stained glass windows decorated the clapboard sides of the sturdy building. There were wide doors to fling open in welcome. Over the years, Jane had noticed travelers taking snapshots of the church. In winter, dusted with snow, it looked like the model for multitudes of Christmas cards.

"Morning, ladies," Fred Humbert greeted them as they neared Fred's Hardware. On a small table on the sidewalk just outside his store, Fred was arranging an overstock of hammers, pliers and paring knives next to what he called "Oops" paint—those quarts and gallons of custom paint mixtures that had not been quite right.

"Morning, Fred." Alice paused to look at the paring knives.

"Who buys these cans of paint, Fred?" Louise tapped a fingernail on top of one of the cans. "And whatever do they use them for?"

"Makin' stripes, I reckon. You see somebody with a house with every board painted a different color and they probably got it from me."

"The idea has potential," Jane commented.

Fred chuckled. He had known these three his entire life. In fact, Alice had helped to deliver his younger daughter, Jean. "If you ever decide to paint a striped house, let me know. I had quite a little trouble learning how to use my new paint-mixing machine last year. There's a lot more where these came from. Maybe Ethel Buckley's place will need a spruce-up one day soon." He referred to the carriage house by the inn, where their aunt Ethel had lived for the past ten years.

"We'll remember that, Fred, but don't hold your breath." This was a private joke between them. When local resident Thomas Percy had painted his house bright yellow, Ethel had gone on the warpath, wanting to collect petitions to have him repaint it in a more "decorous" color. Then when the sisters had painted the inn in historically appropriate colors, rather than repainting it its long-time peach shade, well . . . !

Fred nodded and smiled. He knew Ethel well, since they served together on the church board. Fred once said, "When God told you ladies to pick up your cross and follow Him, I think He meant Ethel."

Jane, remembering, laughed in spite of herself.

Alice moved a little closer. "You're looking a little tired. Have you been working too hard lately?"

Fred laughed and put his arm around Alice's shoulder and gave her a squeeze. "It's the price a good-looking, brilliant guy like me has to pay, I guess."

"It's that ruckus the church board is having about spending the memorial money, isn't it?" Alice also served with Fred on the board of Grace Chapel, two voices of reason in an always well-intentioned, sometimes eccentric, often contentious assemblage.

Fred rolled his eyes. "You'd think we could agree on *something*."

"Lloyd just likes to know we're doing the right thing. And Aunt Ethel likes to support him."

"It's pretty hard to make a mistake buying hymnals, Alice. You don't need three surveys and a vote from the congregation to figure it out. Remember when we decided to change the carpet? We might as well have tried to do brain surgery in the Assembly Room."

"We'll pray about it," Alice assured him.

"Too bad God has to expend so much energy on the church board," Fred said. "Seems like there are places that need attention more." He grinned and tipped an imaginary hat off his sandy-colored hair. "You ladies have a good day, now."

It was only a few steps farther to their destination. Jane took a deep breath as they neared the Coffee Shop. "No matter what bakery or bistro I visit, none of the smells are as good as the aromas coming out of this place."

Alice inhaled. "They've got coffee cake today. And caramel rolls."

"Can you sniff pie, Alice?" Jane inquired, amused.

"I'm working on it," Alice replied as she turned into the doorway of the Coffee Shop. "It's an art, you know."

When the sisters walked in, the other customers stopped and looked up from what they were doing, whether it was reading the weekly *Acorn Nutshell* or arguing over who would pay a bill. The room broke into a pleased hum when the coffee drinkers recognized the Howard sisters.

"Jane! You're looking good." That was from Lloyd Tynan, Acorn Hill's ebullient mayor, who greeted people as though they had just returned from a long trip.

Hope Collins waved a dishrag their way. "Hey, Louise, sure enjoyed hearing you play at the chapel." Hope appeared to have had a recent battle with a bottle of red hair dye. Her hair color seemed to change as often as the menu.

"Alice," the butcher from the meat market said, "I have a cat that just had kittens, you know anybody who'd give one a good home?"

As Jane listened to the cozy small talk, she felt the tenseness in her body dissipate.

After they had settled themselves in the red, faux-leather booth, Hope arrived with a carafe of coffee, a pot of tea and three slices of luscious-looking blackberry pie.

"Only three pieces left and I figured you'd want them."

"You read our minds, Hope," Alice said kindly, "but . . . ."

"Didn't have room on the tray for your vanilla ice cream. It'll be right out."

Alice smiled and settled into the seat. "Thank you."

"Hope *can* read minds," Louise said as she used her fork on the flaky pastry crust. "Or else she waited on Father for so long she just assumes any Howard who walks through the door wants pie. Good thing, too. I'd have hated to miss out on this."

"Welcome to Acorn Hill," Jane murmured to herself as she settled into her seat. "A place you can always call home."

Rice Pudding

½ cup uncooked rice
1 cup water
2 large eggs or 4 egg yolks
½ cup sugar
½ cup raisins
2½ cups milk
1 teaspoon vanilla
¼ teaspoon salt
Ground cinnamon or nutmeg for top

Heat rice and water to boiling, stir once and reduce

heat to low. Cover. Simmer fourteen minutes or until all water is absorbed. Beat eggs with whisk or fork in ungreased one-and-a-half-quart casserole. Stir in sugar, raisins, milk, hot rice, vanilla and salt. Sprinkle with cinnamon or nutmeg. Bake forty-five minutes at 325 degrees. Stir every twenty minutes. After forty-five minutes top of pudding will not be set and will look wet. Remove from oven and stir again. Let stand to make pudding creamy. Serve warm or cold.

At the end of the recipe, Madeleine had made a lengthy notation:

Don't overbake. I did this once and the entire dish curdled. I had to take pickles to the church potluck instead. How embarrassing—what were people thinking? I substitute some cream for the milk. I love this warm with more cream and sugar or berries. It should serve eight unless Daniel is hungry. Then it serves four.

"Here's a heart attack waiting to happen," Jane chortled, reading parts of her mother's recipe book to Alice in the kitchen. Madeleine's commentary provoked pure delight in her. "*Four* egg yolks! Cream! More cream! The things Mother must have cooked for him! Apparently Father wasn't susceptible to coronary difficulties or cholesterol because he lived to a ripe old age."

Alice gave a small, ladylike but disapproving sniff. "You forget, Jane, that *I* cooked for him in his latter years. He grew to enjoy skim milk and egg substitute."

"Good for you, Alice," Jane said mildly. Alice *had* cared for Daniel most lovingly. She was perhaps the kindest woman Jane had ever known. Yet, Jane felt that there was a distance in their relationship. No one had understood how important it was for Jane to leave Acorn Hill and to try her own wings. Sometimes Jane wondered if Alice believed she had been disloyal to family and community by going to California. If only Alice could understand that staying in Acorn Hill would have meant betraying herself.

"Are you *still* reading that cookbook?" Louise sailed into the kitchen looking dignified with her short silver hair, blue eyes and pale skin and her usual uniform of a cotton skirt and a pastel sweater. "There are others in the cupboard that are much newer and cleaner."

"But this has so much of Mother in it!"

Louise peered over the top of her wire-rimmed glasses. "I know you've longed to find out more about our mother.

Why don't you ask Aunt Ethel? She and Lloyd are coming for dinner. Oh, and our guests called and said that they would be in about nine."

"I almost forgot." Jane bolted out of her chair as though it had ignited beneath her. Alice arrived home from work in time to witness Jane's levitation.

"Hi, girls, what's going on?"

"We're having dinner guests and I haven't even thawed meat." Jane wailed.

"Too late now," Louise said. "What are you going to do?"

Jane's gaze fell on the recipe book. "Make rice pudding."

"Oh dear, that will hardly be enough for Lloyd," Alice worried. "You know how he eats."

"Don't worry. I've got soup bones on the stove. I was making consommé. I'll just add a few vegetables. There's still a loaf of homemade bread in the freezer. I'll whip up a few appetizers to take the edge off Lloyd's appetite."

"It has quite an edge, all right," Louise said. "And it contributes to that shelf he has for a stomach."

"To lengthen thy Life, lessen thy meals," Jane quoted with a smile. Next to the Psalms, the most quotable statements she knew came from Benjamin Franklin, her favorite Pennsylvania hero.

None of them had quite figured out the relationship between their aunt Ethel and Lloyd Tynan. Friendship?

Companionship? Soul mates? Whatever it was, they were nearly inseparable, and they invariably aided and abetted one another in confusing facts or passing on gossip. Since Ethel lived only steps from the inn and popped in as regularly as the bird out of a cuckoo clock, Jane had quickly gotten to know the foibles and idiosyncrasies of her father's younger sister. It was an education she was not sure she completely welcomed.

"How many vegetables?" Alice frowned. "No rutabaga, I hope."

"As many vegetables as you'd like. And no rutabaga. Why do you ask?"

"I ran into Rev. Thompson on the way home from the hospital. I hadn't planned to, but impulsively, I asked him to join us for dinner. I don't think he enjoys rutabaga."

"Alice! Do you really think that was a good idea?" Louise asked.

"I'd somehow forgotten that Aunt Ethel and Lloyd would be here. Oh dear, she is always so critical . . . and now it's too late."

"I think it's a perfectly wonderful idea," Jane assured her sister. To herself, she added, "Fireworks. I *love* fireworks."

Chapter Two

"Brie?" Jane held out a small platter to Lloyd. On it were an assortment of crackers and a warm, melty round of pale cheese covered with caramelized onions, pistachios and cranberries.

He eyed it suspiciously, his face growing pink above his bow tie. "What's 'bree'? And what are those red lumps?"

"Cheese. And cranberries. Try it, it's delicious."

"Have you got any of that cheese in a can? You know, when you press the nozzle the cheese squirts out?"

"Try this. If you don't like it, I'll bring out some cheddar." Jane sensed that everyone was holding his or her breath, waiting for Lloyd's decree. If Lloyd didn't like it, Ethel would probably refuse to try it also. Jane could see that Rev. Thompson was watching the cuisine showdown from across the room.

The pastor was dressed in dark slacks and a sports jacket. His leather loafers were the exact color of his belt and a bit of silk fabric peeked out of his jacket pocket. He reminded her of the successful businessmen for whom she had catered in San

Francisco. It was hardly surprising that Ethel had doubted his abilities at first. Grace Chapel had never before seen the likes of the smooth, sophisticated Rev. Thompson. Ethel's model for acceptable pastors for "her" church was her brother.

Jane's father, in his later years, had been a bespectacled teddy bear of a man who loved socializing in the Coffee Shop and playing second fiddle to his giant tabby Wendell. She glanced at the new minister with his meticulously groomed dark hair, sharp hazel eyes and well-bred, Bostonian manner.

Poor Rev. Thompson had had an uphill climb with Ethel.

"That's an odd choice of artwork in the powder room," Ethel said in a strangled voice as she returned to the living room. She had retired to wash her hands before dinner. Now her face was red.

Jane and Alice locked eyes across the living room. They had been waiting for this.

"Odd?" Jane said innocently. "I chose it because it suits the house perfectly. It's a print of a painting by John William Waterhouse, a well-known Pre-Raphaelite."

"But the woman has no clothes on."

"That's because the woman is a *fish*, Aunt Ethel. It's hardly a seductive picture. Everything *strategic* is covered. The painting is titled *The Mermaid.*"

"Really, Jane, you may have gone too far with your 'arty' ways. There is appropriateness to consider."

"I've always consider fish and mermaids to be appropriate around water," Jane said cheerfully. "And, if you noticed, the seashell collection you gave Alice decorates the shelf beneath the print." Jane had let both whimsy and creativity run amok in the powder room, and every guest commented on the delightful Victorian seashore ambience she had created.

"Well, I don't want to talk about it now, in *mixed company*." Ethel puckered her lips and nodded her head in the direction of Rev. Thompson as if to say that they had, at all costs, to protect the poor minister from Jane's indiscretion.

"Good," Jane responded cheerfully. She had no doubt that the subject would come up again. "Let's eat."

She almost laughed aloud at Lloyd's and Ethel's relieved expressions when they moved to the table. The comforting tureen of soup and simple bread were familiar and reassuring after their foray into Brie.

"What a feast!" Rev. Thompson looked over the table admiringly. Madeleine's large white soup tureen had been positioned in the middle of the table. Steam still rose off the crusty bread Jane had heated and placed on a thick wooden board for cutting. Butter glistened in ceramic pots. Freshly laundered white napkins, stiff as cardboard, were folded into pleated wings at each place setting. Jane had made edible topiaries of crudités for either end of the table.

"Will you pray?" Alice asked Rev. Thompson.

He began, to murmurs of assent. "Dear Heavenly Father, thank You for warm friends, good food and gentle hearts. Join us at this meal and in every moment of our lives. Amen."

Ethel cast a doubtful look in his direction before telling Lloyd in a deafening stage whisper. "Daniel always prayed longer."

A flush rose from beneath the collar of Rev. Thompson's shirt. As Jane passed him a bowl of soup, she whispered, "And the food always got cold."

"Salt or pepper, Rev. Thompson?" Alice interjected smoothly.

"Both, please, and for the record, will you all please just call me Ken or Pastor Ken if you must. That whole 'Reverend' moniker is much too formal."

Lloyd and Ethel stiffened with disapproval, and Jane was tempted to throw a bun at them from across the table. Instead she bit into it to stay silent. Much as she wished it were not so, she felt as much a visitor in this household as Ken Thompson and should probably mind her manners.

"Mighty good food, Jane," Lloyd said, his bow tie quivering with pleasure beneath his fleshy neck. "Even that 'bree' stuff wasn't half bad. Cranberries, though, I could take or leave them."

"Jane's mother was a wonderful cook," Ethel informed

Pastor Thompson. "Oh, the fun we used to have around her table. Louise, do you remember when you and Alice were little and your mother insisted on having a costume party on New Year's Eve? We all came as characters from *Alice in Wonderland.* Your father was the Mad Hatter and your mother was Alice. She'd made matching dresses for our Alice and Louise. You girls looked just like princesses." That statement sent the sisters into a spirited conversation as to whether their dresses were cerulean or azure, a fine line of distinction, Jane supposed, but obviously important nonetheless.

"What were you, Mrs. Buckley?" Rev. Thompson asked.

Jane steeled herself for more of the inevitable reminiscing, the sharing of small, inside jokes and visions of the mother she herself had never seen. No matter that she was pleased that her mother had been so beloved in this family and no matter that the others had every right to remember Madeleine this way, it still hurt her heart to know she could never contribute to these conversations, never really know the woman her mother had been.

Ethel, for once in her life, was not forthcoming.

"Ethel? What did you come as, honey?" Lloyd encouraged. "The Queen?"

She mumbled something no one heard.

"What did you say?"

Ethel looked annoyed and slightly embarrassed, as if

the party had been only yesterday. “I came as the White Rabbit,” she said.

Jane and Pastor Thompson both choked at the same time but each recovered gracefully with a sip of water. The image of Ethel as the White Rabbit was definitely hard to swallow.

“It was wonderful,” Alice recalled. “She dressed in white and wore a colorful vest and Father’s old wire rims . . . .”

“And Mother made a pouf of white yarn for her tail,” Louise finished.

“Aunt Ethel flew through the house saying, ‘I’m late, I’m late, for a very important date. . . .’”

“You needn’t go into it any further.” Aunt Ethel pressed her lips together prissily. “Madeleine made me do it. She was such a rascal.”

“I’m sure you were a really cute rabbit, honey,” Lloyd assured her. He paused, bread in his beefy hand. “Now would somebody pass the butter?”

Jane escaped to the back porch while the others were finishing their coffee. The fresh air and the darkness cocooned her in silence. She rubbed her eyes, pulled at the clip in her hair and ran her fingers through the thick dark drape around her shoulders.

What had made her think that this was the place to

come to heal? Granted, she no longer thought of her ex-husband every moment, but that was only because the hurt was occasionally replaced by hearing Louise, Alice and Ethel talk about the mother she had never known and by how set apart she felt here. Little had changed in all the years she had been away. Memories—or her lack of them—followed her everywhere these days, like her own personal rain cloud, hovering overhead.

"Are you all right?" Ken Thompson's rich voice cut the shadows and made her jump.

"You startled me!" Being caught feeling sorry for herself, Jane blushed in the darkness. "Are you already done with your coffee?"

"I'll have more when you come in. Right now I didn't want to listen to the others complain about one of the finest cups of coffee I've had in ages."

"Too strong?"

"Your aunt said she wouldn't sleep all night."

"Oh, Aunt Ethel is not nearly so delicate as she'd have you believe."

"She is 'delicate' like Hoover Dam is delicate," Pastor Thompson said with a chuckle. "She could be shut down, but not without a lot of effort." Jane could practically feel him redden, even in the dark. "I shouldn't have said that."

"It's the truth. In fact," she paused to choose her words

carefully, as Pastor Ken was always concerned about being misconstrued, "I like you better when you're a little irreverent, Reverend."

"And I, you." He shifted from one foot to the other. "Sometimes people forget that pastors are human too. Our standards are set high, and a slip of the tongue . . ."

"Your jokes are safe with me. And I'll never tell Aunt Ethel you said she didn't like my coffee. I'll let her tell me herself, which, of course, she will."

"Thank you."

"I'm sure they all would prefer that I wave a teaspoon of coffee over the pot and call it good." A chuckle escaped her. "It's just one of the many things they disapprove of where I'm concerned."

"Not disapproving, I'm sure, only unfamiliar with at present." He put his hands on the balustrade and stared into the dusk. "Sort of like me."

"I apologize for Aunt Ethel. No one will ever live up to the standard of my father. She adored her big brother."

"And I'm a highly flawed replacement." A chuckle drifted on the air.

Jane rolled her shoulders and willed them to relax. "This is a wonderful place, Acorn Hill, but I'm beginning to believe what Lloyd says is true. 'Acorn Hill has a life of its own away from the outside world, and that's the way we like it!'"

"Not everyone thinks that way." Pastor Thompson turned and leaned against the porch railing.

"True, but they're the 'newcomers.' They've lived here less than thirty years. I'm beginning to believe that the residents of Acorn Hill even breathe personalized air."

She was growing uncomfortable with the intent expression in his eyes. He was seeing more than she cared to reveal. "Would you like some more coffee now?"

He was silent for a moment, as if judging whether to pursue or retreat from the conversation. Jane relaxed when he nodded and smiled. "I'd love another cup."

"Where have you two been?" Ethel asked. "Louise is going to play for us."

She and Lloyd were sitting on a Victorian settee in the parlor like two robust lovebirds on a perch. Alice had gathered three Victorian Eastlake chairs close to the instrument for the performance.

"Sit down, sit down," Alice fluttered. "She's going to play something she's composed herself."

"It is not an earthshaking event, Alice," Louise demurred, but pink points of excitement highlighted her cheeks. As she began to play, Jane closed her eyes and allowed the music to wash over her.

Louise was as good as any concert pianist that Jane and Justin had ever heard in the Bay Area. And they had heard a number of them, including the performing musicians at the gallery openings they frequented.

Justin. The music reached a crescendo as his features flickered in her mind. His warm brown eyes, just the memory of them, could pierce her heart. How could she have misjudged anyone so badly? How dare she consider trusting her judgment again?

The crashing finish of Louise's composition brought Jane back to the present and to the warmly appointed room. Louise's cheeks were as pink as the roses Craig Tracy had sent from Wild Things.

"Bravo! Bravo!" Lloyd leapt to his feet in a move more graceful than Jane had thought possible. Clapping enthusiastically, Ethel followed.

"You should write an original score for Acorn Hill's next Fourth of July celebration." The Fourth of July was a major event in the life of Acorn Hill, surrounded as it was by so much of the nation's history. For Lloyd even to suggest it was quite a compliment. The only occasion that could possibly surpass it, Jane had heard, was the Potterston Art Festival, which was part state fair, part art show and part food-tasting event. There were carnival rides, talent shows, music and a parade, not to mention a swarm of state and local politicians.

Jane smiled when she saw Louise wince. Louise liked to

think of herself as a scholarly artist. Trained at a prestigious conservatory in Philadelphia and accustomed to teaching precocious students, Louise would profit from being able to relax a bit and compose something that could potentially involve a marching band.

To help Louise by changing the subject, Jane announced, "I have a surprise."

She disappeared into the kitchen and returned with a small silver plate filled with chocolate confections in tiny fluted paper cups. "Truffle, anyone? I made them myself."

It shocked them all when Ethel put her hands to her cheeks and sudden tears welled in her eyes.

"Aunt Ethel, are you all right?"

"Truffles! I haven't had homemade truffles in years. Madeleine used to serve them at all her dinner parties. That was such a long time ago. . . ."

Jane's culinary achievements had never before given her such satisfaction. She felt a thread, thin and tenuous as a single strand of a spider's web, form within her, a fragile link to her mother. "It's her recipe, Aunt Ethel. From a book I found in the basement."

Almost reverently, Ethel took a bite of a truffle and closed her eyes. A dreamy expression drifted across her features. "*Just* like Madeleine's. Maybe even better."

It occurred to Jane as she replenished the plate that it

was the first time since she had returned to Pennsylvania that she felt truly connected to Acorn Hill.

She saw Lloyd and Ethel, still bubbling about the truffles and the music, to the front porch and waved them into the night. Lloyd would walk Ethel the short distance to the inn's carriage house, the place Ethel had called home ever since the death of her husband Bob. She was chattering and nodding her head as they moved off, her bottle-red hair silvery in the moonlight.

Closing her eyes, Jane drew in a breath of fresh night air. No matter how many times she had tried to remember the fragrance of the air here in Acorn Hill while she was in San Francisco, she had never quite managed it. And the sounds. Or, more accurately, the lack of them. She tipped her head and listened. A small animal, a cat most likely, stirred in the shrubbery. Somewhere in the distance she could hear the engine of a car. And the porch itself creaked slightly as she moved her feet. It was surprising how noisy the silence could be.

Is this what life would be like without all the big, crashing events and issues that seemed to drown out everything else? Could it be that life in a gentle place such as this was as full of richness as the silence was tonight? It seemed hard to believe, but, having no other good option at present, Jane was willing to give it a chance.

"Thank you." The soft voice blended with the night air in such a way that Jane was not surprised to hear it. She turned to greet Pastor Ken as he joined her on the porch. "Your dinner was delicious. And the truffles . . . well, surely that's obvious."

"Maybe you should say a prayer that Lloyd isn't sick in the night from eating so many. They're very rich." Jane leaned her hips against the porch rail and linked her arms across her chest.

"It seems to me that he's had practice eating too much of something rich before this."

"Do you like it here in Acorn Hill?" she inquired. "Lloyd, Aunt Ethel and all?"

"More every day. Your father's shoes are big ones to fill. Some days I wonder if I'm up to the task, other days I have hope that I am." He leaned against the porch column and studied her. "And you? Are *you* growing to like it here?"

"I grew up here," Jane murmured, as if that answered the question.

"Yes, but I have a sense that you're just as much of a stranger here as I am. Maybe I'm being presumptuous, but somehow I'd place you in the rank of newcomer, like me."

There was truth in that. Jane just had not realized that it was obvious to anyone but herself. Before she could answer, Pastor Ken straightened and reached out a hand to shake hers.

"Thanks again, Jane. Goodnight."

Feeling unsettled by the evening, Jane didn't want to go inside quite yet. Ethel's response to Madeleine's recipe had disarmed her. Since the moment she had uncovered that dusty book in the basement, her mother had been taking form in her mind and heart. Having parties, coaxing the always contrary Ethel to appear as the White Rabbit, tail and all, making truffles that could fifty years later still bring tears to her aunt's eyes. She had not realized until now that she had imbued her mother with all sorts of characteristics, perfect, lofty traits, none of which spoke to the real woman. To Jane, Madeleine was some kind of misty, benevolent angel she had never had the privilege to know. Now she was coming alive, here in the house she had known so well and not entirely in the way Jane had imagined. To her surprise, everything about returning to Acorn Hill held a hint of the unexpected.

She picked up the coffee cup she had carried out of the house and curled into one of the white wicker rockers. The mug was warm against her palms and the rocker invited her deep into its embrace. Louise had sewn ruffled floral cushions for the chairs and porch swing in true, fussy Victorian mode. Left to her own devices, Jane would have chosen something with simpler lines, but Louise had insisted, and she was the one doing the sewing. Jane closed her eyes and tuned in to the remarkable peacefulness of the night. The sounds of crickets chirruping and mosquitoes droning around the porch light lulled her into a semi-awake state.

Despite the sense of always having to prove herself to her family, Jane knew on a deeper level that this was where she needed to be right now. Granted, at first it had felt like escape from the memories of her troubled marriage, but it didn't take long to realize that shelter from that pain was not what she was seeking. She was strong; surely she could handle what was tossed her way. It felt as though what she really sought was herself.

A rustle in the shrubbery bordering the lawn brought her to attention. While Louise and Alice had argued for something more practical, Jane had insisted that there be a hedge of rose bushes. What was a Victorian home without a plethora of roses inside and out?

A rabbit? Probably. They had been into the pot of herbs Jane had been growing outside the back door. Her answer had been to grow a second urn of herbs in the sun porch, a highly satisfactory solution for both her and the rabbits.

Suddenly the shrubbery spoke. "*Yeow!*"

That was certainly not a rabbit. Jane jumped to her feet and moved to the edge of the porch. Body tense and ready for flight, she peered into the darkness where a slender man with straight dark hair was doing battle with a Rose Fairy bush. "*Ow. Ow. Ow!*"

"You'll never win. You might as well back off," she informed the unexpected visitor.

"*Me agarro el zapato.*" The voice was musical and, in spite of the sorry condition of its owner, tinged with pleasant laughter. Her Spanish was a bit rusty, but she was sure he had said, "It grabbed my shoe."

"*Es necesario llamar al policía?*" She hoped she had just asked if it were necessary to call the police.

"No! No, please. But my shoe . . ." He bent to pick it up and plunged his arm into another thicket of barbs. "*Ow!*"

"Serves you right for sitting in my rose bushes. What are you doing there?"

The figure came closer to the light of the porch. He was slender but strongly built, with dark eyes and a sheepish expression on his face. He began picking twigs out of his hair. He was a Hispanic man. Jane felt as if she recognized him from somewhere. Then she realized that the stranger resembled a number of her former much loved employees at the Blue Fish Grille in San Francisco.

"Is it necessary for me to call the police?" she demanded again, this time in English.

"No, please. No." He began to back away, and as he did so, he said in heavily accented but perfect English, "It is just so pretty here, the big old house with all the lights on. I just wanted a closer look. Someday I would like a big house that shines with light."

"Wait a minute!" Jane frantically tried to place him. "Who are you?"

But he was gone, absorbed by the night.

Reluctantly she left the porch and returned to the kitchen where Louise and Alice were tidying up. The stranger had piqued her curiosity, but Jane knew that it would upset her sisters if she told them that she had met someone stomping through their hedges to look at the parlor lights.

Louise and Alice were huddled together over the inn's ledgers, talking in that same, soft tone they so often used when speaking to each other. Sometimes Jane believed that, as children, they had developed a secret language meant to keep their little sister out of their business—and had continued to use it right into adulthood. Most of her childhood memories were of Alice and Louise either bossing her around or doing whatever they could to keep her from tagging along. She supposed, looking back, that it was a perfectly natural thing to do, but for a little girl who already felt very lost, it had left its mark.

"There you are," Louise said. "We thought you had already gone to bed."

"With guests still not checked in? I hardly think so." Jane took a dishtowel from her sister's hand. "But why don't you let me finish up?"

Louise's features softened. "Thank you, Jane. I admit I am tired. Entertaining sometimes does that to me."

"Especially when it's Lloyd and Aunt Ethel." Jane scrubbed harder than necessary on a dessert plate. "Those two are meant for each other. I suppose we should be happy that Aunt Ethel has Lloyd to expend some of her energy on—otherwise, we'd never get a thing done."

"I've never understood how two people could be so different," Alice said. She put the leftovers in the refrigerator and returned her apron to a hook on the wall. "Father was as sweet and easygoing as anyone could be and Aunt Ethel . . ."

"They could have sent her back for a gadfly and made a good swap," Jane muttered. "But she's ours, God love her."

"And He does," Alice said with a smile. "And all of us. Praise Him for that." She came toward Jane and gave her a peck on the cheek. "You're a blessing to us, Jane. The meal was lovely. We couldn't have the inn without you."

Jane smiled softly at her sister. Alice, so tender, so faithful, so trusting. She wanted to make the inn work, because it meant so much to Alice—to all of them, really.

"Do not forget to put out the coffee cake," Louise called back over her shoulder as she headed upstairs to bed. "And set the timer on the coffee pot. Our guests may want to get up earlier than we do."

"Doubtful," Jane commented as she looked at the big Seth Thomas clock on the wall. "It's already eleven o'clock. I hope they check in soon." She glanced at the guest book. "Where are they coming from, anyway?"

"England," Alice offered

"Well, no wonder they're late."

"Not *today*, dear. But they said they were 'on holiday.' I suppose that means not adhering to a time schedule. Do you want me to stay up with you?"

"Of course not. It's only eight o'clock in San Francisco," Jane laughed. "I wouldn't even have eaten dinner yet there." A pang of sadness reverberated within her. Those unexpected reminiscences triggered the pain that had the most impact on her. But that was her past. This was her present. She had chosen it and she would make it work, just as she had when she left Acorn Hill for the first time. If nothing else, she had the steely determination that had gotten her this far.

Louise and Alice said goodnight. Jane listened to their disappearing footsteps on the staircase, and when the kitchen was quiet, she refilled her cup and pulled out Madeleine's recipe book. She took it to the front room and curled into a chair to stare at the pages. Truffles. Divinity. Caramels. Fudge. Crystal-cut hard candies that her sisters liked to call "stained glass." Toffee. Candied grapefruit peel. Sugared pecans. Her father had always had a sweet tooth. Now Jane knew how he had cultivated it.

She had dozed off some time after midnight and when she awoke, Wendell had draped himself over the arm of her chair like a tabby pelt. He did not even wake up to the sound of rapping at the front door, and for a moment Jane didn't know where she was. Or, as Lloyd might say, "did not know if she was afoot or on horseback." Jane did, however, have the presence of mind to scoot out of the chair without disturbing the giant cat and put her mother's book on the side table before greeting her guests.

Framed in the screen door were a large man with straight dark hair, two chins and an umbrella. His trousers were hitched high on his middle so he resembled Humpty Dumpty. Next to him was a petite lady wearing an explosion of plaid. "We're George and Muriel Fairchild. So sorry we're late," the gentleman said. "Car troubles."

"We have a good garage here in Acorn Hill," Jane offered as she opened the door to the inn's newest guests.

"No need. We've got it fixed." He looked around the foyer and eyed the grand staircase to the second floor with apparent relief and pleasure. "Look at this, Muriel!

What lovely woodwork . . ." He turned a full three hundred and sixty degrees to admire every inch of the entrance hall. "Remarkable." He peered at Jane. "You do know the history of this house, don't you?"

"Absolutely. Won't you come in? Would either of you like a cup of tea?"

That awakened something in the woman in plaid. She responded in a strong English accent. "Oh yes, my dear. Please! I think I should perish without it!"

"Two of your specials and one guy who wants to know why there's no veal on the menu." Pedro, Jane's beloved headwaiter, poked his head into the gleaming Blue Fish Grille kitchen and gave her a grin.

She rolled her eyes and asked, "What did you tell him?"

"That our head chef doesn't believe in eating anything raised with such cruel and inhumane treatment and he shouldn't either." Pedro's black eyes danced with mischief.

"Now that you've said what I think, what did you actually tell him?" Jane slipped chicken breasts wrapped in Gruyère and prosciutto onto a warm plate and ladled the cream sauce on top.

"It is the Grille's policy not to serve veal, and that tonight's special was not to be missed."

Jane finished adding garlic mashed potatoes formed in a paper sleeve to look like a small tower, piped cinnamon squash roses around the perimeter of the plates and garnished them with parsley and an array of edible flowers. When she was done the dishes looked more like art than dinner. "Good job. There you go."

She watched with satisfaction as Pedro disappeared through the stainless swinging doors, knowing that with one taste of what her employees fondly called "Jane's Too Good Chicken," the veal would be forgotten.

Suddenly Pedro burst back through the doors, disapproval on his features. "We can't serve this! No one eats chicken for breakfast! Don't you know how to cook oatmeal? And abruptly, instead of smiley-faced Pedro, Jane's Aunt Ethel was there holding the platter while a gloom-and-doom chorus made up of Louise, Alice, Lloyd and two complete strangers dressed in plaid chanted the refrain, "Can't you cook oatmeal? Not even oatmeal?"

She sat bolt upright in bed, eyes wide, heart pounding. It took her a moment to regroup. Then she fell back onto the pillows not knowing whether to laugh or cry. These crazy dreams were recurring less frequently now, but they still troubled her when they came. Could she truly find peace and comfort in this quaint inn, or would she be forever dreaming of the city life she had left behind?

Chapter Three

The sun was just creeping over the horizon when Jane took a cup of coffee to the back porch. She loved those silent, mysterious moments of dawn when the sky was neither light nor dark and even the birds seemed to hold their breath for one brief moment before the sun broke. Then the cacophony of bird sounds burst forth, including the crowing of the rooster who lived on the first farm outside of town, beyond the inn on Chapel Road.

"Early morning hath gold in its mouth," Jane murmured. Cupping the mug with her hands, she let the warmth seep into her palms as she watched nature's spectacular show. Again Ben Franklin had hit the nail on the head.

She recalled her father's fondness for quoting Shakespeare. As a child, she, too, wanted a quotable source and old Ben, whom they studied in every grade because he was a Pennsylvanian himself, had seemed the logical choice.

"You do put on a good show, God," she commented into the stillness. "I give You that." Her faith walk—or "faith stagger" as she often put it—was ragged, but she had never doubted that something this beautiful had to be created by the Divine. She had not reflected much about faith one way or the other in the past few years. It had become more of a good idea than a lifestyle to her, but being here had opened doors with exceedingly rusty hinges. It was about time.

She mulled over her breakfast menu. Something showy, she thought, since George and Muriel Fairchild were today's only guests. The fresh juice was squeezed and waiting. The blackest, strongest coffee of the day, Columbian, was already ground and fresh brewed. The cream and sugar cubes were waiting. Later, she would make another pot fixed to the Fairchilds' liking; some guests didn't like coffee stout enough to hold a spoon upright. There were eggs and apples in the refrigerator, chunky slabs of bacon from the butcher shop and plenty of maple syrup. It was the perfect morning to try one of her mother's recipes. Jane drained the last drop from her cup, stretched cat-like and was ready to begin her day.

Squinting at her mother's German pancake recipe, Jane decided to double it. The dish would resemble what was often called a "Dutch Baby," an impressive dish she had often used at brunches. She had no doubt about trying the new recipe on her guests. She had come to believe Madeleine's notations in the old book were the most accurate barometers of success. Her emphatic notation after a homemade sauerkraut recipe, *One could wipe out the entire church community with this foul concoction,* rang true. So her notation beside the pancake recipe, *Puffy, pretty and delicious,* was good enough for Jane.

German Pancake

- 3 eggs
- ½ cup flour
- ½ teaspoon salt
- ½ cup milk
- 2 tablespoons butter, melted
- 2 tablespoons butter, softened

Heat heavy skillet in 450-degree oven until very hot. With wire whisk, beat eggs until blended. Sift flour, measure and sift again adding salt this time. Add flour mixture to beaten eggs a little at a time and beat after each addition just until mixture is smooth. Add milk in two additions and beat lightly after each. Lightly beat in melted butter. Use the remaining two tablespoons of butter to grease bottom and sides of skillet. Pour batter into skillet. Bake at 450 degrees for twenty minutes. Loosen pancake from skillet and slide onto serving platter. Serve with melted butter and a sprinkle of powdered sugar or pan-glazed apple cinnamon slices.

Pan-Glazed Apple Cinnamon Slices

2 tablespoons butter

2 apples, peeled, cored and sliced

2 tablespoons sugar

½ teaspoon ground cinnamon

Melt butter in frying pan. Add apples sprinkled with the cinnamon/sugar mixture. Cook over low heat. Stir occasionally until apples are glazed and tender. Spoon into center of baked pancake.

This will fill one pancake. I double this if I double the recipe.

Quickly calculating the amount needed to double both recipes, Jane peeled apples and heated and filled the old eleven-inch skillet handed down through the generations from Jane's grandmother. It was so heavy she wondered how a slim, willowy woman like her mother had managed to lift it. Of course, *she* was doing it, Jane reminded herself, and if Mother didn't double the recipe, she would have used an eight-inch skillet.

She heard the Fairchilds entering the dining room just as she slipped the pan into the oven and glanced at her watch. Perfect. They would just have time for juice and coffee before the presentation.

She joined Alice and Louise who were visiting animatedly with their guests.

"Good morning." She greeted their guests and refilled the coffee cups. The pair, despite a short night of sleep, looked remarkably fresh and alert. Mr. Fairchild, in a blue denim shirt and khaki trousers—again hitched above his waistline—wore a digital camera around his neck and a bright smile. His wife had forgone plaid for a shirtwaist in powder blue and a beaded string to which her reading glasses were attached. Neither of them would win "Year's Best Dressed" any time soon, but they did look approachable and eager to visit.

"My, my!" Muriel eyed the table that Jane had set with rose floral china, napkins with a lacy edge and pale pink crystal goblets. "Your table is lovely." Her voice was unexpectedly wistful.

"I must say, I'm thrilled to be here," George added, not nearly so concerned with tableware as he was with Pennsylvania itself. "I've been a fan of Benjamin Franklin all my life. Did you know that he is the only person whose signature is on the Declaration of Independence, the

Constitution *and* the peace treaty with England?" George's face was suffused with joy.

"I'm sure I must have heard it. . . ."

"*And* he discovered the Gulf Stream while sailing here from England! How remarkable. I really don't know if daylight savings was such a good idea, however. . . ."

"You'll have to excuse George," Muriel said, giving her husband an indulgent little smile. "Even on vacation he can't keep from bursting into a lecture. A professor to the core, my George."

"That's good," Jane said. "I could use a little refreshing on Pennsylvania history myself. I've only moved back to Acorn Hill recently."

The timer on the stove rang and Jane moved quickly to the kitchen. She opened the oven and pulled out the pan to sprinkle cinnamon and sugar onto the pancake and then returned it to the oven to bake for two more minutes. Then she pulled it from the oven and slipped it onto a serving platter to carry into the dining room.

Highly satisfactory gasps of pleasure greeted her creation. Jane loved the way it appeared—a puffy, golden masterpiece that sank into a tasty dish, part omelet, part luscious pancake. The aroma wafted into her nostrils and she felt her own mouth water. As Louise cut the concoction into five wedges and began to serve, Jane returned to the kitchen for the sizzling pan-glazed apple slices and the honey butter she had whipped together with butter, honey, whipping cream and vanilla.

"There's maple syrup in the cruet. Help yourself."

As she returned to the kitchen again to collect fresh fruit and a bowl of marshmallow-yogurt topping, she could hear sighs of pleasure from the other room. *Music to a chef's ears*, she thought.

"Divine!" Muriel announced when Jane returned. "Absolutely divine!"

"Won't you join us?" George gestured to an open chair. "Please?"

"Thank you. I believe I will."

As she gathered another plate and silver from the sideboard, Louise and Alice rose from the table.

"I have an early lesson today," Louise said, "so if you will excuse me. . . ."

"And me." Alice stood. "We have a staff meeting at the hospital." And they were off again, leaving Jane to run the inn.

When her sisters were gone, Jane turned to the Fairchilds. "What are your plans today?"

"A tour of the town. It's very picturesque. Do you have any recommendations about where we should go first?"

Jane hesitated for a moment. Opening the inn had caused a brief tempest in the teapot of Acorn Hill. Some of the residents and even a few of the shopkeepers were not terribly eager to become tourist attractions. Jane therefore liked to recommend the shops that had supported the inn's presence. If they meandered into the others, although they would be welcomed, Jane knew there could be an undercurrent of reservation about "the strangers."

"Why don't you stop at the florist shop, Wild Things, first? Craig not only does beautiful floral arrangements,," Jane said, "he also carries an interesting line of gifts and art." Craig would welcome the Fairchilds warmly. Not a native of Acorn Hill, he enthusiastically accepted the idea of tourists in town.

"And stop by Grace Chapel. The door is always open. In fact, all the churches here are old and unique. The Methodists meet in a lovely brick edifice on the corner of Hill Street and Village Road. And don't miss the Presbyterian Church on Berry Lane. It was built by a local stonemason before the turn of the century. His great-grandson now plays the pipe organ in the same church."

"I'm glad I have my camera, Muriel. I think I'll be taking lots of pictures." George practically pawed the floor, eager to forge ahead with the day.

"And stop by Time for Tea. Wilhelm Wood has the most amazing collection of teapots. Most are for sale, but there are several unique ones from his own collection on display."

"Do they serve an afternoon tea there?" Muriel asked.

Jane shook her head. "He just sells the leaves and accoutrements."

"In England we have tea every day. Such a genteel custom." Muriel was obviously disappointed. "It's a tradition that the United States doesn't fully embrace, a proper tea. Too bad you don't do tea here at the inn. It's the perfect setting." She looked at the gleaming mahogany dining table, chairs in pale green and ivory damask and the fragile creamy lace at the windows. "Simply perfect."

"Come on, Muriel, come on, we haven't got all day." George had his hand on the doorknob.

"I know, dear. It's just that I'd forgotten how much I missed it until I'd mentally revisited the custom."

Jane, observing Muriel's disappointment, blurted, "If you come back at four o'clock, I'll see what I can do."

Now where had that come from?

Jane waved the Fairchilds down the steps and onto the sidewalk. It was not part of the inn's policy to give the guests a meal other than breakfast. Now she would have to run to the stores if she were going to have anything to serve her guests.

"Where are you off to?" Louise dropped a stack of sheet music onto the kitchen table and wiped a stray bit of hair from her eyes when she returned from her lesson. "It is warm out there."

"To the bakery. I seem to have opened my mouth too wide and got a foot stuck in it."

"What does that mean?" Louise took a pitcher of peach tea from the refrigerator and poured it into a glass Jane had icing in the freezer.

"Muriel Fairfield was waxing eloquent about having a 'proper tea' in England and she sounded so homesick for it that I said I'd pull something together for this afternoon."

How Louise managed to raise her eyebrow nearly to her hairline Jane would never know, but it was a source of constant fascination to her. That had been Louise's signal of surprise or disapproval even as a young girl. Perhaps Jane was so aware of it because she was the one who had surprised Louise or garnered her disapproval most often.

"It won't be hard. And we *did* mention it once early on."

"And decided against it because of the extra cost. Money does not grow on rosebushes, you know."

"Darling Louise, I promise, the guests will eat bread and water for the rest of the week." Impulsively, she gave her disapproving sister a peck on the cheek. "See you later."

Immediately upon leaving the house, Jane had the strong

sensation that she was being watched. She looked to the rose hedge, but there were no stray men hiding there. It wasn't until she reached the driveway to Grace Chapel that she realized who it was studying her so intently. A small girl—she looked to be about eight years old—was standing in the drive, leaning against a pathetically rusty bike. Her eyes, an intense blue that was almost alarming, followed Jane's every step. The little girl wore a thin cotton shorts set that looked a size or two too small. Her feet were bare and her legs scabbed and tough looking as armadillo hide.

"Hello," Jane greeted her.

She had nearly passed by when the little girl responded. "Hullo. You've got pretty hair."

Pausing, Jane studied the pale blonde mop that, if it were properly combed, would be a cloud of lemon-colored curls. "So do you."

"It's got snarls." The child picked up a clump of curls to demonstrate. "Mama says I'm big enough to comb my own hair but it hurts to comb these." She dug into her pocket and pulled out a small plastic comb, a giveaway with the name of some business printed on it. "See?"

"What's your name?" There was something irresistibly appealing about the child, tangled hair, shabby clothes and all.

"Josie. But sometimes my mama calls me 'Cornflower.'"

"I can see why." Jane couldn't help smiling. "Where do you live, Josie?"

She pointed in the direction of an area of town where some shop owners had apartments for rent over their stores. "We just moved here from Philadelphia. When Daddy left, Mama said we had to find a cheaper place to live so we came here. Mama's lookin' for a job." The child so matter-of-factly spewed personal information that Jane was taken aback. Then she remembered herself at this age and realized that she had probably been little different. With Daniel in his study and her older sisters off doing other things, Jane had spent a lot of time hanging over the porch railing, waving at passersby and initiating conversations—just like Josie.

"It was nice to meet you, Josie. I wish I could stay and visit but I have some shopping to do."

"That's okay," the little girl said, but Jane saw a significant droop of her shoulders. Then they straightened. "Maybe I'll come visit you someday. You live in the big spooky house, don't you?"

Jane had never heard it described quite that way before, but to a child the old mansion might indeed look "spooky." Then, before Jane could respond, Josie slid onto her decrepit bike and with a spray of gravel headed toward home.

As Jane approached Hill Street, she saw Sylvia Songer coming out of Fred's Hardware.

"Hello!" Jane called out. Sylvia was one of the people she liked most to run into around town. Though she was as chary of newcomers as the rest, she and Jane had a special bond. Fabric. And art.

And an artist she was. Jane recognized it in the simple shirtwaist Sylvia wore, and guessed the hours she had undoubtedly spent sewing tucks and stitching buttonholes. She had even embroidered a bumblebee on the cuff of her sleeve and appliquéd a bouquet of flowers on the hem of the skirt. Probably no one but Jane realized that Sylvia had made it herself.

"Aren't you pretty today!"

Sylvia's pale features lit as Jane spoke. Her pleasure gave way to a blush. She put her hands to her cheeks. "It's the worst thing about redheads," referring to her pale, strawberry blond hair. "We turn pink both indoors and out."

"Anything new come in?"

"Not until tomorrow." Sylvia dropped her gaze shyly to the ground. "You could come in late tomorrow and see things as I unpack them."

A warmth flowed through Jane until she, too, felt pink in the cheeks. How good it felt to have someone reach out to her for a change. "I would love to come, but you'll have to put me to work—unpacking, checking invoices, loading shelves. . . ."

"That's not necessary," Sylvia demurred. "But . . ."

"You could use the help."

"It's my own fault," Sylvia said frankly. "When I go to market, I lose my mind. It's like walking into a treasure chest—ruby, jade, emerald, every hue of rose and green, buttercup yellow—the fabrics are a sensory overload. I want to order them all."

"*Ummm*. I know exactly what you mean. You know the passion I have for vintage fabrics. As artists, Sylvia, we feed on color."

She blushed again. "*You* are an artist. I'm a seamstress with a little fabric shop."

"We're going to have to talk about that, m'dear. You're much too modest."

"I don't want to bore you or take your time. You work so hard at the inn."

"And I *am* fifty years old," Jane finished for her.

Sylvia blushed. "I didn't mean it like that. I'll never see forty-five again myself. Besides, you look fifteen years younger than your age."

Jane grinned and flexed the muscle in her arm and paraphrased an early feminist. "And, my dear, this is what fifty looks like now. I'll be by late tomorrow. Don't open those boxes without me!"

Her steps were lighter as Jane walked toward the Good Apple Bakery. It hadn't occurred to her until now how isolated she had been in Acorn Hill. In San Francisco she had a vast well of friends to dip into. Here she had been so busy reestablishing her relationship with her sisters and working in the inn that she had barely noticed her lack of friends.

"Who had deceived thee so often as thyself?" Ben Franklin had asked. *No one,* Jane concluded, and it was time to stop. At times Acorn Hill residents could be a bit stuffy and reticent, but they were also salt-of-the-earth people. She was determined to find that particular seasoning in every one of them.

Feeling lighter in spirit than she had in weeks, Jane queued up behind Viola Reed at the Good Apple Bakery where Viola was scrutinizing the trays in the pristine display case through the bottom half of her bifocals.

"Looking for the perfect cookie?" Jane inquired as Viola nearly bumped her over in her effort to bend in half and examine the bottom row of filled teacakes, sugar cookies and cake doughnuts.

Viola, who was wearing a long chiffon scarf around her ample neck, flung one end of it over her shoulder. "We're having a reading tonight. Didn't Louise tell you? What do you think would go over best? Cherry bars? Biscotti?" She eyed the case again. "The Russian teacakes look nice today."

"She must have forgotten," Jane responded smoothly. Louise and Viola were soul mates of a sort, both having an aversion to most fiction written in the past twenty years. "Trash," Viola had deemed it, and she sold it in her shop most unwillingly. Only in Acorn Hill would a reader have to *beg* to buy a book from the only bookstore in town. If Viola could interest her customer in a classic, there was no way she would let that customer leave with a bestseller. Sci-fi novels and their readers never darkened the doors of Nine Lives Bookstore.

"Why don't you serve éclairs? I can't make them any better myself than the ones they sell here." For Jane, who had also done a stint as a pastry chef, that was high praise indeed.

"*Hmmm*. I think you're right. Éclairs it is."

While Viola was completing her transaction, which, typically, she made as complicated as possible, Pastor Thompson entered the bakery and fell in line behind Jane.

"I didn't think you'd cross the threshold of a bakery, Chef Jane." As usual, he was meticulously dressed. Jane wondered if he had ever worn a wrinkled shirt or a pair of scuffed shoes. A flash of her father came to mind, bespectacled and informal, a sprinkling of cat hair on his clothing.

"I'm a chef in a hurry today," Jane responded. "Besides, I learned early on in the restaurant business, if you don't have time to make it yourself, find those who make it almost as well as you do and buy theirs."

"Business must be hopping at the inn." He was dressed

casually today. Casually, at least, for him—in chino pants, and an unstructured yellow jacket over a crisp white shirt.

It was no wonder, Jane thought, that the older residents of Acorn Hill initially had been a bit suspicious of this newcomer to their church. Her father had worn three colors his entire life—navy, black and white. Jane remembered the year she had sent him a red knit sweater for Christmas—and how happy he had been with the delighted response he had received from a transient when he gave the sweater to the man.

Even the associate pastor of Grace Chapel, Henry Ley, never varied from his uniform of tan pants and white shirts. Naturally, those under twenty-one thought Pastor Ken was the best thing since the Palm Pilot and cell phone.

"I accidentally opened my mouth and offered to pull together an English tea for our new guests at the inn this afternoon."

Just then Viola pulled away from the counter like an SUV backing out of a small parking space and left Jane next in line.

"Any loaves of cocktail rye bread? Scones? Tarts?"

Clarissa Cottrell, owner of the Good Apple, frowned. Clarissa was tall and thin. No one worked harder than she. After the Good Apple closed for the day, you could always find her down on her knees scrubbing floors until they gleamed, sanitizing bread racks or relieving the windows of sticky fingerprints.

"One miniature loaf of rye left, no scones and some cherry tarts."

"That will have to do," Jane said, a little disappointed. She had really been hoping for lemon tarts and anything that resembled a scone so she would not have to bake. She heard Ken clear his throat behind her.

"Need any help taste-testing for this maiden voyage of the typical English tea?"

She paid for her purchases and turned around. "Are you volunteering?"

"A man has to do whatever he can for his flock. Look at me now. I'm here for three dozen glazed doughnuts for tonight's youth group since I can't be there to lead them."

"Do you know anything about tea?" Jane asked, amused.

"Darjeeling, Gunpowder Green, Earl Grey and the Prince of Wales. My grandmother was British." He chuckled at Jane's startled expression. "You expected me to simply say orange pekoe when I'm trying to impress you with my cosmopolitan knowledge?"

"Consider me impressed. Will you join us at four? Muriel Fairchild will regale you with stories of your grandmother's birthplace, I'm sure."

He patted his pocket and pulled out his Palm Pilot. Fleetingly Jane recalled her father's notepads from the now long-gone feed store and the stubby pencil he sharpened himself with his pocketknife. With the tiny stylus, Ken poked at the screen until his schedule appeared. "Free as a bird. I'd love to come."

"Punch us in then."

"I'll be there."

The grocery store didn't yield all that she had hoped for. There was no fresh parsley, chives or watercress. Jane did, however, find a lovely pot of lemon curd and two fine, fat cucumbers. She met Lloyd Tynan at the checkout line where he was waiting impatiently to pay for a can of coffee and some frozen TV dinners.

"Mighty nice meal we had at your place. Mighty nice." He examined her basket with a critical eye. "That's a small order. Must mean you don't have any guests today." He said it with such hope in his voice that Jane almost laughed aloud. In Acorn Hill, an empty inn was a good inn, according to Lloyd.

"Sorry to disappoint you, but we do have guests. A lovely couple on their vacation."

"*Harrumph.*" Mabel Torrence, a widow and new employee of the store, shook her head as she began ringing up Lloyd's order. "Got enough people here already, it seems to me. Don't know what you want to have more for. We'll be tripping over them until they take over. Next thing you know, they'll be holding elections. Fine people like Lloyd here will be voted out of office, and we'll be replaced by a shopping mall. Tourists will be the death of us. Just you wait and see."

"My, that does sound appalling," Jane commented mildly, rather enjoying Mabel's doom-and-gloom prediction. "I hope you can hang on to your political office when the time comes, Lloyd. I'll vote for you, I'm sure."

Lloyd looked slightly befuddled. Although he agreed in principle with Mabel, even he couldn't imagine a scenario quite that dire anywhere in the near future. So he did what he'd always done when a conflict between constituents arose. He mumbled an inaudible reply, said his good-byes and hotfooted it out of the store. It was the tactic that had kept him in office for so many years.

The first few times Jane had encountered reluctance, suspicion or outright hostility about the inn, she had questioned her sanity about coming back to Pennsylvania. Now knowing that there was far more bark than bite in the citizenry, however, Jane had begun to enjoy deflecting their comments. She gave Mabel a wide smile, thanked her profusely and walked out of the store humming.

As she returned to the inn, she noticed a man sitting on one of the many park benches strategically placed around Acorn Hill. His head and shoulders were hunched; his hands were clasped limply between his knees. Without even seeing his face, Jane knew it wore an expression of dejection. Her heart went out to him. Oddly, she felt as if she knew him, this disconsolate stranger. The sun glinted off his black hair as he moved his hands to his face, never lifting his head.

Abruptly Jane realized that she *did* know him. He was the visitor in her shrubbery the night before. Torn between stopping to talk and her responsibilities at the inn, she finally submitted to the draw of the inn.

She had her thoughts focused on other matters as soon as she entered the back door of the house.

"There you are!" Louise red-faced and flustered greeted her. "The phone has been ringing off the hook ever since I walked in. We have new reservations booked for the next two weeks. Sylvia Songer called from Sylvia's Buttons, something about fabric the two of you had discussed."

"I'll look at the reservations book later. For now, can you help me in the kitchen? I have to get started on the tea."

"That's actually a meal, isn't it? Meat or fish, breads, sweets . . ."

"That's considered a high tea. *This* is an afternoon tea, and the food is less heavy and there are more sweets." Jane rolled up her sleeves both literally and figuratively to get to work. Louise did the same. "Will you find a recipe for scones in one of my books and organize the ingredients for me?"

"Why don't you use Mother's recipe? I imagine it is in

that old book you found. She used to make the best scones. She liked them with raisins but Father always preferred them plain. Alice and I, of course, wanted them with blueberries."

"Mother used to make scones?"

"Of course. She made them for us and for parties. She loved parties."

Suddenly, Muriel's tea took on a whole new meaning.

Without another word, Jane went to the cupboard and withdrew her precious book. She found the recipe with Madeleine's typical notation. *So good even the church treasurer loved them!*

Tea Scones

1½ cups flour
⅓ cup sugar
2 teaspoons baking powder
½ teaspoon salt
½ cup raisins
1¼ cup heavy cream
2 teaspoons lemon zest, optional

Combine flour, sugar, baking powder and salt. Make a well in center of mixture and add raisins, three quarters cup cream and lemon zest. Stir until crumbly and use your hands to knead dough into a ball. Work the dough gently and do not over-mix. Pat or roll dough into a half-inch-thick circle and cut into six to eight wedges, or using a lightly greased and floured three-inch biscuit cutter or the rim of a glass, cut into rounds. Cut close together to make as few scraps as possible. Dip cutter in flour often to keep dough from sticking. Push scraps of dough together; firmly pinch edges with fingertips. Pat this into another half-inch-thick circle and continue to cut. Space one inch apart on lightly greased baking sheet. Brush scones with additional cream and sprinkle with sugar *or* combine one egg and one tablespoon milk. Brush onto scones. Bake at 450 degrees for fifteen to eighteen minutes until golden brown. Serve warm.

Madeleine had added as a note: *Yum. Use nothing but cream!*

Jane could not agree more. Cream had been out of favor with cardiologists for a long time, but rumor was that fat was coming back into popularity. She hoped that boded well for her scones.

In her element, Jane moved with precision through the steps of making scones. She loved the texture of foods in her hands and was unabashedly happy to toss the mixture together until it made a compact ball, to roll the dough into a circle, cut smaller circles with the rim of a water glass, reroll and cut again. Then she covered them with a thin damp cloth and set them aside. She mixed fresh strawberries that she had with sugar and put them in the refrigerator.

The clotted cream was more of a problem. Traditionally, making it was a twenty-four hour affair, but Jane whipped a cup of heavy cream with a couple of tablespoons of confectioner's sugar and then folded in a half cup of sour cream. Chilled, it would be every bit as good as the British version.

"May I help you with anything else?" Louise asked. Jane had almost forgotten that her sister was in the kitchen handing her measuring cups, spoons and bowls just as a surgical nurse might silently and efficiently assist a surgeon at work. It occurred to Jane that she and Louise made a surprisingly good team. This was a brand-new concept for her. Growing up, Alice and Louise had been more like bossy young mothers. Not only had Jane lost Madeleine in her life, she had also missed the experience of simple sisterhood.

"Let's take a little break." Jane went to the refrigerator and took out a pitcher of lemonade. She raised it toward Louise with a questioning glance.

"Yes, please." Louise pulled up a stool and sat down. "It would help to get off my feet for a moment. Oh . . . you spilled. Be sure to clean that up. . . ." her voice trailed away, and then she said, "Oh dear, I just spoke to you like I used to talk to Cynthia."

"You do that quite often," Jane commented softly as she handed her sister a glass. "I wonder if you even realize it."

"Do I?" Louise's voice was faintly remote. "It seems I raised both of you, so I suppose it comes naturally."

When are you going to start thinking of me as your sister instead of your child? Jane silently wondered.

Alice and Louise had mothered her so long they didn't even realize that there was another way.

"What have we in the way of day-old bread? I bought some cocktail rye at the Good Apple, but crustless white bread with avocado, Dijon mustard and chives would be delicious. Butter it lightly, add the filling and cover with a second slice of bread. Cut the sandwiches into triangles. I'll do cucumber sandwiches and a few with thinly sliced tomato and fresh basil. We can put them on the serving tray now and cover them with a damp napkin."

Louise looked impressed.

Jane opened the refrigerator and frowned. "Where did all my basil go, anyway?"

"You are like a general fighting a war when you get into the kitchen, aren't you?" Louise commented. "You remind me of myself when I am putting together a piano recital. Or Alice a skit with the church youth group."

"I suppose you're right. I am accustomed to running big kitchens. Perhaps I don't have to use quite so much firepower to throw together a small tea. It's just that it's my first—and I didn't exactly have time to plan."

"You and Cynthia remind me a great deal of one another," Louise said matter-of-factly as she trimmed bread crusts with one of the wickedly sharp knives Jane insisted upon.

Jane stared at her sister. Louise's daughter was one of the lights of her life. It hardly seemed possible that she could resemble her maverick, artsy aunt in any way.

"Oh yes. Cynthia approaches life much the way you do. She flings herself into it, like a lemming into the sea . . . or is that what lemmings do? I guess I have never really known. I am not much for small animals of any sort. Not that I am totally opposed to Wendell, mind you, but . . ."

"Louie! What on earth are you talking about?"

Louise put down the knife and studied Jane. "You both have . . . panache . . . élan . . . an innate elegance. Sometimes it makes me feel rather dowdy in comparison."

If a window had been open, a breeze would have blown her over. Jane sat on the tall stool beside the counter and attempted to take in what her sister had said. "You? 'Dowdy'? Music, literature, education? I always considered *you* the erudite, literate one in the family."

"I can read, yes," Louise said with a smile as she finished putting tops on the sandwiches. "And play the piano. But I cannot paint and I am only a passable cook." She held up the tray of sandwiches. "But these do look lovely, if I do say so myself."

Once again taken aback by Louise's comments, Jane regrouped by keeping her hands busy with the sandwiches.

At that moment, the back door flew open and Alice scurried in, her arms full of mail and a teetering stack of books from the church library. She dropped them on the counter and a dusting of flour flew into the air. "My, those are heavy!"

"Studying for a test?" Jane eyed the books: *Youth Group Activities for Church Leaders, What About Our Children?* and *Games, Skits and God.*

"Planning session. We need to keep it lively for the kids."

"Alice, you are a dear. Those kids do not know or appreciate how much you do for them." Louise said.

"But I know how much He does for *me*. It's so little to give back. By the way, I ran into Pastor Thompson at the hospital. He said he was coming later for tea. When did we start serving tea? And what time is it?"

"At four. I only wish I'd had more time . . . ."

"I attended an afternoon tea when I was traveling abroad," Alice recalled as a soft, pleased expression stole across her features. "So lovely. The finest silver and linen—and such a vast selection of teas!"

"Silver and linens! Thank you, Alice, I might have forgotten! Could you pull a couple small tables into the parlor and set them with the linen and silver? The new linens are in the bottom drawer in the buffet in the dining room."

"It is a good thing that I just polished the silver," Louise commented.

"And china teapots. Do we have any?"

Alice raised an eyebrow. "Do we *have* any? There's Mother's entire collection."

"What was that?" Jane wasn't sure she had heard Alice right. Again, she felt that odd feeling, the one that startled her every time something she had not known about her mother came up. Why had they spoken so little of Madeleine to Jane when she was a teenager?

"You didn't know? She loved teapots. Father said her friends gave her one every year for her birthday. They are on the top shelf of the cabinet in the butler's pantry. We never used them after Mother died . . . ." Alice's voice snagged as she remembered exactly *why* Jane could not remember and had not been told.

"No wonder I didn't know," Jane said, discreetly ignoring Alice's distress. "I never got to cleaning out that cabinet because I needed a ladder to get up there." Jane put down the knife she had been using to slice tomatoes and cucumbers and gestured to her sister. "Is there something to climb on around here?"

The ladder was short and old. Jane could feel the wood creak as she climbed the three steps to the top. She hoped that the glue and nails that held it together would survive her weight. Just in case, Louise and Alice poised, one on either side of her, bracing themselves against the rickety contraption.

Buy new ladder, Jane reminded herself as she opened the narrow row of doors just under the ceiling, *if I don't break my neck on this one first*.

The risk was definitely worth it. The doors opened upon a perfect row of teapots, some simple, some so beautifully painted they belonged in a gallery. There were all shapes and sizes, colors and designs. "These are spectacular!" As she reached up, the ladder wobbled.

"Just get what you want and come down," Louise ordered in the voice she used for piano students who did not practice between lessons. "Alice is a nurse, not a miracle worker. If you fall, she'll never get you patched up." A nasty creak from the ladder itself emphasized her point.

Jane chose four pots, one festooned with roses, another with a tree branch filled with tiny blue and yellow birds, a simple white Haviland china piece and a black one filigreed with gold. Carefully she handed them down to her sisters.

"*Now* we're ready!" Down from the ladder, she ran her

finger over the smooth surface of the pot. She glanced at the clock. "If I hurry, I still have time to make some cream puffs before we need to boil the water. Louise, Alice . . ."

"Chopin, Beethoven, Liberace, the Three Tenors or Kenny G?" Louise called from the parlor where she was studying an array of compact discs.

"You choose." Jane flopped into one of the chairs. "I've made more than my share of decisions today." From this vantage point, she could see the lawn and gardens outside. "Oh rats!"

"I hope not," Louise said without missing a beat.

"Look at the flowerbeds. If we don't get the weeds out, they'll choke the plantings. Before we know it, the only color around here will be dandelion yellow. Sometimes I don't even know where to start."

Even Louise sighed then. "It is a little overwhelming, isn't it? How did Mother and Father keep it so beautiful, I wonder. And our grandparents before that?"

"Probably by not trying to run an inn. And when Father was alive, the Grace Chapel's handyman did this yard too. Maybe we should hire someone to work here. Much as there is to do, we could use someone at least three days a week."

"And pay him with what?" Louise demanded. "We are not making buckets of money, you know, and will not for a while."

"I'm less concerned about money than I am my aching back and the eyesore we'll create if we don't do something. Which reminds me . . . the oddest thing happened last night after you both went to bed." Jane started to tell the story of the man in the shrubbery, but the grandfather clock in the hall began to chime. Four o'clock. Jane straightened. "I can't host a tea looking like this."

She took the stairs two at a time and flung herself into her room, pulling at the shirt she was wearing.

"Now what?" She stared inside her closet. She pulled out a bright, flowing orange tunic with matching leggings. No use being shy now. If the conversation lagged, they could talk about her choice of clothing.

The room about her had a pleasantly disheveled appearance—discarded clothing, recipe and gardening books. Several pieces of framed art were stacked along one wall to be rotated with Jane's mood. Today, facing out, was a sketch of a jungle cat lazing sleepily in the African sun.

As she collected the heavy strands of her hair and began anchoring them into a beaded clasp that she had made herself, she glanced out the window. George and Muriel were dutifully trotting up the sidewalk with Rev. Thompson just behind. They were three minutes late. Thank heaven for small favors.

Chapter Four

They were gathering at the bottom of the stairs as Jane descended. She had chosen the right color for making an entrance, she decided, because Louise's eyebrow was acting up again and Alice's mouth was puckering. The Reverend Thompson was beaming ear to ear at the sisters' responses. Theatrically, she glided the rest of the way down the stairs like a bright ball of orange light, grinning to herself.

Jane had not completely figured out what drove her to tweak her older sisters' sensibilities like this, other than the fact that she would enjoy a major "loosening up" in her family. Had their mother lived, Jane thought, things would have been very different. Deep in her heart, an understanding was budding. Her kinship with her mother was growing daily. It was she who most resembled Madeleine in both interests and personality, and she felt somehow obligated to put lightness back into the family.

Louise graciously showed the guests into the parlor, which glimmered in the bright afternoon glow. The dropped crystal chandelier, the collection of antique glass vases and even the eyes of the porcelain doll collection Alice had showcased on a three-tiered, nineteenth-century, carved burl walnut table sparkled with welcome and light.

"Oh." Muriel paused in the doorway in wonder. "How absolutely lovely."

Alice had done her job well. The lace-covered tea tables were appointed with glistening china and silver. She had collected roses from the garden and put them in tiny bud vases at each place setting. Even Jane was impressed. She had overseen professional staffs that could not make a room look more charming than this. This house was made for tea parties. How odd that it had not occurred to her until now. Obviously Madeleine had known it years before.

"You did this for us?" Muriel Fairchild's voice had a breathless quality. "I didn't imagine. . . ."

Jane put a hand on her arm. "Actually, we didn't imagine either. It happened almost by itself. We didn't have time to think about details, and it came together on its own. We should be thanking *you* for the idea."

"Too gracious, too gracious," Muriel muttered as her husband seated her at one of the tables with a flourish. Things were going swimmingly—swimmingly that is, until they heard a clatter at the front door and the screen door creaking open.

"*Yoo-hoo! Yoo-hoo!* Anybody home?"

Ethel knew perfectly well that *everybody* was home—

including the guests and Pastor Thompson. From her vantage point in the house next door she could practically hear the clocks ticking at the inn. Although she clearly had not been planning to attend a tea party until she discovered it was being formed, her hair was perfect. Jane knew Aunt Ethel slept on a silk pillowcase in order to keep her "do" intact between her weekly beauty parlor appointments. In her wake trailed Lloyd Tynan.

"Uh oh," Jane murmured.

"Now Jane," Alice whispered. "There's always room for one more."

"Not one more with Lloyd's appetite."

Jane mentally tallied the sandwiches she had made. They would have to keep an eye on Lloyd to make sure the other guests got their share.

After introductions were made, Alice seated the Fairchilds, and Jane maneuvered Ethel and Lloyd to Rev. Thompson's table. "I'll join you once we've served. Here comes Louise with the tea now."

"Those little pots are wearing coats!" Lloyd, his corpulent bulk squeezed onto a chair made for someone half his size, observed in amazement. "A coat for a teapot? I've never seen such a thing."

Jane peeked at Louise and smiled. Her eyebrow was practically hairline height.

"It is a tea cozy," Louise explained. "Once the pot is heated with water, emptied and dried, it is ready for the tea and boiling water. To keep it a proper temperature while it steeps, I wrapped it in a cozy."

"I think that's probably the craziest thing ever," Lloyd muttered. He began keeping his opinions to himself, however, after Ethel kicked him under the table.

"My, oh, my, silver strainers too." Muriel picked up the tiny strainer by her plate. "And you said you'd never served a tea before."

"We discovered them with the teapots. They were my mother's." As Jane said it, another tenuous thread connecting her to Madeleine formed in her heart.

"You knew, of course, that it was Queen Victoria who promoted and sanctioned the tea ritual," Muriel said. "And naturally her subjects eagerly followed. I believe the Queen developed the habit of taking tea in the afternoon because she loved sweets. Since Victorians, especially the wealthy nobles, ate a big breakfast, a light lunch and a grand supper around nine in the evening, it was the perfect break in the day. So wise of the queen . . ."

Lloyd and Ethel looked impressed by all this information. If a queen approved of having tea, perhaps it was not so frivolous after all.

"I believe it was one of her ladies in waiting, the

Duchess of Bedford, perhaps, who introduced it to her. She was the one who started having tea and cakes in her room. Soon, she was inviting other ladies to join her in her dressing room. Once Victoria heard of the idea, she loved it so much that by the late 1840s she was having daily afternoon teas too.

"But I go on too much," Muriel said. "Tell me what exciting thing has happened in Acorn Hill since we arrived."

"I heard today that someone from Acorn Hill had a new baby at the hospital in Potterston. Can you tell us who the lucky parents are?" Louise inquired of Alice. "Or is it confidential?"

"Somebody named Bartholomew. I'm not familiar with the family so they must not live in town," Ethel said briskly. "Baby girl. Six pounds, eleven ounces. Twenty-three inches long. Dark hair."

"Have they chosen a name yet, Aunt Ethel?" Jane inquired, unblinking. How *did* her aunt do it? She collected gossip so quickly that it barely had time to happen before she was spreading it.

"Mikayla, Makayla, Mokaylo, one of those made-up names people seem to like nowadays. Whatever happened to good, solid names like Gladys, Bernice . . . ?"

"And Ethel," Lloyd added.

"I can't imagine," Pastor Ken cleared his throat and put his napkin to his lips. Jane bet that he was struggling not to laugh.

"Prince of Wales or Gunpowder Green?" Louise asked Lloyd when she came around with the teapots.

Lloyd glanced nervously at Ethel as if to say that Louise was now rowing with only one oar in the water, a crayon short of a box or, Jane's particular favorite definition of insanity, a French fry short of an order.

"Perhaps you didn't hear us discuss the teas when I first poured. The Gunpowder Green is very delicate and thirst quenching. The Prince of Wales is . . . what did you say again, Muriel?"

"Bright, with a dash of oolong. I find it delicious."

He picked up his china cup and thrust it in the direction of one of the pots. His thick hand made the porcelain cup look like a child's. "That one."

"Good choice," Muriel trilled. "The Keemum character makes the Prince of Wales so delicious."

Looking stricken, Lloyd peered into the bottom of his cup as if searching for the poor prince's body.

As Ethel, too, began to study the bottom of her cup, Muriel said, "Did you know that tea gowns became the most exquisite and expensive dresses in a lady's wardrobe?"

"Why did they name a tea 'gunpowder'?" Lloyd muttered.

"Has the council figured out what to do with the memorial money yet?"

The discussion ping-ponged between the guests until Jane realized she was attempting to keep track of three separate conversations. She was glad when George spoke louder than the others, drawing the attention solely to himself.

"We stopped at the florist shop this morning," he said. "It's an impressive place. A town this size is fortunate to have such an asset."

"An expensive asset," Ethel said. "I'm appalled at what Craig Tracy charges for something you can grow in your own backyard. I'm afraid he just doesn't understand a small town very well, being a newcomer and all. He's so different from the rest of us."

Different like me, you mean, Jane thought.

At least Ethel was an equal opportunity insulter. She has managed with her unthinking pronouncements to insult half the people in the room. Quickly Alice changed the subject. "I saw a letter from Cynthia in the mail. How is my lovely niece?"

"According to her letter, she's editing a wonderful new book, something about a duck who flies up and down a chimney into a little boy's room."

"As legend has it," Muriel continued, "tea was invented by a Chinese emperor in 2737 B.C., when leaves accidentally blew into his pot of boiling water. . . ."

"Your daughter is a book editor?" George perked up. "Does she work on textbooks?"

"Lloyd said Fred Humbert's daughter was home last weekend. I've forgotten where she goes to school."

While the conversation was ricocheting around the room, Jane leaned closer to Pastor Ken. "I had the oddest thing happen here the other night."

"Oh? A problem?"

"Not really. I was out on the porch enjoying some night air and discovered a man in our rose hedge."

He grew serious. "Did you call the police?"

"No. I thought of it, but the fellow took off. I talked to him for a moment. He speaks Spanish as well as English."

"What did he look like?" Pastor Ken frowned until his eyebrows nearly met over the bridge of his nose.

"Dark haired, small-boned . . . it was rather dark." She told him about their brief exchange.

"I had a fellow of that description stop at the church the other day. Unfortunately I couldn't talk to him for more than a moment, as I was about to counsel with a couple to be married in Grace Chapel. From what I gathered, he'd hitched a ride from somewhere in Texas and ended up here in Pennsylvania. He looked a little lost so I asked him to come back."

"Did he?"

"Not yet. I think I'll look into this."

"He didn't do any harm," Jane assured him. "It was just . . . odd."

From there, the conversation galloped from one subject to another and Jane was lulled by the homey chatter. She had begun to consider what it was she would make for breakfast in the morning when the conversation drifted into more disturbing territory.

"Looks like your foundation is in need of patching again," Lloyd said.

"Wasn't that checked while we were working on the house?" Alice asked in surprise.

"I asked them to," Louise assured her. "They said that it was in decent shape and did not need to be shored up. Of course, they did not tell me what sort of regular upkeep measures we should take."

"How old is this house?" Lloyd asked. "A hundred years, maybe. It's no shocker if it needs steady upkeep. I check the foundation on my old house a couple times a year. I fill in any cracks or splits and it's doing just fine. Anybody been down there and notice anything?

"Such as . . ." Louise said carefully.

"Crumbling grout mostly. Yes sir, you got to keep on top of the foundation," Lloyd's eyes lit at his little pun. "Nothing that ruins a house faster than ignoring steady upkeep."

God was right about building a house on a firm foundation, Jane mused. Her own foundation had begun to crumble in the past few years. *On the rock of Christ I stand, all other ground is sinking sand.* Is that how the old hymn went? Here she had begun to feel that solid footing of faith return tenfold.

"We haven't really sorted through the basement yet," Alice offered. "Jane was down there briefly. Did you see any crumbling?"

"No, but I was preoccupied."

"Well, somebody should be checking. I can tell you what I use to seal my own basement. Maybe you can hire someone to do it for you. I'd rather do that than one day have to lift the whole house and put a new basement under it."

"Oh dear," Alice murmured and shrank into her chair.

Jane understood her sister's reaction. She followed the ledgers as well as Louise and Alice. There was no way that the inn was running on its own right now. It took both Louise and Alice supporting it with their outside work to keep things on an even keel. Louise had suggested accepting a couple of additional piano students after seeing what it cost to buy the new washer and dryer.

On the other hand, Lloyd was the Acorn Hill equivalent of Chicken Little. If everyone listened to him, the sky was falling every few days. Jane was quite sure that whatever Lloyd said could be taken with a grain of salt.

As a chef, Jane was not willing to cut corners on the food they served, but without telling either sister, she had started to pay for half of the groceries out of personal funds.

No matter how carefully they watched the budget, the inn was expensive to run. What is more, they dare not scrimp in the building stage of the business, when people were trying it out for the very first time. Good first impressions were vital to a new restaurant, Jane knew, and the inn was no different.

She was relieved when the conversation drifted away from the inn and back to the delicate sandwiches and sweets she had served. The compliments flowed so freely that she was not even offended at Ethel's ultimate pronouncement.

"Well, I think a tea is too much work," Ethel announced after eating her fill of sandwiches and sweets. "Now you have more linens to wash and iron, all those bread crusts you sliced off are wasted, not to mention what you must have given to Wilhelm Wood for this fancy tea. Why, I'll bet you just funded another one of those trips he's always running off on." But it couldn't have been too bad. She asked for two scones to take home for breakfast in the morning.

Everyone turned to her except Lloyd, who was making the last of the tarts disappear.

"Seems to me that we're to live a simple life. None of this hoity-toity nonsense."

Completely unruffled, Mrs. Fairchild looked pityingly at Ethel. "Well, I say it was perfect. The best I've had in America—anywhere but England, in fact. And it runs a close second even there."

George, dabbing at his mouth with the corners of his napkin, bobbed his head in agreement. "You should be serving an afternoon tea here every day. A big money maker, I'm sure. With food like this, you could charge whatever you wanted."

Ignoring Ethel's soft *harrumph*, Jane caught Alice's eye, then Louise's. "But what would be a *fair* price for a service like this? Something that would ensure a steady flow of customers?"

The figure George threw out took them aback. He chuckled at the astonished faces in the room. "And worth every penny of it, I might add."

Jane had experienced those proverbial "light-bulb moments" before, but this time her head truly lit up with new possibilities for the inn.

"Muriel, George, perhaps we could visit a little more about this later?" Jane felt her sisters' eyes boring into her. They were thinking exactly what she was thinking. *Potential.*

The food depleted, her gossip spread and an adequate number of people insulted, Ethel deemed the party finished. She thanked Jane at the door in her typical hook-in-a-marshmallow fashion.

"It was lovely, dear. You really do have your mother's art for cooking. I'd serve those scones with more cream and strawberries, though." She held up the pair in the napkin. "A little dry otherwise, I think. By the way, did you have any leftover cream?"

While Alice was retrieving cream from the kitchen—two scones' worth—Lloyd pumped Jane's hand in gratitude. "You are far and away the best cook in Acorn Hill." A little clearing of Ethel's throat had him add, "Except for your auntie here, of course. Since you moved to town, I've gained a bit of weight. We're mighty grateful for your hospitality."

Jane smiled and took his beefy cheeks between her palms. "Thanks, Lloyd. That was nice of you to say."

Blushing, he backed out the door and down the steps.

Louise was more than a little angry as she cleared away dishes while the guests continued to visit. "Didn't that woman ever listen to one of her own brother's sermons on gossip or a critical spirit?" Jane put her own tray of dishes down in the kitchen and shrugged. "Now I'll have to go and make apologies to the Fairchilds and Rev. Thompson," Louise's look softened, "and you."

Jane's heart warmed. "Thank you, Louise, for understanding. I can handle Aunt Ethel, but I appreciate your noticing what was going on. And you do make the most gracious apologies. I'm sure our guests aren't as upset as you are."

"I certainly hope not." Shaking her head, Louise glided out of the kitchen.

Ethel reminded Jane of that line, "I washed my hair and I can't do a thing with it." Ethel was their unruly gift of nature and none of them seemed able to do a thing with her either. She wondered if Madeleine had been able to keep her in line—or if Ethel had been a different woman before her husband Bob Buckley died. She had never been terribly curious about Ethel. She wondered if anyone ever had.

"Fearfully and wonderfully made. Your works are wonderful." The scrap of Psalm 139 came to her unbidden; it was one of the Psalms her father loved most. Ethel, too, was fearfully and wonderfully made. Jane decided she would make an effort to remember that next time Ethel opened her mouth.

When she returned to the parlor, the conversation had turned to things more interesting than Ethel's unending spew of information about everything and everyone in Acorn Hill.

"That was wonderful, Jane. I have no room left," Rev. Thompson rubbed a hand across his flat stomach. "I'll have to be carried home."

As Jane thrust the plate of truffles in front of him, she said, "These are small. They'll slide into the cracks between the other food."

"I don't know. . . ." He looked doubtful about putting one more thing in his stomach.

"I'll try one," George offered. "If it's anything like the rest of the food here, it's got to be good."

As they chatted, Muriel reached out and picked one of the truffles in gold foil from the tray beside her.

Dreamily, she asked, "Where did you get those chocolates?"

"I made them—from my mother's truffle recipe."

"My dear, professional chocolatiers would be green with envy. They are divine. Candy like this should have exquisite wrapping and be sold from its own shop," Muriel commented. "But perhaps I should try another, just to make sure. . . ."

As the laughter erupted over the taste-testing comment, George rose. Muriel brushed creases from the front of her skirt and stood as well. "We hate to run, but we purchased tickets for the local musical revue in Potterston and we'd best get going or we'll be late."

Pastor Thompson mentioned the ladies' Bible study and rose, too.

When everyone had taken his or her leave, Jane, Louise and Alice sat once again, this time staring at each other in mild astonishment. It was Alice who finally spoke.

"That was the best party in this house since Mother died. Jane, you have her touch."

"But what am I supposed to do with it?" She felt nervous and edgy inside, not at all like she had just pulled off a successful social gathering. In fact, she felt totally off-kilter, as if there was something left to do, and she had no idea what.

"Don't 'do' anything. Just enjoy your success," Alice said.

"But look what we learned about the foundation of the inn," Jane countered, feeling a touch of despair. "Tea parties are one thing, keeping a solid footing is quite another. I don't want the first floor disappearing into the cellar one day when I'm not looking."

"Lloyd always exaggerates," Louise said calmly. "Whatever he says, you can divide in half and then believe part of that. Besides, isn't there some way one could benefit the other?"

"You heard what Mr. Fairchild said about the tea. Is it possible. . . ." Alice trailed off hopefully. Then she straightened in her chair in a take-charge manner. "We'll pray about it."

Jane bowed her head as she had done so many times before in this house. Prayer was her father's first plan of action. Alice and Acorn Hill were nudging her back to that too.

"Dear Heavenly Father," Alice began, "thank You for bringing Jane back to us. And thank You for allowing us this wonderful home into which we can invite guests and show them the hospitality and love of You in us. I've prayed about this a long time, Lord, and the inn feels as though it's Your answer, but we're puzzled, Lord. Where will the money come from to keep it going? Forgive us for our worry, Father. Help us to remember that You provide for all Your children in Your own time. Show us what's next and give us the strength and will to do it for Your glory. Amen."

The turbulence within Jane had subsided by the time Alice stopped praying. In fact, a deep sense of peace had overtaken her. There *was* nothing to solve at this moment. Jane felt sure that a door would open for them when it was time. She laid her hand over Alice's folded ones. "Thank you." Hardly enough appreciation for a reminder of who she once was, Jane thought. Something that she thought had died was springing quickly to life inside her.

"Are you coming?" Louise asked Jane.

"Where?" Jane had tidied the kitchen, laid out a snack for the new guests who were checking in that evening and settled herself in a chair with a sketchbook. If she was going to help Sylvia tomorrow, she wanted to have some new collage ideas or clothing designs in mind in case some bit of fabric caught her eye.

"To Nine Lives, of course. Viola is having a reading tonight from the next selection that the book club will discuss. She's hoping to entice a few more people into the fold. We have to support her, naturally."

Naturally. It had not even occurred to Jane to support Viola's literacy attempts, and she supposed she should be ashamed of herself for that. Her chair was so comfortable . . . .

"I'll see you there," Louise concluded, giving Jane no option to refuse. "I promised to help Viola set up chairs. Don't be late."

"I'll be there as soon as the new guests check in. According to their reservations, both should be arriving soon."

"Is it three rooms tonight?"

"Yes, the new guests are a young couple who were married over the weekend, and the other is a single woman. That's all I know."

"Honeymooners," Louise said with a smile. "How delightful. It's good to see people happy and in love."

Louise, Jane thought later as she heard a car pull into the driveway, hadn't recognized the irony of her statement. They were, after all, a household of three single women, one divorced, one widowed and one never married.

She found a pair of human lovebirds nested on the front porch when she answered the door. The couple, holding hands and giggling, could barely take their eyes off one another long enough to look at her. The young woman's face was pink and glowing with whatever her new husband had just whispered in her ear.

Jane cleared her throat.

"Oh, hi, uh . . . I'm Tim McPherson and this is my . . ." he stumbled a bit on the word "wife."

"Theresa." She thrust out her hand to shake Jane's. Jane was caught by surprise by the firmness of the woman's grip. "What a beautiful place! The town is a picture postcard and this house, well, it takes my breath away." She smiled and Jane realized that neither Theresa nor Tim was as young as she had first assumed. It was Theresa's businesslike demeanor that had signaled that perhaps this was no early twenties pair of newlyweds. They were nearer to thirty, if not already on its other side. It was love that made them both appear brand-new.

"Welcome to Grace Chapel Inn. I'm Jane, one of your hosts." She stepped aside and held the screen door for them. "Come in."

"Awesome!" Tim breathed. "Look at this woodwork . . . and the stairs. That is an amazing banister."

Satisfaction warmed Jane as she watched him. Sometimes being so utterly familiar with the house made her forget just how beautiful it really was. She had slid down that banister a few times in her childhood, but that had ended when her father discovered her doing so. She had also been guilty of writing her name on the underside of the stair lip where no one else would notice. She wondered if it had survived the renovation. The pictures she had drawn of her sisters, stick figures with coils of hair, were still on the inside of what had been her bureau drawer. It was the first thing she had checked when she had started unpacking her things in her old room. Though she remembered the minutiae, it was good to be reminded of the bigger picture.

"Here's the room you'll love, Tim. Look at the books." Theresa was standing in Daniel's study, eyes wide. The room invited sitting. The mossy green walls and russet colored chairs mounded with tapestry throw pillows fairly called out with invitation.

"Those were my father's," Jane explained. "If you're into apologetics, Greek, Hebrew, the classics or the history of Israel, it's the place for you. There's also a shelf of bird books. You're welcome to use this room to read. It's a cozy cave in here. Or take the books upstairs. You can just leave them in the room when you check out."

She noticed Theresa looking at a copy of *Jane Eyre*. "If you want a better lit place to read, you can also use the sun room. Come, I'll show you.

"Let me show you the sideboard in the dining room," Jane offered when the tour of the first floor was nearly complete. "I like to have a few things on hand in case the guests like a midnight snack." In her head she ran down the list of offerings she had put out that evening. *Fudgie brownies and carrot cake on a dome-covered serving plate, pretzel sticks and mustard, mini-muffins and whatever was left from the afternoon tea.*

"Do we have to wait for midnight?"

"This place is amazing," Tim mumbled between bites of muffin.

Theresa licked her fingers to get the last morsel of brownie. "We're just lucky we found it. It was purely by accident, you know."

"Oh," Jane's ears perked. "And how was that?"

"Someone at my office knew someone at church who knew someone whose relative lives in Acorn Hill. Apparently they'd mentioned it in passing, something about why on earth a little place like Acorn Hill would need an inn. That's what caught my attention. Tim and I wanted a complete change of scenery. We thought an inn in a little town would be perfect, and here we are."

Ruefully, Jane nodded. It figured. This bit of business had come by way of a complaint from locals about the inn. *All things work together for them that love God.* He was obviously rounding up business for them even in backhanded ways. Alice in particular spent a good deal of time praying about that very thing.

Even so, it might be wise to consider more options in advertising, Jane reflected. She had suggested a more aggressive advertising campaign, but her sisters turned it down. What seemed common sense to her was commercialism to Louise and Alice. Of course, neither of them had much business experience.

"You should be getting the word out about this great place. Do you advertise much? Of course, if you get crowded, then you might not have room for us."

At 7:59 P.M. Naomi Hopper called to say she had been delayed and would be in late. Fortunately, or unfortunately, depending on the way Jane chose to look at it, there was still time to get to the bookstore for the reading.

All but one of the chairs in a semicircle in front of the podium had already been taken when Jane arrived. She slipped into it and tried to will herself invisible as Viola gave her a disapproving stare. Being late was almost as grave a trespass in Viola's eyes as reading science fiction.

As Viola began to read in her loud and dramatic stage voice, Jane mentally escaped and began to look around the room. It was a lovely little bookshop, really. There was not an empty space on any of the wooden shelves, a tribute to Viola's eagle-eyed approach to organization and order. Each section was clearly named—Travel, Regional, Autobiography, and so forth. The floors were carpeted with a rubber-backed brown carpet that muffled noise (a pet peeve of Viola's) and hid any dust or grime carried in on customer's shoes. The walls, what little one could see of them, were a pale taupe color and hung with portraits of Viola's top ten list of authors, including Kipling, Poe, Charlotte and Emily Brontë, Dickens, Shakespeare, Twain and her one nod to a contemporary author, Billy Graham.

The one section missing from view was the contemporary novel. Those, Jane knew, were kept on the nethermost shelves in a rear corner. Only a serious shopper who desperately wanted a beach read or thriller would even be able to find them. According to Louise, and much to Viola's dismay, the residents had outfoxed her and books were flying off these shelves.

She could smell the coffee brewing and a hint of warm cider in the air and wondered exactly how long one could expect to listen to Viola perform.

Viola's voice gave out before Jane's patience.

She was second at the coffee line, behind Hope Collins from the Coffee Shop. "I didn't know you were a book fan," Jane said. "Do you come here often?"

Hope gave a small, ladylike snort. "I do, but it hasn't been easy. I just love romance novels and whodunits and you know how Viola encourages those. It's like pulling teeth to get a book out of this place without a lecture."

"I'm surprised you can always find what you want

here," Jane said mildly. She didn't see Viola and romance novels coexisting in peace.

"Everybody can find the books they want here because of me," Hope said proudly. "Want to know how I did it?"

Jane was definitely curious.

"I told Viola that, if she didn't order the books that I and lots of others liked, I'd go on-line and order them at a discount and sell them at the Coffee Shop. *Hoo-wee*. It didn't take but a couple days and I had everything I wanted. It's worth it to me to pay a little more to buy from Viola. I love having the bookstore here." Hope lowered her voice to a whisper, "Now she orders five of everything I ask for. They're her best-sellers, but she doesn't want that to get out."

Jane held her hand in the air Boy-Scout style. "The secret is safe with me. Scout's promise."

As Hope took her coffee and cookie and headed for the door, Craig Tracy edged up beside Jane. "Nice to see you here," he said.

She noticed the relief in his voice at a completely friendly face and translated Craig's "you" into "another outsider, someone with whom to commiserate." Craig had moved to Acorn Hill some years ago, not nearly long enough to make him an insider with the born-and-raised citizens of the community.

"Selling lots of flowers?" Jane took a sip of coffee.

"Remarkably, yes. Too many funerals at the Presbyterian

church but—to compensate for those—a number of weddings for the Methodists. Grace Chapel has been pretty quiet except for altar flowers. And there's been a rash of new babies born at the hospital in Potterston. They're always good for sales."

Jane liked Craig. He was clear-headed and sensible, and he knew just where he stood with the community—and it didn't bother him a bit. She also enjoyed his artistry with flowers. He was as talented and creative as any florist she had seen elsewhere.

"Can you get me some edible flowers?"

"I can't say I've had a big demand here in Acorn Hill. You're the first to ask actually. What kind do you want?"

"Carnations, daylilies, gardenias and roses. How much do you have to order at a time? If I can only have one or two of them, I'd take carnations and daylilies. I found a curious recipe for carnation vinegar for fruit salad in my mother's cookbook. I'm eager to try it out. And I'm thinking of doing some fancy cakes." She didn't want to mention the teas just yet. "Wouldn't that—and gardenias—be lovely?"

"I'll see what I can do. Since flowers that are specially grown as food can have no pesticides or other chemicals used on them, I'd have to check on availability. Would English daisies or nasturtiums do?" Craig looked at her with undisguised pleasure. "You have no idea how exciting it is to think of doing something creatively different. Sometime, would you allow me in your kitchen when you're decorating a cake?"

"I haven't had a student shadow me in years. I'd like that very much."

Business and pleasure combined and done, Jane moved toward the door but was waylaid by Ethel.

"I'm glad to see you here, Jane, absorbing our local culture. It will be good for you to strengthen your roots here."

Jane had the image of herself as a tree in the Enchanted Forest, wearing a chef's hat and wiggling her root-like toes deep into Acorn Hill's rich earth. "Yes, well . . ."

"But you can't leave yet. Have you said hello to Patsy Ley?" Ethel took Jane's hand and towed her across the room to where the associate pastor's wife was standing, sipping cider.

"Patsy's been working with the Sunday school youth, haven't you, Patsy? And she's done a nice job too. You're particularly good with the younger girls, I hear."

Patsy and Jane simply stared at each other, not having to talk, as there was no way to get a word in edgewise until Ethel sniffed out a more interesting conversation and wandered off.

"Patsy," Jane began, a little unsure how to say what she was thinking. "I met a sweet little girl today, about eight years old, who said she and her mother had just moved to town. I was wondering if . . ."

"I'll bet that you've met Josie," Patsy said with a smile.

"How did you know?"

"She rides her bike around the church parking lot for hours on end. Her mother told her it would be safe there, out of traffic. Poor little thing is there nearly every day while her mother works. It's a hard situation. Henry usually takes his lunch to the church so he can work over the noon hour. I've been packing extra, and he and Josie eat together sometimes."

Jane was touched by their compassion. "Is there anything I can do? She's a remarkably sweet child."

"I'll keep you in mind. Her mother has agreed to put her in our Sunday school and they're both very excited about it. We'll see what comes of that."

As Jane headed toward the refreshment table she heard, "Hi, Jane." It was Fred Humbert's wife Vera. "Quite a social event, huh?" Vera's blue eyes twinkled and her round face broke into a grin. A fifth grade teacher, Vera loved a party and was an all-around good sport. Her class was one of the most popular at school. She planned field trips to everywhere from the fire department to the bakery, where she bought everyone the treat of his or her choice. When the fifth graders were studying Pennsylvania history, she made Fred dress like Benjamin Franklin and give them a speech on the early days of the United States. And when they studied plants and flowers, Craig Tracy always turned up with a bouquet of flowers for the teacher and a lecture for the students on the history and properties of each flower. Spending fifth grade with a teacher other than Vera was a grave disappointment for the students at Acorn Hill School.

"Too bad Fred had to miss it," Jane commented, knowing full well that he was probably relieved to be at a church board meeting instead of being at Viola's. She had watched Ethel scoot out of Nine Lives moments before in order not to miss the entire meeting. Ethel had every confidence that Grace Chapel could not run without her input.

"What did you think of the reading?" Vera inquired.

"Ah . . . interesting. Very interesting."

"You didn't listen either, did you?" Vera said with a grin. "But I do love to watch Viola on stage. She's Ethel Merman and the Marx Brothers rolled into one."

"Bizarre as that image is, I think you could be right."

When another teacher walked up and began to talk standardized testing with Vera, Jane wandered off, right into the path of Wilhelm Wood. Jane and Wilhelm had forged a friendship based on his love of San Francisco and California in general and his appreciation for fine dining. Widely traveled and well-read, Wilhelm was adept and highly practiced at small talk.

"I met some of your guests," he began. Tall and blond, with hair that was thinning and gathering an occasional streak of gray, Wilhelm was an imposing figure. He always appeared to have freshly stepped off a page in the men's section of someone's new fashion catalogue. Even in his so-called "sweats," which were likely purchased on Rodeo Drive in Beverly Hills, he appeared more dressed up than most men in their Sunday church clothes. "Lovely people. How was your afternoon tea?"

"I'm toying with the idea of having it become a regular thing. What do you think?"

"I think that's great. When you get some brochures printed, bring them by the store. I'll give them to my customers. Everyone who comes into my store likes tea."

Brochures? She had not got that far with her planning, but it was a good idea.

An idea occurred to Jane. "If I do this, could I give out your card? What people taste they might want to take home with them."

"Brilliant!" He glanced around the room where several of the die-hards were clustered. The rest of the group appeared to be dispersing. "Want to talk about it on the way home? I'm going to walk around the block just to get a little exercise."

Saying their good-byes on the way out the door, they burst into the crisp night air. They were laughing and chatting as they came to Sylvia Songer's shop. A light was still burning in the window.

"I think I'll just drop off here," she said to Wilhelm.

"Thanks for your company." Jane approached the front door of the shop and knocked on the mullioned windowpane. She could see Sylvia in the workroom at the back of the store, holding swatches of fabric up to the light and then arranging and rearranging them on the huge cutting table in the center of the room. Knocking harder, she called out. "Sylvia! It's me."

Sylvia came out of the back room looking alarmed and patting her head to locate the glasses that were perched in her hair. When she saw who it was, her shoulders and expression visibly relaxed.

She unlocked the front door to let Jane inside.

"You're out late."

"I keep forgetting that nine-thirty is late in Acorn Hill," Jane said with a laugh. "The gathering at Nine Lives just broke up. I was on my way home and saw your light. Besides, you're up 'late' too."

"You won't believe my good luck. A lady from Potterston was here today." An overjoyed smile split Sylvia's usually solemn face. "She had inherited an old house with trunks and trunks filled with scraps of cloth and what she called 'old junk.' Jane, it's the mother lode of antique fabric and clothing. I told her how valuable it was and that she should keep it, but she had no interest whatsoever. She wanted to know if I'd buy the whole lot, which, of course, I did. Come and see."

Visiting Sylvia was a bit like entering an oversized dollhouse. The small rooms had floor-to-ceiling shelves that housed hundreds of bolts of fabric. Then there were floor racks of more fabric, quilting and sewing books and equipment. There was a dizzying jolt of color on every wall. Jane could not help reaching out to finger some of the lustrous satins and buttery soft flannels as she made her way to the workroom.

She gasped when she saw what was spread helter-skelter across Sylvia's worktable. There was enough velvet and lace to make a dozen quilts. The colors of the fabrics—ruby red, brilliant jade, midnight navy, purple—were a pirate's bounty of gem tones. But what excited Jane most was the astonishing collection of vintage garments—stacks of them.

"Can you believe it?" Sylvia said with awe. "I told this woman that she had some very valuable clothing, but she said she wanted to be rid of it all."

Jane picked up a flapper dress with hand-beaded flowers twining across the front. When the fringe shimmered, she noticed that even at the hem, under the fringe, were sparkly black beads.

Sylvia draped the matching scarf across Jane's arm. "This is the real thing, probably worn once or twice. Isn't it fabulous?" She reached into the pile and pulled out another dress. "Look at this one."

It was a cotton dress in splashy colors of green and teal. Silver, gray and blue fish embellished with sequins swam along the hem of the dress. "Amazing," was all Jane could muster.

With a flick of her arm, Sylvia spread the skirt wide. "This is a hundred-and-ninety-inch hem. Can you imagine? Vintage 1950s. Look at the self-covered belt. They were big then." She began burrowing in the pile only to pull out a brocade suit with a mink collar. "Three pieces, all intact. And there's more."

"You could have a fashion show," Jane said. "And open a vintage boutique."

"I have no idea what I'm going to do with this, but right now I feel like a kid in a candy shop." Sylvia looked at Jane shyly, her fair skin a bright pink. "I was hoping you could help me."

"Help you what?" Jane was rubbing her hand over the ribbon weave fabric of an old designer suit.

"Figure out what to do with all this. You're an artist. Ethel talks about your work often."

Jane was fairly certain she did not want to know what Ethel had said. "I've had my phases—oil painting, acrylics, watercolors, pencils, you name it. I sculpted for a while too. The most recent thing I've done is make jewelry."

"Anything with fabric?"

"Collages and a little clothing design, just for the fun of it. I did some vests for a boutique once. That's about it."

"That's it? That's more than I'd expected. Ethel said that you were a very contemporary artist."

"I'll bet." Jane smiled. "To Ethel, anything after Michelangelo borders on contemporary. But I'm a chef now. And chief cook and bottle-washer at the inn that my sisters and I hope to run in the black some day." She sighed. "I've let a lot of the things I love to do slide."

"Then it's time to start again," Sylvia said eagerly. "And what a perfect place to begin."

Jane fingered a piece of jade velvet. "I did take a class in costume design to help out a local theater group. In fact, I designed and sewed all the costumes three years running."

"And?" Sylvia asked.

"And I *loved* it." Jane laughed. "I hadn't had so much fun in years." She looked longingly at the bounty of color spread across Sylvia's shop. Maybe this *was* the diversion she needed. "Oh, all right. I'll help you do . . . what *is* it exactly that you want to do?"

Sylvia clapped her hands together and bounced on the balls of her feet like a girl. "I don't know. But I know we'll create something wonderful."

Jane breathed in Sylvia's excitement. Why not? She could easily work on projects at the inn. Sylvia's shop was just a short jog away, and she needed a friend, one of her own. Her sisters kept telling her that she needed to get out more, that she would stagnate if she buried herself at the inn both day and night. As she had found in the past, the more creative she was in another part of her life, the more creative she became in the kitchen.

"When do we get started?"

Sylvia looked helplessly about the room. "As soon as possible."

"As I said before, I'll be over tomorrow evening to help you unpack your new shipment of fabrics for the store and make more room for this stuff. We can talk as we work." Sylvia's beaming face told Jane all she needed to know. It was the right thing to do, Jane thought, even though it made little sense in the current scheme of things. When things didn't make sense in her life, she remembered Alice, so wise compared to her, who would say, "It's God talking. Just listen."

Well, she was listening now. Somehow she suspected He had a hand in this. It really felt as though here, in Acorn Hill, God was more active and more obviously present. Or perhaps, it was that she had finally started to listen for Him.

Her mind whirling with thoughts of God's prodding and Sylvia's projects, Jane walked toward home but found herself not at the front door of the inn but rather at the pathway to Grace Chapel. She glanced at the inn. There were no new cars in the driveway, and light was beaming from all the first floor windows. It would not hurt to go inside, just for a minute.

The moment she walked inside, a feeling of restfulness descended upon her, a knowledge that, no matter how far she traveled, this building signified home. Her faith, her father, her family were all part of the very atmosphere of this place. The interior was cool, as it always seemed to be when the chapel was empty. The life of the place was the fellowship of its people and the worship that they offered. She walked to the front of the church, taking in every carved and painted detail as she went.

The walls were a creamy white but always seemed to glow a hazy pink, perhaps reflecting the rich red carpeting of the aisle and the altar area. The wood was old with a patina so warm and rich that it begged to be stroked.

She ran her hand gently across the top of a pew, then sat down and stared at the front of the church. Memories came flooding back. Her father, in the pulpit, weaving one of his marvelous sermons, somehow drawing in the congregation with an anecdote of his growing-up years on the farm, and, before he was done, convincing them in his simple way that proof was everywhere of God's love and the saving grace of Jesus. Jane had always marveled at that. Her father saw God and His grace everywhere—in the birth of a calf, the ripening of the harvest, the lowly chicken that laid its egg, and, most of all, in people. As a child, she had loved the stories, and as she had matured, she had recognized the profundity of their message. An ache gripped her heart. Daddy gone. A mother she had never known. A failed marriage. A life she would not return to. At fifty she felt little different from the way she had at eighteen, searching for a way when it all seemed so hard.

Curiously, as she sat there, her heart lightened. Flashes of the inn kept intruding. She, Louise and Alice working amicably together. Madeleine's cookbook. Ethel's story about being the White Rabbit. The afternoon tea.

Life *was* hard, but there was so much to be thankful for in it. Jane felt a sense of relief spread over her. This part of her life was just another beginning. She had recreated herself before. Here was the *opportunity* to do it again.

A tiny scraping sound at the rear of the church caught her attention as the hairs rose on the back of her neck. It had not occurred to her that she might not be alone. Her father had always insisted that the chapel be left unlocked. "If people need a church, then they're welcome here. Where will they go if we send them away? 'For the Lord your God is gracious and merciful, and will not turn his face away from you, if you return to Him' (II Chronicles 30:9, RSV). He is our example."

She glanced behind her into the shadowy darkness and wished she had flipped on a light other than the one controlling the dim sconces on either side of the altar. Nothing.

She turned back to face the altar but could not shed the feeling that she was not the only person present. Slowly, she turned back again and stared into the darkness. The pews appeared vacant. Then she heard it again.

Setting her jaw, berating herself for being so silly as to come into any empty building alone, even if it was in Acorn Hill, and reminding herself that she should be far more street-smart, she stood up. Cautiously, she walked toward the back of the church.

She was almost upon him before she saw the slender, dark-haired figure in the last pew. He was bent in prayer, his eyes closed, his head bowed. She noticed his lips moving and a slight swaying in his body as he prayed. It was the same elusive man that she had seen in her shrubbery. Ready to solve the mystery surrounding him, Jane opened her mouth to speak, but stopped herself. He was obviously talking to the One he needed to talk to. Quietly, she walked to the door and slipped through it.

Chapter Five

There was a new car in the driveway, Jane noticed, as she approached the house. When she entered the foyer, she found Alice and the owner of the vehicle.

"Jane, this is Naomi Hopper."

Thin and nervous, Naomi could barely unclench her hand enough to shake Jane's outstretched one. Her fingers felt cold and stiff, as though they had recently been submerged in ice water. Her lips, pinched and colorless, only added to Jane's notion that she was partially frozen and needed some serious warming.

"Hello, we're happy to have you with us, Miss Hopper."

"*Ms.* Hopper," the woman said quickly.

Jane gave the uneasy woman a broad smile. Their new guest was obviously extremely tense. Jane hoped that a stay at the inn would relieve some of her stress.

"Ms. Hopper has come from Minnesota. She isn't sure how long she's staying, but I assured her that we don't have her room booked again for some time." Alice sounded pleased. If this guest stayed, there would be more money in the coffers to help pay the bills. Alice yawned delicately, shielding her mouth so that their guest would not see. Jane, however, didn't miss it.

"Why don't you go to bed, Alice? Let me show our guest to her room."

"Oh, that's not necessary." Alice looked weary. It couldn't be easy working at the hospital, doing all the volunteer work she did, and still putting in hours at the inn.

"Shoo, Alice. I'm going to have a cup of tea and I'd like to invite Ms. Hopper to join me." She turned to the woman. "What do you think?"

"Actually," the woman took a deep breath and sighed a sigh that sounded as though it had come from the soles of her feet, "I would absolutely love a cup of tea."

"See?" Jane made a scooting motion with her hand. "Go to bed, Alice. Sleep well."

"If it's not too much bother, that is." Ms. Hopper made the statement sound like a question.

"Not a bit. Especially if you're willing to have it with me in the kitchen." This poor woman needed the relaxed atmosphere that Jane's special domain would provide.

"That would be perfect."

Jane led the way, switching on the overhead light as she entered the kitchen. A wave of satisfaction flowed over her as she looked around. Granted, it was not the kitchen she had left behind at the Blue Fish Grille, but Jane had managed to make it her own. Her block of surgically sharp knives on the polished counter, a peg board on the wall containing her collection of cooking tools, and in the tall, glass-paned cabinets an array of Madeleine's china made it an imposing work area. But the pièce de résistance was Madeleine's enormous wooden chopping block dominating the middle of the room. Jane had sanded the old giant until her hands were raw, and it was in first-rate condition. Her father did not cook anything that required a lot of chopping and so had used it for a stand for his microwave. When she had first arrived, she had not even realized what was beneath its red and white checked tablecloth. As she had sanded, she had run her hands over every gouge and scratch, imagining her mother cooking for her family.

"Oh," Ms. Hopper breathed, "how lovely."

Jane filled the stainless steel kettle and put it on the burner to heat. Then she took out a teapot, filled it with hot water from the tap, and set it on a tray with two cups and saucers.

"A professional chef?" Ms. Hopper asked.

Jane, holding a sugar bowl filled with sugar cubes, nodded. "Yes. By the way, may I call you Naomi?"

"By all means. I should have said that immediately. I guess I was just a little . . . overwhelmed . . . when I arrived. I'd been driving all day and then, to find myself at this lovely place ..." She struggled to collect her thoughts. "Tell me about being a chef."

"Sure. Although it's not all that interesting. It's mostly about chopping, slicing, dicing, sautéing and cleaning up. Would you like something to eat? I have a few things left from tea."

There were the truffles and plenty of brownies and toffee bars. When Jane turned off the ceiling light and they were seated across from each other at the kitchen table, the warm glow of Jane's ceramic chef lamp, a roly-poly chef in a white uniform wearing a tall hat and carrying a tray of entrées, lit the room. Justin had given it to her; it tickled Jane's fancy. All the years she had shared with Justin had not been bad ones. Jane leaned back in her chair. "Actually, my first love was art, which I've managed to incorporate into my profession. When I graduated from high school with a scholarship to art school, I left Acorn Hill and moved to San Francisco. I started cooking to make money during school and then apprenticed with a pastry chef for a year. Later, I went to a small but wonderful culinary program in the heart of San Francisco. It was relatively easy after that. The last few years out West I worked in two incredible restaurants." As they sat together, she noticed that Naomi's face had grown less stony and that her shoulders had relaxed. Jane felt her heart inexplicably aching for this stranger she knew nothing about. "How about you?" she ventured.

For a moment Jane thought she had asked too much. Stricken, Naomi looked as though she wanted to pull up a drawbridge and retreat. "I'm nothing much, really. No particular talents, although I do like cooking. I spent many years working in bookstores and libraries. I suppose you'd say my specialty is reading. There's not much call for that in the job market these days."

"So you're looking for a job?"

"Yes," she sighed.

Jane moved the silver tray of sweets toward Naomi. "Have a truffle. There's nothing like a good dose of chocolate to clear the mind."

Naomi smiled. "Is that medical advice?"

"From a chocoholic it is. Try one."

Naomi bit into the truffle and her eyes floated closed. "Oh my. I feel my brain clearing already."

"It's my mother's recipe."

"Your mother is still living?" Naomi asked hesitantly.

"No. In fact, I never knew her."

"I'm sorry." Naomi appeared completely genuine. "What was her name?"

Surprised but not offended, Jane answered, "Madeleine."

"How pretty." She picked up another truffle and held it in the palm of her hand. "Truffles by Madeleine."

"So tell me more about this job hunt of yours," Jane was relieved to see some color return to Naomi's cheeks.

"What can a fifty-four-year-old woman with no college education, no special training and very little savvy find to do in this fast-paced world?" Naomi sounded lost. "I feel like a chick pushed out of its nest. I'm not sure I'm ready to survive on my own."

Jane's antenna perked up. "*Pushed* out of the nest?" She'd had some experience with that herself.

Naomi began to nervously flatten the gold foil from the truffle and re-pleat it again. "My husband left me. I tried everything I knew how to do to get him to come home, but he wouldn't even listen to me. Now he says it would be a 'good idea' if I found somewhere else to live. He wants to sell the house and divide the money between us so that we can be 'completely through' with each other." A tear spilled onto her cheek. "I'm not ready to be 'through' with anything."

Jane felt the piercing in her own heart; she also experienced a brief sense of gratitude. Though Justin had left her, it was she who made the decision to put her life in San Francisco on hold and to return to Acorn Hill.

Not knowing what else to do, Jane poured more tea. Muriel Fairchild was right. They *should* serve regular teas at the inn. Tea, chocolate and conversation made a sweetly medicinal balm for the troubled soul.

"I didn't mean to unload on you. You have no idea who I am, and you must have hundreds of guests who pass through this wonderful place. Please accept my apology."

Hundreds of guests? I wish!

"I've been driving for the past three days, in circles mostly, and haven't talked to anyone. It just spilled out. I know you have no idea what I'm talking about, but there's something about you that makes me believe I can trust you."

Jane took her hand and held it, saying nothing, weighing words in her own mind. "Actually I do know what you're talking about," Jane said quietly. "All too well. My marriage recently ended." Perhaps God's hand guided Naomi to their doorstep.

"I'm sorry. Now I've brought up your painful memories too." Naomi's face was suffused with misery. "Why can't I just keep my big mouth shut?"

Jane gently squeezed her hand. "You're being harder on yourself than anyone else could ever be. And it's okay. I'm coming to terms with what happened between Justin and me, just as someday you will regarding your husband."

"I don't see how that's possible." Naomi's voice was forlorn.

"I didn't either," Jane admitted, "but it's happening. Slowly, to be sure, but happening." And, as she said it, she knew it was true.

"What happened?" Naomi's voice was so soft that Jane could barely hear it. "Never mind, it's absolutely none of my business. Forgive me."

"Justin is also a chef. A very good one. He's worked for several years at an exclusive place and garnered an excellent reputation as an all-around reliable man to have on staff. His restaurant regularly gets written up for its good food. Two years ago I began to work at the same establishment."

"And that was the problem?"

"Yes and no. I'm more of an innovator than Justin. I like to experiment with flavors and textures. I enjoy creating new presentations for meals. I suppose that's the artist coming out in me. Anyway, the reviewers went wild for a while, saying how the restaurant had somehow gotten a 'pick-me-up' and that the food was better than ever. Justin never said anything, and everyone assumed that he had been the instigator of the new ideas, so I just let it ride. Then I got an offer to go to a new restaurant, something more cutting edge, and I jumped at the chance. I thought it would be better for our marriage if I was out of his way."

Jane refilled her teacup and dropped in two cubes of sugar. Why was she telling all this? Maybe it was the vibration of understanding pulsing between them or the ready compassion in Naomi's pale blue eyes.

"And that didn't work?" Naomi asked softly.

"Not the way I expected it to." Jane shook her head in wonderment, even now. "The place took off. It became the hottest eatery around. People were waiting weeks, even months, to get a reservation. We added an extra early seating for dinner just to accommodate some of the rush. In fact, for an enormous price—which, unbelievably, customers were willing to pay—they could eat in the kitchen and watch me and my staff prepare meals. We answered questions, chatted and made jokes as we worked." Jane chuckled. "That propelled us to work even harder. We didn't want anyone going out and saying our foods were less than fresh or the kitchen untidy."

"Oh my."

"My employer is—was—a trendsetter. Young, ambitious, bold—and completely willing to let me do anything I wanted in the kitchen. I suppose I was tired of Justin's rules and ways, so being out from under that, I let loose. I tried every fun and funky thing I'd ever conceived of. Our specialties included a bison prime rib with a citrus glaze and horseradish mashed potatoes. I garnished main dishes with edible flowers. We painted pictures in vanilla, chocolate and raspberry sauce on dessert plates. I hired one young aspiring artist, a college student, to do only that. Every plate brought to a table would be different, roses on one, balloons another.

"Of course, the food was fabulous even without the extra bits, always the freshest the buyer could find. If anyone complained even slightly, the meal would be on the house and everyone at the table would get free desserts. The décor was eclectic and very hip, the music was always excellent—musicians between gigs from the show-business scene. It was a fun place for everyone from customers to staff."

"How wonderful for you." Naomi tentatively reached for another truffle. "Or was it?"

"That's where the 'yes and no' comes in. I was having the time of my life. They paid me well and let me have my way in the kitchen without question. The reviewers loved us. I got more press in that brief time than I'd had in my earlier career."

Jane stared into the bottom of her teacup, noticing that a few tiny flakes of tea had escaped into the cup despite the strainer. "And Justin hated every moment of it."

Understanding dawned in Naomi's eyes. "He was *jealous.*"

"It ate at him like a cancer. He couldn't get it out of his mind that his wife got more attention than he did." It had been ugly. Jane shook her head sadly. "Nine years of marriage and I *never expected that.*"

"What happened?" This time it was Naomi who got up and turned up the heat under the kettle.

"Nothing, at first." This was the first time Jane had told anyone the entire story, and now that she had begun, she did not seem to have the will to stop. "Then it started to get to him. Friends and peers of Justin's were commenting on my success. I'm sure none of them ever dreamed how deeply and fiercely this affected him. Every friendly jibe about Justin's having to 'keep up,' or congratulations about his 'talented wife' was another hack at the cords that held our marriage together."

"So you left him?"

"Oh no. I had no idea what was going on in his head. If he'd talked to me, even once, I would have gladly done what I could to save my marriage. Working at the Blue Fish Grille and doing all those creative things was a lark for me. I knew I'd burn out sooner or later. If Justin had even hinted that my work was hurting our marriage, I would have quit. Nine years of marriage was worth more to me than some newspaper reviews. But he never said a thing. He just withdrew. I attributed that to his busy schedule. He hadn't hired another chef after I left, and I assumed he was taking the brunt of the load himself."

Jane raked her fingers through her hair and then gathered it so tightly it pulled at her scalp. She hated the helpless feeling that telling her story stirred up in her, but there was a catharsis too.

"What he was really doing was seething with anger and resentment that I was getting all the great reviews. He took it as a personal affront. Odd, because no one ever said a bad thing about his restaurant. It wasn't until I discovered that he'd been calling reviewers to 'thank them' for their reviews of his restaurant and mentioning that *he* was the one suggesting those innovative ideas to me, that I really knew anything was wrong."

"How awful," Naomi murmured. "He betrayed you."

Jane nodded. "After that, story after story began to surface about things he'd said or ideas for which he'd taken credit. I discovered that to hear him tell it, I was nothing more than a trained monkey in a chef's hat, doing *his* bidding. Finally, people began to wonder why, if he was so creative for *my* restaurant, he wasn't implementing some of that in his own. When his boss called him on it, he had to admit that he'd had nothing to do with my success. He barely escaped losing his job and was told that if he *ever* pulled another stunt like that he could leave."

"Serves him right," Naomi said, indignantly.

"Of course it did, but he blamed me for 'nearly ruining' his career. He never took responsibility for his own actions or apologized to anyone—not even me. Not that I wanted an apology—what I wanted was time to talk things out, to repair the damage, maybe to apologize to *him* for not knowing him better. But he didn't give me the chance. He just walked out and left me."

"No wonder you came back here," Naomi said.

"It breaks my heart to think about it, but he's no longer the man I married. Maybe there is some truth to 'male midlife crisis.' Something in Justin certainly snapped." Saying it out loud made Jane realize how true it was. There were two Justins—then and now. Somehow this made it easier for her to understand what had happened.

It was Naomi's turn to take Jane's hand. "Thank you for sharing that. I'm sorry about your loss, but I'm ashamed to admit that somehow I no longer feel so alone."

"Don't worry about it. Frankly, I feel lighter than I have in ages. It reminds me that I was pretty much an innocent in what happened. I didn't set out to make him feel underappreciated, insignificant or worthless. I thought he'd be proud of me and happy for what my new position could provide for us financially. Was I wrong!"

"And here you are, running the most lovely bed and breakfast I've ever seen, taking in strays like me and making them feel almost human again. Bless you." Naomi's eyes welled with tears. "Bless you."

After she had shown Naomi to her room, Jane returned

to the kitchen. She filled Wendell's water bowl and gave him his nightly treat before pulling out the ledger in which they kept their financial records. She sat down at the table, curled her legs beneath her and stared at the pages. There was a new entry, one that hadn't been there the day before. She recognized Alice's handwriting and saw the transfer slip from Alice's checking account to that of the inn. Jane's shoulders sagged. Her sister had moved the lion's share of her paycheck from her own account into the business.

No wonder Alice had announced earlier that she was "simply out of the mood" to go on a four-day weekend she had planned with friends. She had used the money to shore up the inn instead. Jane was more than willing to take on most of the work, but Alice and Louise had been footing too many of the bills—and saying too little about it. The inn needed to be more profitable. She thought back to what she had told Naomi about letting her creativity loose and just seeing what happened. Maybe she was going to have to do that again.

At three in the morning, it occurred to Jane that she had made a mistake dredging up all those things about Justin and by looking into the inn's ledger just before bedtime. The inn was still holding its own financially, although she was eventually going to need some income other than what the inn could pay her, which was, to date, nothing. Granted, she had no personal room or board expenses, but she wasn't willing to go forever without subscriptions to gourmet magazines, pricey saffron for the kitchen or the silver and crystal she used in making jewelry.

She squeezed her eyes tightly shut and tried to block out the notion that she was never, ever, going back. San Francisco was, to her mind, the most beautiful city in the world. She was not the kind of woman to run from conflict or difficulty, but something had called her here to Acorn Hill. She had experienced a sense of being *led* to this place. "That's God talking," her father would have said. And she believed it was true. His presence felt very strong these days, as if breaking loose from her life in California had opened a space for Him to enter. But sorting it all out was daunting—not to mention exhausting—at 3:00 A.M.

When she finally slept, she dreamed of Justin pointing a finger at her as she walked along the piers of San Francisco. He wagged it at her and said, "Go away. This is my town now." If Justin disappeared from her midnight imaginings, then the inn would present itself, calling out like a living thing, for paint, for new gardens, for ongoing repairs, just like a demanding child. Jane awoke. Deciding that she would not be intimidated by either a mean-spirited man or a vocal house, she sat up and snapped on the light.

In years past, she might have picked up a sketchbook and done some drawings until her eyelids grew heavy again, but now that held little appeal. Something inside her had broken when she had discovered Justin's disloyalty, and now the idea of sketching seemed more work than fun. Had she allowed him to take that away from her, too? Jane slid beneath the covers up to her nose and berated herself for bringing up the subject with Naomi.

I should have known better. It wouldn't have mattered to her if I hadn't told her about me. But she seemed so sad and alone. I couldn't let her sit there and think I didn't understand. Father would have sat there all night if he'd thought it would help. He was close to You, Lord, so he knew what was pleasing in Your sight. It didn't really take all that much on my part to settle her down—

With a start, Jane realized she was praying. *Lord, what am I supposed to do? I don't believe in divorce but Justin would have to meet me in the middle on this, and he's already told me that won't happen. Besides, Louise and Alice need me here. Neither one actually knows how to run a business—or cook much more than the basics. And there's such a strong feeling of Mother and Father here. I'm searching, Lord, but I have no idea what it is I should find.* Jane yawned and reached up to turn out the light. *Maybe I'll just let You figure it out. . . .* And within moments of saying that, she was sound asleep.

In the kitchen a few hours later, Jane had been surprised to hear footsteps on the stairs before eight o'clock. Muriel and George had already left very early to go bird watching with a take-out breakfast Jane had packed the night before. The other guests must be early risers as well. She finished making coffee and mixed the batter for chocolate waffles. Quickly, she plugged in the Belgian waffle-maker and began to whip egg whites to fold into the batter.

Chocolate Waffles

MAKES SIX WAFFLES

2½ cups flour
1½ teaspoons baking soda
¾ teaspoon baking powder
¼ teaspoon salt
2 cups buttermilk, room temperature
4 eggs
3 tablespoons butter, melted and cooled
4 ounces(4 squares) semisweet chocolate, melted and cooled

Combine flour, baking soda, baking powder and salt. Set aside. Preheat Belgian waffle iron. Pour buttermilk into a medium bowl. Separate eggs, blending yolks into buttermilk. Place whites in a medium bowl. Set aside. Add butter and chocolate to buttermilk mixture; mix well. Add flour mixture to buttermilk mixture, stirring until blended (will be thick). Beat egg whites with electric mixer on high speed until stiff peaks form. Fold egg whites into batter with a rubber spatula. Pour three-quarters cup batter onto center of hot iron for each waffle. Bake four to five minutes or until evenly browned. Serve immediately with maple syrup or whipped cream and raspberries.

"Everyone is up early today." Jane said as she entered the dining room with a pot of coffee in one hand and a plate of fruit in the other. She felt as if she were intruding on the newlyweds, who had their eyes locked together in a melting gaze.

Naomi, too, appeared embarrassed at the emotion glowing around the pair, but her color was better this morning. She didn't look quite so much like a deer in headlights as she had last night, though the deep furrow between her eyebrows had barely lessened. It was written on her face that her heart was broken.

Alice appeared in the doorway looking crisp and professional in a white nurse's uniform. Louise, not far behind, wore her own skirt-and-sweater-with-pearls uniform.

"These are fabulous," Tim announced.

From the corner of her eye Jane observed Naomi make a grand show of eating by moving food around on her plate but rarely taking a forkful to her mouth. She was uneasy about the drawn, almost haunted look in the woman's eyes, but had no idea what to do about it. Be kind to her, Jane decided, that was all there was to be done right now.

"How long are you staying?" Theresa asked Naomi after the waffles, whipped cream and raspberries were gone.

"I . . . I'm not quite sure yet. Maybe as long as they'll have me."

Alice looked up from clearing the table, her eyes sparkling about anticipated income. At this point she would consider a more permanent guest or renter just to make sure the bills were paid on time. Jane knew that one of her sister's strongest values was reliability. Steady-as-she-goes Alice always did what she had said she would. Being late with bills did not sit well with her.

Jane was glad that Naomi might stay. She liked the quiet woman with the sad eyes. God had put Naomi and Grace Chapel Inn together for a reason.

As they rose from the table, Naomi faltered. Tim reached out to her to keep her from falling. Clutching the back of her chair with one hand to steady herself, Naomi swept a lock of hair from her eyes with the other. "How silly of me! I must have slipped. Thank you, Tim."

"Are you all right?" The young man ignored Naomi's unconvincing explanation. "Were you dizzy?"

"Oh, maybe a little. Excited, I suppose. I'm not accustomed to being treated like a queen as I am here. But I'll get used to it, don't you worry."

None of them believed a word of it, Jane realized, but because Naomi was so adamant about feeling fine, they carried on as if nothing were wrong.

"What are you up to now?" Louise walked into the butler's pantry just as Jane pushed a stool toward the high cupboards.

Jane turned around and put her hands on her hips. "Do you know that's exactly what you used to say to me when we were young? 'What are you up to now?' 'What have you done now?' and, my all time favorite, 'What are you thinking about? Daddy won't like it.'"

"We were a bit overprotective, I suppose. Alice and I both thought we had to be mother hens with . . . circumstances as they were."

"Oh, Louise, I know it was difficult for you, too. But all I wanted from you and Alice was to be my big sisters."

"But what *are* you looking for in the cupboard?"

"We were pretty hasty when we retrieved those teapots. I wanted to see if we'd missed anything." Jane mounted the step stool.

"Don't fall—" Louise caught herself. "I just did it again, didn't I?"

Jane's laughter floated down from the ceiling. "Actually, since you caught yourself, I'll admit that I'm glad you don't want me falling."

"Indeed," Louise said dryly. "We'd have a much harder time getting repeat business if either Alice or I had to cook."

As Jane turned to smile down at Louise, a glint of porcelain shoved far back in the cupboard caught her eye. Standing on her tiptoes, she reached to pull it out but hesitated at the sound of rattling pottery. "Louise, get me something higher to stand on, will you?"

"I thought you said you did not want to fall." Louise had perched her glasses on her nose and was looking up at Jane.

"*Louise!*"

"Oh, all right. Fortunately, Alice is working today. She can check you into the hospital when you arrive." Louise left for the kitchen and returned with the high stool on which Jane usually sat to peel potatoes.

"Perfect. Slide it in next to me." Jane stepped onto the higher surface.

"Limber as a monkey," Louise commented. "How do you manage? You behave like a woman half your age."

"Running, weight-resistance training, all the things you haven't seen me do much since arriving here. As soon as I get a moment to myself, I'm going to start exercising again. What on earth?" Jane's fingers reached a smooth round ball with what felt like little stems on it. She grabbed it and withdrew it from the cupboard.

"Our teapot!" Louise was thrilled. "I thought that had been discarded years ago."

Jane stared at the miniature porcelain pot. It was no more than six inches high and equally wide. It was white, with tiny pink rosebuds decorating the sides, and it looked exactly like one of the big teapots Jane had unearthed earlier.

"It had a lid. Is it up there still? And the cups?" Louise was obviously delighted by the discovery.

"Just beyond my reach, I think. If I stand on my tip-toes . . ." One by one, Jane was able to withdraw an entire tea set, six tiny cups and saucers, six slightly larger dessert plates and even a minuscule creamer and sugar bowl. When—unassisted—she scrambled down from her perch, Louise was already setting up the tiny set.

"Thanks for protecting me on the way down, Louise."

"Now, now, Jane, first things first. What memories this brings back. I'd completely forgotten this existed until just now."

"I don't remember it at all," Jane ventured.

"No, you wouldn't. Alice and I quit having tea parties after Mother died. She was the one who loved them so, and after she was gone, well, it just didn't seem the same. I can hardly wait for Alice to see this."

Again, Jane was struck by the disconnect she shared with her sisters. Their lives were broken into two parts, Before Mother and After Mother.

Louise, engrossed in her own memories, suddenly gave a gasp. "I have forgotten the time. I promised Pastor Ken that I'd go over some music with him for church. I am going to be late."

"Run along," Jane said. "There's nothing much to do here right now anyway."

"I will make up the beds when I get back," Louise promised as she singled out a stack of music on the table and tucked it into the crook of her arm.

After Louise had departed, Jane studied the tea set intently, imagining how it must have been to be a child attending one of her mother's fanciful teas. She carried the set to the kitchen and gently washed it in sudsy water and dried it with a soft towel. The porcelain glinted in the sunlight.

Impulsively, Jane picked up the phone and dialed the number she had added to the bottom of the list that hung on the wall.

"Hello, Josie? This is Jane. I was wondering if you'd like to come for tea."

With the deed done and the hour set, Jane felt a little foolish. What had inspired her to invite an eight-year-old girl to join her? What would the child think? Or her own sisters, for that matter? But then Jane reconsidered. Josie was home alone every day while her mother worked. Ever since she had seen the child, she had wanted to do something to help without appearing intrusive. Besides, they would have fun. And what better reason was there for an invitation than that?

"This is *cool!*" Josie sat across from Jane as they "took tea" in the parlor. Her big straw hat was slipping off the back of her head, and the dress they had found in the attic and put on over her T-shirt and shorts was sliding tipsily off one shoulder, but Josie was determined to remain poised in her costume. The child determinedly kept her pinky finger in the air as she managed her teacup.

Josie used four spoonfuls of sugar before she was satisfied with the taste of the tea that had been deliberately made on the weak side. Jane was glad Wilhelm wasn't here to see what she had done to his favorite Earl Grey. It had taken Jane twice as long to figure out what both might wear for the party than it had to put together a few appropriate treats—peanut butter and banana slices on crustless bread, strawberry jam on crackers, and cookies from the cookie jar she kept out for guests. She had settled on a lime green straw hat with a gigantic brim and a neon yellow sundress that she had bought on impulse at a consignment shop near Beverly Hills.

"Can we do this again?" Josie asked hopefully. "Maybe my mom could come too?"

"I think that could be arranged." Jane held a teapot in her hand. "More?"

"My mom never gets to go to a party," Josie confided. "She said she used to, but not any more."

"Why not?" Jane asked carefully. She didn't want to pump the child for information, but Josie had piqued her curiosity.

"She only works now. She says times for parties are past." Josie pondered that statement. "But if they're past, how come *we're* having one?"

"Maybe she feels that *she* can't go to parties because when she isn't working she needs to rest."

Josie wrinkled her nose. "It's no fun." Then she gave a sigh that seemed to originate deep within her. "I wish my mom could go to a party, too." Jane watched, fascinated, the play of emotions that flitted over the little girl's face. "But," Josie finally concluded, "the only way she'd go to a party any more is if she could work there too."

It was upsetting to see the disappointment on the child's face and hear the resignation in her voice.

"Tell me more about your mom," Jane encouraged. "Something fun."

A grin swept over Josie's face. "She's silly. When I cry, she goes to the cupboard and gets our jar of tears."

"A jar of tears?"

"Yeah. She collects my tears in her jar, even though the jar is always empty. She says she might need something salty one day."

"What happens when she gathers your tears?" Jane asked.

"I giggle. It's *funny*. It's no fair either. I never get to cry very long before Mom makes me laugh again."

Jane's heart was touched.

"And when we run out of groceries before payday, we make 'silly soup.'"

"What's that?"

"We look in the refrigerator and the cupboard, and use whatever we have that would go into a soup. Mom lets me mix it up. My favorite is tomato sauce, rice and broccoli. Sometimes we have leftover chicken or beans too. Once we made it with boiled potatoes, milk and tuna fish. One time it wasn't very good, though."

"What was that?" The idea of mother and daughter concocting a ridiculous soup to make even poverty fun, gripped at Jane's heart.

"Bouillon cubes, pork and beans and a tomato." Josie wrinkled her nose again. "Too watery." She leaned back in her chair and smiled happily. "My mom is cool."

"Yes, I think you're right. Your mom is *way* cool."

Josie giggled. Then she fell silent, as if pondering some deep question. "Why do you get to have parties all the time?"

The question took Jane by surprise. She *did* have parties all the time. First the restaurants, now the tea parties—how had she missed that delightful bit about her own life?

"I'm very lucky, Josie. What I do for a living is *make* parties."

Josie looked longingly at Jane. "I wish my mom could work for you."

After Josie left, Jane decided to walk to Grace Chapel. If Louise was playing, then she would listen for a while. As formal as Louise could be, she played with a vitality and dynamism that was irresistible.

It was interesting to note, Jane thought, as she walked the path to the church, that each of the Howard girls had a God-given gift quite unlike the others. There was Louise with her music, herself with her art and cooking, and Alice with her ability to heal spiritually and physically. She was sure that both Louise and Alice had maximized their gifts and shared them with the world. She wasn't so sure about herself, however. What more could she give? This time she was going to leave the answer to God.

The church organ was silent. The empty nave glowed like a jewel, colored by the light that passed through the stained-glass windows. She walked purposefully to her favorite window and sat down so that the light, as it filtered through the colored glass, dappled her legs and arms with color. It was the depiction of Christ the Shepherd cradling a tiny lamb in one arm. *The Lord is my Shepherd, I shall not want. He makes me to lie down in green pastures. He leads me beside still waters; He restores my soul. . . . Even though I walk through the valley of the shadow of death, I will fear no evil. For thou art with me; thy rod and thy staff, they comfort me. . . . Surely goodness and mercy will follow me all the days of my life* (Psalm 23, RSV).

She could practically hear her father's strong, confident voice. *Have faith in Him, Jane. He'll take you where you need to go. Even though it may seem dark and frightening, He is beside you.*

"Then where were You when Justin and I fell apart?" she

murmured. But then she admitted that she had thought less and less about God during that hectic, exhilarating phase of her life with Justin—the gallery openings, the restaurants, the delighted food critics, the glory before the collapse. It occurred to her that God *was* there; she just hadn't noticed. She shook her head. Here she was making excuses for God when she had no excuse for herself.

God never moves away from us, Jane, but we do move away from Him. Her father's words and memory were so near in this building.

"Jane?"

She looked up to see Pastor Thompson, his handsome face creased with concern.

"Hi." She was pleased when he sat down in the pew in front of her and rested his arm on the back to face her.

"Anything I can do?"

"You're doing it." She felt no urge to say more, and he demanded no explanation. They had rapidly built a comfortable friendship. Quick, witty, intelligent and straightforward, they had fallen into a relaxed camaraderie that had little to do with age or gender. It was more of a matching of souls.

Finally she spoke. "I came looking for Louise. I thought I might catch her playing the organ."

"You just missed her. She was going to stop at Nine Lives to say hello to Viola before going home."

"Ah. The mystery is solved." She felt a languorous sense of comfort as she warmed herself in the sunlight through the windows.

"Is everything all right? If I'm overstepping my bounds, please tell me straight out and I'll remove my 'pastoral hat.' There are times I simply want to sit here, too. I usually choose the window depicting the baby Jesus in the manger. I think of what went before. Mary, pregnant, probably in labor, riding a donkey all day, finding nowhere to rest once they stopped for the night. Joseph, scared silly by what he'd undertaken—a woman, nine months pregnant, who insisted she was carrying the child of God. When things seem too much, it reminds me that with God you can have peace in even the most difficult circumstances."

Jane stretched her arms and legs, grateful for his gentle reminder of her blessings. "Next time I'll try out the baby Jesus window."

When Pastor Thompson smiled in response and moved to stand, she put her hand on his arm. "You don't have to go. Unless you don't have time to stop and rest, that is. It's good to talk with you. It reminds me of the conversations I used to have with my father. His favorite window was that of the Ascension. 'Such hope,' he'd say. 'I can hardly wait to follow Him.'" She looked at the minister. "I suppose that's why it's easy not to mourn my father. He's living his dream-come-true."

"And what are you living?"

"Not my dream-come-true yet, but I've realized lately that I'm not living a nightmare any longer either." Encouraged by his silence, she continued. "God is easier to find here. Things seem simpler, less confusing. I wonder if the bright lights of the big city blinded me to what is really important. I didn't know how far I'd strayed spiritually until I came back here." She paused, gathering her thoughts. "Granted, there's a lot that needs change. I had my priorities out of order for a while. I had put God somewhere in the middle of the list, after Justin and the restaurants. Working so late on Saturday nights became my reason for skipping church on Sunday. It wouldn't have been impossible to find a service at another time, but I didn't do that often." She sighed. "Do you think God can forgive someone who's put Him 'on hold'?"

"Have you read the Old Testament lately? He allowed his children to wander forty years in the wilderness."

"Well, I haven't quite had my forty years, but it seems like it." She smiled at him fondly. "Thanks for reminding me."

"By the way," Pastor Thompson said as he stood up. "I did some research for you on that fellow, the one in your rosebush."

"And?"

"His name is Jose Morales. He likes to be called 'Joe.' Joe has been doing some work on a dairy farm not far from here. He admitted to me that many nights he sleeps on a couch in the office attached to the barn and often has to use a garden hose to bathe. I don't think his employer realizes that he's homeless. Joe offers to stay there as 'night watchman.' Weekends he walks or catches a ride into Acorn Hill to make it appear that he actually has a home to go to."

Jane unconsciously put her hand to her heart. "What a proud man he must be—and how sad."

"I caught up with him here one day. He comes to pray. I think he's spent a night or two sleeping in a pew. My guess is that he makes his rounds among us—the Methodists, the Presbyterians and the bus station, sleeping a night here and a night there. He's also been seen at the truck stop outside of town. They have showers there."

"What are we going to do about it?" she asked, surprised that she had said "we" instead of "you."

"I've been thinking about talking to the pastors of the other churches, but if one of them is unhappy with the situation I'm afraid Joe will lose a sleep station."

"Is there a room somewhere? It wouldn't have to be much bigger than a closet to be better than what he's got."

Pastor Thompson raked his fingers through his perfectly groomed hair, and Jane realized how much this plight of Joe's was upsetting him. "I've been working that question into all my conversations lately. 'Any place someone could rent a room?' 'Anything?' And so far, nothing."

"It really feels awful to know there's usually an open guest room at the inn, and I can't offer him a place to sleep. But we do need to keep the rooms open for guests." Jane chewed on her lower lip. "There's got to be a way. Let me think about it. And pray."

"Two heads and two sets of prayers are better than one." Pastor Thompson looked at her with gratitude in his eyes. "Thanks for joining my team."

She winked and grinned. "I hear it's the best in town."

Sylvia sat on a small stool in the back of her shop inventorying her latest purchases. Vintage dresses and fabrics were strewn about the room. As usual, she had a tape measure draped around her neck, a nest of pins poked through the front of her sweater for easy access, and reading glasses and a pen propped in her pale red hair.

"Looks like you're having fun," Jane commented, enjoying the colorful chaos around her.

"Bliss. Sheer bliss." Sylvia looked up at Jane from her low perch. Her eyes were glowing.

Jane spread open her hands. "I'm here to help. Tell me what you want me to do."

"I was just about to start folding fabric. I moved some seasonal fabrics to the sale table out front so I'd have room for this. Let's put greens in one pile, blues in another and so on. I'm itching to do a velvet crazy quilt as soon as I make sense of this."

"What *are* you going to do with all this cloth?" Jane picked up a piece of velvet that felt buttery soft in her hands.

Sylvia's expression grew wistful for a moment. "If I could, I'd love to—" Then the dreaminess vanished as quickly as it had come. "Oh, never mind. I'll probably just look at it for a while, sew some of it into quilts to sell in the shop, or organize a class and sell it in kits."

Jane put her hands on a stack of fabric and leaned forward. "But if you could do what you'd *love*, what would that be?"

Sylvia looked at Jane wistfully. "I don't get to do that, so there's no use talking about it."

"Who says?" Jane demanded. "What fabric police stopped in here and wrote you a citation for doing something creative? If anyone is monitoring creativity, they'd better stop at the inn next—I've got recipes that would get me thrown in jail."

The ridiculousness of the statement took Sylvia off

guard, and she began to laugh. She stood up and gave Jane a hug. "You're a breath of fresh air, do you know that?"

"California smog, you mean. So what is it you'd love to do?" She lowered her voice. "You can tell me, I'm reliable." Then Jane pantomimed locking her lips and throwing away the key.

"Want some coffee?" Sylvia asked. "This may take a while to explain."

"So what you really want to do is fabric art," Jane reiterated as she sat across from Sylvia, "and have a showing just like watercolor or oil painters might have."

"I know it sounds odd, but look at these clothes. Fashion is art. Just as there are periods, such as Impressionism, in art history, so there are periods in fashion. You can look at a dress and say 'fifties' or 'turn of the century' and others will know what you're talking about. But these few dresses are just a tiny part of what I'd love to share with people. What I'd really love to showcase are my quilts and wall hangings."

Jane glanced around the shop. There were quilts on every wall, from fluffy baby blankets with white bunnies to masculine plaid flannel throws, each a sample of what could be made with patterns and fabrics from Sylvia's store.

"Not those. The ones I make for *me*." Sylvia moved a rack of clothes left for alterations aside, and Jane saw another cabinet. Gently Sylvia removed a small quilt about the size of a landscape one might hang in a living room. "Like this."

Jane's jaw dropped as Sylvia held up the piece. It was artwork, pure and simple; intricate, detailed designs were sewn into every corner of the piece. It was silk, a contemporary rendition of the outspread wing of a swan over blue water. A single majestic bird hovered on the water nearby as if waiting for its mate to join her. Jane took a step backward and squinted. Imagining it hanging on a wall, she knew it could hold its own in a gallery. The detail was exquisite, down to the gold and silver threads with which it had been sewn.

"Sylvia, this is amazing. How long did it take you?"

"Months," Sylvia admitted. "But I didn't work on it all the time. I had others going, too." She pulled out a quilt that resembled a Mondrian, fiercely contemporary with its straight lines and bright colors.

One by one, she pulled out an array of wall hangings, each more intricate and lovely than the last. She could have covered every wall of the inn with her designs, there were so many. And there were jackets finely beaded in ornate patterns, fashion dolls, even fabric jewelry. Finally she said, "This is what I make for me."

"Spectacular! Have you had art school training? Your designs are stunning."

Sylvia blushed so red her hair seemed faded in comparison. "Yes, well, no. I mean . . . I guess you could say I had a little training. I took a class by mail."

"Either that was some class or you are extremely talented."

"It was all my mother could afford," Sylvia explained. "She knew I had talent, but she had no idea how to help me with it. She did the best she could, and I know that she gave up things she wanted to pay for what I got."

"Have you shown these to anyone else?"

"No." Sylvia turned her head away from Jane's intent gaze. "I would never do that. People would think I'm silly, spending all my time cutting apart pieces of fabric and then sewing them together again."

"Isn't that what you do when you make alterations on your customers' clothes?"

"That's different . . . sensible. This seems frivolous."

"Do you believe the painting I've done or the jewelry I've made is *frivolous*?"

"Of course not. But not only are you an artist, you're a chef."

"That's right. Is it any less frivolous to spend hours decorating a cake or setting up a buffet that looks beautiful only until the first portion is taken?"

"I never thought about it that way."

"Beauty and creativity come in lots of forms, Sylvia. This is yours."

Sylvia sat down on a chair. "I suppose it is."

Jane pulled up a second chair and faced her. "I don't know very much about you, Sylvia. I'd like to know more."

Sylvia grew uncomfortable again. "Oh, there's nothing to know really. I've lived a pretty dull life."

It was going to be like pulling teeth, Jane realized, but she was going to hear Sylvia's story even if it took all week.

Jane loved to shop in Fred's Hardware. It was a flash from the past to walk through the door. In addition to carrying paint, nails, hammers and the like, Fred had a smattering of everything else. Garden supplies filled one corner, small appliances another. There were a few toys, mostly miniature tractors and cars, puzzles, games and baby dolls as well as an assortment of what Louise called "junk": jacks and balls, chalk for hopscotch, magic tricks, paddles with a ball attached by rubber band, Chinese finger puzzles, wax lips and other trinkets that might appeal to a child. Everything on that shelf was marked fifty cents and, according to Fred, was the single shelf with the biggest turnover in the store.

There were rakes and shovels, out-of-season Christmas

lights, cleaning supplies, hunting knives, a barrel of packaged caramel corn mixed with candied nuts—and her own personal favorite, the inexpensive boxes of chocolate-covered cherries that only appeared before Christmas in other stores. Fred, however, managed to keep them on hand year round.

As she stood, looking around, the top of Fred's head appeared as he ascended a flight of steps accessed by a trap door in the floor by the counter. "Still using that old basement, I see."

Fred looked up and grinned. "Old habits die hard. Besides, I've got everything just where I want it down there. Good shelves, labeled and sorted. Why mix myself up by moving things around now?" He grinned. "At least that's what I tell Vera every time she nags at me to move stuff upstairs to the attic."

"Attic?"

"That's probably too fancy a word for it." He dug into the barrel, pulled out a bag of caramel corn, opened it and offered some to Jane. "More like a hole under the eves, but years back one of the past owners must have stayed up there. There are a table and chairs and an old cot."

"I'm sure a lot of buildings in Acorn Hill could tell tales. There's a lot of interesting history in this part of the country. Just think how many stories are likely still left untold."

"What can I do for you today?" Fred inquired, remembering that he was running a store.

"Do you have any cookie cutters? Small ones?" She had been hatching ideas to have Josie and her mother over for tea, and she knew Josie would love tiny, decorated cookies.

"I believe I do." Fred knew exactly where to go. He pulled a cardboard box off the shelf and held it out to Jane.

"These are perfect, Fred."

"I think they were for making animal crackers or some such. Never sold. Vera told me nobody makes their own animal crackers. Live and learn, I guess."

"Will you put them on our bill?" Fred kept a monthly tally for the inn, and on the last day of the month either Alice or Louise arrived with the checkbook to settle up.

"How about bringing me a couple of those cookies when they're done?"

"It's a promise."

As she walked toward the inn she saw Joe plodding down the road toward her. He looked exhausted and dirty. She was about to call out to him when he saw her. Like a frightened rabbit he scurried off to a side street and out of sight.

"Do you know much about Sylvia Songer, Alice? How long has she had Sylvia's Buttons?"

They were preparing their dinner in the kitchen, and now Alice's brow furrowed in concentration. "Now that you ask, I'd have to say not much. She's been such a blessed fixture here for so long that it never occurred to me to ask her many questions." She frowned. "And I've always thought I knew everyone in Acorn Hill so well. . . ."

Then Alice's face lit. "I do know that she's one of our most faithful churchgoers. If Sylvia isn't in the third pew from the back, left side, just under the stained-glass window depicting Stephen the Martyr, she's either ill or out of town."

"She moved here years ago from Potterston," Louise offered as she spread placemats and put out the everyday dishes. They were from her marriage to Elliot, and Jane knew that Louise was sentimentally attached to them. "It seems to me that I once heard something about a single mother raising her. What I do know is that she can work magic with a needle and thread. I would guess she can double the length of a garment's life—repair it until it falls apart and then turn it into a quilt for Grace Chapel's missions."

Magic. Her sisters had no idea what Sylvia was capable of. Jane could not get the sight of Sylvia's beautiful creations out of her mind, or the fact that she had hidden them away again before anyone else could see them. *How could a woman so talented keep herself under wraps?* Jane wondered.

⊖

She was still thinking about Sylvia the next afternoon. When the inn was quiet, Jane put several "Aunt Sally" cookies—ones that Madeleine had indicated were her favorites—and a canister of peach tea she had purchased from Time for Tea into a small bag and started for Sylvia's Buttons.

Clara Horn, one of the biggest gossips in Acorn Hill and a friend of Aunt Ethel, was leaving the store as Jane arrived.

"Doing some sewing, Clara?"

"Doll clothes for some little ones. Sylvia even has patterns. She runs a fine store, that one, and who'd have thought it possible?"

Jane inclined her head. "What do you mean?"

"Oh, you know, the way she grew up and all."

Usually Jane avoided Clara because she wasn't interested in all the gossip the woman made it her duty to spread, but this felt different somehow. "No, I don't know."

Clara's eyes lit like beacons. "Well, let me tell you . . . ."

By the time Jane entered the store she was reeling with information and guilt.

Sylvia greeted her and took the bag Jane offered. "What's this? Those wonderful molasses cookies with hard white frosting? And peach tea? You can drop in anytime."

"You may change your mind after you hear what I did," Jane warned. "I'm afraid I was snooping into your affairs."

"Well, that couldn't be much of an investigation, Jane. My life's an open book."

"And Clara Horn read it to me."

"Clara—the source of all knowledge, some of it accurate, most of it not. Why don't you tell me what she said, and then I'll tell you what really happened."

"She said you grew up in Potterston. That your family . . ."

"Was just my mother and myself. We were very poor—so poor, in fact, that I remember a winter spent mostly in the library because our house was practically unheated. We'd go home at night and hurry into bed with our coats on. But . . ." Sylvia pondered for a moment. "When I look back on it, there were blessings. In the library, I'd go through every book that had pictures. *Every* book. When I got into the art and fashion collection I thought I'd died and gone to heaven. I'd get those little slips of paper and stubby pencils they provided by the card catalog and draw and draw and draw. Finally the librarian—God love her—found me out and gave me a writing tablet." Sylvia smiled at the memory. "She said she didn't have time to be refilling the depleted paper bin."

"So you attribute your early interest in art to a winter in the library?"

"Several winters, actually. Even when Mama worked, we didn't dare burn much fuel—just in case she might lose her job. She cleaned houses during the day and washed dishes for a restaurant in town over the dinner hour. I've never known anyone to work harder than my mother. She sewed, too, all my clothes and all her own.

"*She* is the main reason I do what I do. We'd go to rummage sales and consignment shops every week. She taught me to look for good-quality fabrics and colors that made a pretty palette. Sometimes I'd just look for buttons or trim, depending on what was for sale. That's how the name 'Sylvia's Buttons' came to be. Then we'd carry our treasures home and sort them out.

"The one thing Mama never let go of was her little old sewing machine. She had me draw patterns on newspaper and cut them out. For a penniless child, I had some of the nicest clothes at school."

Sylvia's expression grew dreamy. "She was always dressed beautifully, too. If people didn't know our situation, they never would have guessed we lived in poverty. For the price of thread and a can of oil for that machine, she made us look like princesses."

"Remarkable. Simply remarkable."

"People started to wonder where we got our outfits, and Mama started getting requests to sew clothes for other people. She said it was pure pleasure to sew on fabric that hadn't been cut out of the middle of something else. And we bought new buttons and trims. Eventually she had enough business to find a better place to live. When we had a real sewing room, she taught me to help her. I'd sew on buttons and hem skirts, and before long I could set in a sleeve or make a bound button hole as well as Mama." She swept her hand around the room in an expansive gesture. "And look at me now."

"Where is your mother now?"

"She still lives in Potterston and she still sews, mostly alterations and the occasional quilt. She sends all the complicated requests to me." She nodded toward a rack holding four velvet evening gowns. "Bridesmaids' dresses, for example."

"A happy ending then."

"Yes, I suppose it is." Sylvia's expression became serious. "We haven't known each other long, Jane, but what you feel always shows on your face. Something is on your mind."

"I was just thinking about Josie and her mother Justine. They live here in town. They don't sound much different from you and your mother."

"Poor?"

"Definitely."

"Desperate?"

"Probably."

"Lonely?"

"I'd guess." Jane told her about the tea party with Josie, and then asked, "Do you think I could do something to help without giving the impression that I pity them? Josie's mom is a hardworking, honest young woman who's had some bad times. I'd like to reach out to her if I could."

"Let me think about it. Sometimes people offered us help, and Mama felt so shamed and small, she would cry. Their attitude made her feel like she would never be any more than she was. Others, though, were more thoughtful in bringing food baskets or sending money anonymously. Of course, Mama always knew who they were or could figure it out. At Christmas she would make scarves and ties for those who helped us during the year, and at night we'd deliver them to mailboxes or doorsteps undetected." Sylvia chuckled. "I think people got more and more generous when they figured out where those ties were coming from. One Sunday dozens at our church had one of Mama's garments on. I think that was her proudest moment."

"Thank you for telling me. And let me know how best to approach Josie's mother."

"I will." Sylvia looked pensive. "And it would be a blessing for me to help a pair like Mama and I were. We knew we were somebody, even when we were nobodies. It's good to help others know that too."

Chapter Six

"What on *earth* have you been thinking?" Louise burst into the kitchen, flung a bill onto the counter and jammed her finger at it until Jane feared that she would hurt it. Louise's complexion showed that she was unusually upset.

Jane put down the towel she had been using to dry her hands and stared at her sister. She had never seen Louise like this. "About what?" She had no idea what Louise was talking about.

"This!" Louise picked up the slip and waved it in the air. "Do you realize that this month's bill from the General Store is triple what we allowed for in our budget?"

"Really? I know I've been cooking a lot but . . . ."

"You've lived a pampered life, never having to worry about money as Alice and I have. Those fancy restaurants you've worked for might let you order whatever foods you wanted, but you can't be careless here. Where is the money supposed to come from to pay this bill?"

Jane hardly heard the question. Louise's initial remarks were still ringing too loudly in her ears. "Pampered life" . . .

"never having to worry about money" . . . "can't be careless" . . . None was a phrase that Jane ever imagined would be applied to her.

The chill in the house had nothing to do with the thermostat.

Grimly, Jane prepared breakfast for her four guests, fighting the temptation to set out gruel, bread and water as a way of showing Louise that she was cutting back her spending. She did, however, go to Madeleine's recipe book for inspiration. Neither of her sisters had complained so far about a dish that she had made from that cookbook.

Very Good Pancakes

MAKES SIX PANCAKES

Under the recipe title Madeleine had written,

I double recipe. Cold pancakes spread with jam are a delicious afternoon treat.

Jane had tried it and she had to agree.

1 cup flour

3 teaspoons baking powder

1 large egg

¾ cup milk (may add ¼ cup more milk for thinner pancakes)
1 tablespoon sugar
¼ teaspoon salt
2 tablespoons butter, melted
Raspberries or blueberries

Stir together flour and baking powder. In separate bowl whisk together egg, milk, sugar, salt and butter. Add to flour mixture. Fold in berries if desired. Butter griddle, heat until drop of water dances on the surface. Use one-third cup batter for each pancake.

As Jane prepared the batter, she reminded herself that she had inadvertently been responsible for causing Louise's tirade.

Granted, she had refused to scrimp on ingredients for the inn, but she had also been paying half the bill from her own pocket. Of course, she had not told Louise or Alice that she was doing so because she did not want to worry them. Unfortunately, this time she had not found the bill herself and so was not able to pay half from her own account and the other half through the inn's ledger before her sisters could know what she was doing. But at this moment what she felt was righteous indignation at Louise's outburst.

Perhaps her hopes for personal transformation had been a dream, Jane thought as she scrubbed forcefully at a nonexistent spot on the counter. What had she been thinking? Coming home to build a bond with her sisters, to learn more about her mother and to allow the steady pace of Acorn Hill gradually to heal her disappointments? *Great concepts poorly executed,* she thought grimly. She and her sisters had never connected properly as children. What made her think that they could manage now, as adults, with such divergent life experiences? Only one bit of knowledge deep in her heart made Jane decide to endure for a while longer. Her father and mother would have wanted it.

She picked up Madeleine's recipe book again. Just the sight of her mother's even handwriting and cheerful doodles on its pages made her feel calmer. There, she discovered another breakfast recipe that was simple yet elegant.

Efficiently she peeled and sliced six large seedless oranges crosswise in quarter-inch slivers and placed them on one of the inn's most beautiful porcelain platters. After sprinkling them with a tablespoon of brown sugar, she lavished on them an entire cup of sour cream topped off by freshly ground cinnamon and two tablespoons of freshly grated orange peel. She held the platter up for inspection.

Perfect. Elegant and simple. Her mother's note at the bottom of the recipe had said it all: "sinfully simple."

Then she got out her own recipe for artichoke frittata.

Jane's Frittata

MAKES FOUR TO SIX SERVINGS

½ pound fresh sliced mushrooms
1 cup finely chopped onions
1 tablespoon vegetable oil
5 large eggs (lightly beaten)
10 ounces frozen spinach (thawed and drained)
12 ounces marinated artichoke hearts, drained
6 ounces grated sharp Cheddar cheese

Sauté mushrooms and onions in oil. Combine them, the beaten eggs, spinach, artichokes and cheese in a buttered one and a half-quart casserole. Bake at 350 degrees for forty-five minutes.

She doubled the recipe, which was tasty, unusual and easy to serve.

Breads and homemade jams, fresh granola, milk and sugar on the sideboard—Jane ticked off the breakfast requirements one by one. Then she took inventory of herself. She had put on the closest thing she had to armor, a clean white jacket and a stoic expression. Clearly, she was not about to flinch under her sister's reproving gaze. She had done nothing wrong. Louise had not even given her time to explain.

If Louise had *asked* her about the grocery bill before she began to rant and rave, Jane would have told her that she personally would take care of the amount of the bill that was over budget. But no, Louise had not given her that opportunity.

She took three deep breaths. She wasn't going to rock the boat just yet, no matter how upset she was.

George and Muriel Fairchild beamed when Jane came into the room carrying the frittata in oven-mitted hands.

"Oh, look! She's wearing a chef outfit." Muriel twittered. "How impressive."

Jane winced. The way Muriel said it, it sounded as though she had dressed for Halloween.

"Wow!" was all Tim and Theresa could muster. Naomi sat straighter in her chair. Alice smiled, but Louise looked far from pleased. She was, no doubt, counting artichoke hearts and tabulating cost.

There were equally gratifying responses to the oranges and cream, and to the baskets of assorted breads. By the time Jane finished serving the frittata, George was holding out his plate for seconds.

Alice and Louise, meanwhile, made small talk with the guests.

"Jane, dear," Muriel said, "you are wearing the most lovely bracelet. Wherever did you get it? I'd like to take some home as gifts."

Jane glanced at her wrist, not even remembering that she had put on jewelry. "This?" She held out her arm to display an unusual collection of antique buttons and gemstones. "I made it. Sylvia Songer has a million buttons around her shop. I just picked some that I thought might be nice together."

"You *made* it?" Muriel looked positively astounded. "It's so clever. I've never seen anything like it. You wouldn't, I mean, of course you couldn't. . . ."

"Sell it?" Jane said. "Of course I would. I'll just make myself something else." She slipped the bracelet off her wrist. "Here, try it on."

Muriel slipped it on her wrist and admired it with pleasure. "I'll take it." She glanced at her husband. "Oh dear. I've purchased myself another gift and still don't have the ones I want to take home."

"I can make more," Jane offered. "If you're interested, that is."

By the time Muriel and Jane had negotiated a sale, George had cleaned up the last of the frittata and the newlyweds were back to gazing into one another's eyes.

When she was sure that everything was under control, Jane retreated to the kitchen and put her starched white jacket back on its hanger. It had felt good to look professional, even for a few moments. The only opportunities she would have to do so here at the inn were the ones she made for herself.

She took a mug from the cupboard and filled it with coffee and an extravagant amount of cream. Alice and Louise could clear the table when the guests were done. She had to sort through the emotions running riot within her. Hurt, guilt, disappointment, anger and amusement vied for her attention until it occurred to her what was really going on. She had allowed Louise to make her feel like a naughty, irresponsible child. But she wasn't a child, nor was she naughty or irresponsible. Somehow, they had to iron this out.

Knowing that she would have to confront Louise sooner or later, she was still happy to put it off when Muriel followed Louise into the kitchen.

"Jane, George and I are checking out this morning. I'd love to visit a few minutes before we have to go."

Jane was on her feet in a flash. "Let's talk in the parlor."

Naomi had already disappeared upstairs when they

walked by the dining room. She behaved like a benevolent ghost most of the time, whispering around the edges of the inn's activity, not really taking part and yet not wanting to be left out. Tim and Theresa were holding hands and looking out the window.

"Sweet, don't you think?" Muriel whispered, as if there were even a possibility that they were paying any attention to anything outside themselves.

"A fresh start in life," Jane agreed. "And two shall become as one."

Muriel eyed her speculatively. "You are your father's daughter, aren't you?"

That statement took Jane by surprise. "Why do you say that?"

"There's a gentle thoughtfulness about you. That's how preachers are, aren't they?"

That made her grin. "Well, Muriel, we'd all like to think so, but I have heard a few fire-and-brimstone types in my lifetime that might not fit into that category."

As Muriel digested that, Jane added, "People tell me I'm a lot like my mother. She was a cook, too, and she loved tea parties."

"That's actually why I wanted to talk to you, to encourage you to make afternoon tea a part of your offerings." Muriel lowered her voice to a whisper, and Jane thought she was about to be given the secret recipe for Coca-Cola or the mysterious ingredient in Colonel Sanders chicken. "And *never* scrimp on the water."

"Ah . . . of course not . . ."

"Your tea yesterday was perfect. You must have used natural spring water, not that dreadful stuff you call *tap* water." Muriel shuddered.

Although Jane hadn't had any complaints about Acorn Hill's water supply, an artesian well that ran sweet, clear and cold, she nodded in helpless agreement.

"The most important ingredient in tea is the water, I think. And if you ever make tea with distilled water, mind my words, you'll only do it once." Muriel shook her head. "What a flat, dull drink that is."

Jane worked hard to smother a grin. Muriel was as passionate about tea as Louise was about the grocery bills.

"Are you ready, dear?" George Fairchild, decked out in camera, umbrella, sun hat and glasses and with a jacket tied by the sleeves at his paunch, fairly beamed at his wife. "Do you know how much history there is to absorb in Philadelphia?" He turned to Jane. "Not that this isn't a wonderful place. Muriel and I will be back again, no doubt."

Muriel shook Jane's hand and as she did so, said, "Remember, *hot* water."

Jane saw them to the porch and waved them off with a

hint of regret. She really did love the people who came through their doors. Sweet and odd, gentle and forceful, brilliant and inquisitive, in love or having just fallen out of it, they came. And all left a gift behind, the privilege of having served them. Perhaps that, she mused, was what her father had meant when he had advised his daughters always to have "a servant's heart."

She returned to the kitchen to find a note on the table.

Please take the artichoke dish off the menu. I believe quiche can be made more inexpensively. No one took a croissant today. Perhaps they should be served only on Sundays.

Louise

She paced the length of the kitchen a few times, all raw nerves and pent-up emotion. Louise was making her crazy. There was no other choice. She had to expend some of her energy or burst. Jane raced up the stairs to get ready.

Knee pads. Wrist braces. Helmet. She checked her equipment on the front porch before venturing down the stairs to the sidewalk. Athletic and strong, she had loved both ice-skating and roller-skating as a child, and had spent hours on the frozen pond that her father had created for them by filling a low spot at the end of the property with water from the garden hose. Already a runner, when she had laced on her first pair of in-line skates, she knew she had found her escape from the pressures of the world. At least for a time, she could outskate them and return refreshed and ready to tackle them again. She had not felt the need to skate in Acorn Hill—until now.

Ethel dropped a terra-cotta pot containing a huge begonia when she saw Jane sail by her house. She did not even notice the pieces of broken clay. Instead, her gaze was fixed on her niece, waving pleasantly and smiling at her from beneath a black-and-teal helmet.

Lloyd, on his way to Ethel's house, was so startled by the racing figure moving toward him that he stumbled backward against a lilac bush as Jane veered around him, dipped in a driveway and propelled herself off the sidewalk and onto the street.

She skated down Chapel Road to Berry Lane, where she waved to Viola, who was putting a small table of clearance books and aging calendars outside the door of the bookstore. Hope Collins was visiting with Pastor Ley outside Time for Tea. They both watched her slack-jawed as she passed.

Haven't these people ever seen anyone on in-line skates before? There have to be some high school students around here that . . .

Of course, a high school student on in-line skates likely would not have attracted any attention whatsoever. It was when a woman the age of a high school student's *mother* flew by that eyebrows began to lift. *Oh well, it's too late now.* She made a left onto Village Road and waved at the gardener of the Presbyterian church. He saluted, a hand trowel to his forehead, touching the bill of his cap.

By the time she made another left in front of the Methodists, who were just coming out of a midweek morning service, and waved at the customers in the Good Apple Bakery, she was feeling much better. Her legs were experiencing the good ache of exertion and her hips, currently unaccustomed to this particular exercise, were crying out for respite.

Jane slowed as she took the right turn off Hill Street and back onto Chapel Road. In the homestretch, seeing Rev. Thompson's bicycle leaning against the back corner of Grace Chapel, she turned in. He was just coming from the back of the church, a Bible in hand.

She angled to a stop just short of the chapel's steps. "Hi. What's up?"

He stared at her in bewildered amazement. "Jane?"

"Ken?" She laughed as she pulled off her helmet and shook out her dark hair.

"Out for a little spin, I see." He shut the door behind him and sat down on the top step.

"Mental health measure." She wiped her forehead with the back of her hand.

"Too many cooks spoiling the broth?"

"It's more like too many sisters in a stew," she responded.

"How is it working out?"

She sensed that he had already read her mind and surmised how difficult this entire sister thing had been. "We've had better times. I thought we'd called a truce, but it's off today, and Louise is ready to do battle with me again."

Wisely, she thought, the minister did not answer.

The chapel, built into a small hill, had a flight of concrete steps that led up to the rear of the main part of the building and another that led into the basement. Jane dropped onto the concrete steps leading to the chapel to join him. The coolness on the back of her legs and the skittering of a stone by her feet suddenly brought back a memory so vivid that she could nearly hear the laughter of playing children and the ringing of the church bell to call them in from recess.

"I used to play a game on these steps. When we were small, Father held vacation Bible school for two weeks every summer. It was a wonderful time, especially since we had the best steps for playing 'Stone School.'"

"What, pray tell, is 'Stone School'?"

"We'd all sit on the bottom step each with a stone in hand. At least six of us could fit at once, more if the little ones were playing. Whoever was 'Teacher' would stand in front of us.

One by one, we'd hold out our hands in fists, the stone in one hand, and the other empty. If she tapped the hand that didn't hold the stone, you got to 'graduate' to the next step. If she picked the hand in which you held your stone, you had to stay where you were. The trick was to make her think the *empty* hand actually held the stone. The first one to the top of the steps was teacher for the next round." As she talked, she could practically see the scabs on her knees and her untied shoe laces. Suddenly, memories of the taste of bologna and mayonnaise sandwiches and Fig Newtons made her mouth water.

"It was a wonderful game, really—very democratic and easy for the little ones to play. The 'big' kids in fifth and sixth grade liked it too." She smiled. "I played a lot of Stone School on these steps."

"You'll have to come over next summer and teach our vacation Bible school children your game."

"Ah, yes, vacation Bible school." She looked at him impishly. "I don't suppose you want to hear about some of our other 'games'?"

"Why does it worry me when you ask that way?"

"I was thinking of the time Father caught a group of us using the gravestones as pretend ponies. We'd crawled up and straddled our 'horses' and were in the midst of yelling 'Giddyap! Hi Ho Silver, Away' when he found us." She rolled her eyes. "I still remember that lecture. Respect for the dead, concern for church and family property and hadn't any of us been raised better than that? I suffered the most. Being the preacher's kid, I was, naturally, the one who really should have known better."

Pastor Thompson laughed, stood and offered his hand. She took it gratefully. Her legs were already screaming in protest over the unaccustomed exercise, warning her that she would pay dearly for this bit of energy release.

After bidding the pastor good-bye, she was able to skate home slowly, having taken the edge off her anxiety and upset. She had even managed to put Louise's words in a perspective of sorts. It had not been the words, exactly, but the tone and the anger that had hurt her heart.

Jane did not even see Ethel until the handle of a broomstick poked out in front of her like a signal arm on a train track, commanding her to stop. Fortunately she could manage her skates or Ethel might have toppled her.

"Just a minute. I have something to say to you." Ethel's cheeks were burning pink and fire blazed in her eyes.

Jane's mind went directly back to the day on the Buckley farm when she and her cousin, eating garden tomatoes fresh from the vine, had dropped Ethel's crystal salt and pepper shakers through the cracks of the bales in the haymow. Ethel, of course, had noticed them missing, and Jane had finally broken under her fierce inquisition and spilled the beans.

Uncle Bob was ordered to empty the square bales from the barn by hand until the family treasures were found, while Jane and her cousin were sent to the chilly "potato room" in the basement of the old farmhouse where last fall's potato crop had been stored. One by one they had to sort through the potatoes, dig out the sprouting eyes, and dispose of those potatoes that hadn't made it through the winter. Jane still remembered the first time a rotten potato had exploded in her hand, sending odiferous slime all over her hands and legs. It made bile rise in her throat just to think of it.

She prayed that Ethel had not been storing potatoes anywhere nearby.

"Where are your propriety, your decency and good manners?" Ethel looked like a redheaded wet hen, puffed up and angry, her eyes dark and beady, beak ready to snap at Jane.

"Fully intact, I think." Jane fought back the feeling of being ten again.

"Look at you! You look like a hockey player." Ethel said that as if there were nothing more hideous on earth to imagine. "A *Howard*, going out in public like that, looking like a great big..." she was at a loss for words "... *beetle*."

Jane opened her mouth to speak, but Ethel was not yet ready to let that happen. "And poor Lloyd. You frightened him so badly he fell into a lilac bush."

She obviously didn't see any humor in the situation.

"He didn't fall, Ethel. He just did this little jitterbug dance and backed into them. I'm sorry I startled him."

Her aunt went on as if she hadn't heard a thing. "The embarrassment of it all!"

It was difficult to be repentant when Jane felt as though she were living in a situation comedy. "I'll apologize," she promised, suppressing a smile.

Ethel glared at Jane. "He's talking about having a law passed that would prevent those awful skates on the streets of Acorn Hill." Still, Ethel was not done. "What would your father have thought? He's probably rolling in his grave right now."

Jane doubted that. Daniel had loved to ice-skate as much as she. In fact, at one time he might have joined her with roller skates. "Aunt Ethel, what would my *mother* have said?"

"Madeleine?" she gave a dismissive wave. "That's probably where you got this foolishness. Your mother was absolutely incorrigible. She would try anything new or different just for the thrill of it. She was always telling little jokes and playing tricks. I can't see why, but she especially loved to play them on *me*."

Imagine that, Jane thought.

"Your mother could be very naughty sometimes. Daniel always called it 'playful' and seemed to enjoy and approve of it. I, of course, had to remind him what was proper."

Of course. Jane, despite her regret about scaring Lloyd, was feeling rather high-spirited at the new bit of information about her mother.

Much to her delight, Ethel confirmed her thoughts. "Your impetuosity came from Madeleine. I know it didn't come from *my* side of the family."

Much to her aunt's surprise, Jane leaned over and gave her a big kiss on the cheek. "Tell Lloyd I'll make him some of Mother's chiffon cake with lemon icing as a peace offering, will you?" Jane skated off with Ethel staring dumbfounded at her back.

Jane's giddy release didn't last long. When she got to the kitchen, there was another note on the counter. Once again, Louise had come and gone. This one was even more upsetting. Now her sister had gone too far. Louise had chosen tomorrow's breakfast menu.

Please make omelets without meat. There are plenty of vegetables in the refrigerator to use up. Please use less cheese. Fancy breads are not necessary. Toast will be fine. Frozen orange juice will suffice, as fresh oranges are high-priced right now. Fruit compote can be made with canned fruits. It appears we have an overstock.

Louise

To Jane, those were fighting words. Louise had thrown down the gauntlet, asked for a duel. *Picking out the inn's recipes? Insisting on insipid foods? Plain toast?* Jane dropped onto a stool and stared at the note. Obviously, despite what her sister might say, Louise had no idea about who Jane was, or the strength of her determination to serve only the very best to her patrons. Jane would happily eat sardines and crackers for a week just so her guests did not have to eat less than the best. And what were she and Louise arguing about food for anyway? Had there been a change in their agreement that she would make all the decisions for the kitchen? What was going on?

Jane went upstairs to shower and change. Thirty minutes later she came back to the kitchen to do what she always did when she was upset—cook.

Chiffon cake with lemon frosting, orange poppy-seed bread, Scotch shortbread, dropped coconut cream cakes, fudge sauce for ice cream. The only thing that stopped her after that was the fact that she had run out of ingredients, containers to put things in and freezer space to store her "creations." But she did have a nice start on sweets for her next tea. Experimenting with different flavoring extracts, such as rum, coconut and almond, she had also started more truffles, which were now cooling in the refrigerator.

Eyeing the bounty laid before her on the counter gave Jane a sense of satisfaction. They were going to need another freezer if she kept this up—or need to have several more teas.

She glanced at the clock as she packed up the last of the baked goods to store in the last bit of freezer space. *After four o'clock.* Jane was glad that there was no tea to be served that day. Not only were her legs aching from skating, but also the arches of her feet were beginning to complain of too many hours of standing.

As she wiped the counter and readjusted the flowers she had salvaged from a dying bouquet, the front door opened. Taking a deep breath, she waited.

There was a lot of puttering going on in the living room. She heard the piano bench open and close twice and a scrape against the floor as it was pushed beneath the keyboard. It would not be long before Louise came to the kitchen for her usual afternoon glass of iced tea.

Oh, Lord, help me with this. Let me know what to say. It isn't going to be easy.

Jane was at the table when Louise entered. Their eyes met and Louise was the first to pull her gaze away. "Hello."

"Hello."

So far things are going swimmingly, Jane thought wryly. "I got your notes."

"Good." She saw Louise stop herself from saying more. "You agree, then?"

"Oh, I didn't say that."

The flash in Louise's eyes looked like mini-lightning. "What does that mean?"

"It simply means I don't agree. It's not necessary to do that because—"

Before Jane could say, "I'll pay the difference out of my own pocket," Louise burst into a tirade. "You've always been headstrong and willful, Jane, but I thought that surely by now you would have grown out of it. We are supposed to be a team here. A *team*. That's why we need to work together to carry off this venture. Or would you like to see all three of us homeless because we've spilled our life's blood into this place?"

"Louise, I had no idea—" Jane began, horrified by her sister's dramatics.

"Of course you didn't," Louise said haughtily. "You never have. You've always been different from the rest of us." With that she turned and left the kitchen.

Jane numbly listened to her sister's retreating footsteps on the stairs. Again, she had been cut off before she had a chance to explain. And again, she had been cut to the quick by Louise's insinuations.

You've always been different from the rest of us.

Louise might as well have told her that she was not even

a part of the family. In her hurt, Jane barely acknowledged the fact that Louise had said nothing except what she already knew to be true. She *was* different. Artistic, independent, given to live life with a sort of rebellious élan, she was not the same. She would not have been content with Louise's stuffy, academic ways, nor with the idea of composing an opera, something Louise had dreamed of doing. If she were a musician, Jane could see herself as a back-up singer for a famous pop soloist or cavorting on stage in a Broadway musical.

It was the same with Alice. While Jane had left Acorn Hill the first day she could and had not looked back, Alice had found everything that was good for her here and had chosen to return home after nursing school.

Still, the truth, as it had come out of Louise's mouth, hurt.

She had to get out for a while. A run? Hardly, considering that her legs were turning to rubber even as she sat. A talk? With whom? It wasn't as if she had had time to make scads of new acquaintances except . . . She stood up and strode out the door, heading for Sylvia's Buttons.

The bell rang on the shop door, but there was no one in sight. Jane meandered through the aisles, pulling out a bolt of fabric here and there just to admire the colors. Seeing them brought back a twinge of longing. When, exactly, had she stopped painting altogether? She had had a studio in the home she and Justin had shared, but at some time, she really couldn't say when, it had become a storeroom for whatever didn't seem to fit in the rest of the house.

The back door slammed and suddenly Sylvia appeared in the doorway, a doughnut in one hand and a cup of coffee in the other. "Hi. It was so quiet that I thought I could get over to the bakery and back without anyone coming in. Did you just get here?"

"About ten seconds ago. Aren't you worried about someone coming into your shop while you're gone?"

Sylvia smiled as she moved enough bolts of fabric to make space for herself on her cutting table and sat down on a high stool. "You forget. You're in Acorn Hill now. Things work a little differently here from where you've come from."

"Now you're beginning to sound like Lloyd Tynan. 'Acorn Hill has a life of its own away from the outside world. . . .'"

"'And that's the way we like it!'" They finished together and laughed.

"Besides," Sylvia took a bite of her sandwich and chewed for a moment, "very few thieves I know want to stock up on quilting materials or bridal lace. The cash register is always empty, mostly because as soon as I get some cash, I pay a bill with it, and everyone knows that."

"I have been away a long time," Jane acknowledged with a sigh. "Maybe too long to think that I can ever really come back."

"Trouble at the inn?" Sylvia reached under the counter, pulled out an unopened bottle of mineral water and pushed it toward Jane.

"Louise and I had words." Jane twisted the cap and it opened with a hiss. "It was all her fault."

"Of course."

"Well, it was," Jane said, "even though I'm not free of responsibility in the matter. If she had just talked with me instead of flying off the handle and scolding me as if I were a naughty child, none of this would have happened."

As Sylvia finished her sandwich, Jane replayed the story, embellishing only slightly on the skating adventure. Sylvia laughed out loud at the part about Lloyd's falling into the lilacs and laughed even louder at Jane's rendition of Ethel's scolding. By the time Jane was done, Sylvia was wiping her eyes with one hand and holding her stomach with the other. Even Jane was laughing.

When they finally got hold of themselves, they sat across from each other in pleasant silence.

"So what will you do?" Sylvia finally asked. "About Louise, I mean."

"I'm not sure. She made me very angry. I've held my

tongue, but I'm afraid if I hold it too long, I may explode." Jane pulled at her hair as she often did when she was thinking hard. "What would *you* do?"

"I'd let it pass." Sylvia gathered the plastic wrap her sandwich had come in and put it in the trash.

"Then you're a better woman than I. Louise had no right to do that, not in that manner, at least."

"I doubt she was thinking about 'manners' when she saw that bill," Sylvia said.

"Then what *was* going on?"

Sylvia's brow furrowed and she grew very serious. "I think Louise is afraid."

That was the last thing Jane had expected to hear. "Fear? Louise? I don't think so. My sister can strike fear into others' hearts, but have it in her own? I doubt it."

"People do odd things when they're afraid, Jane. I know. I've been there."

"What is she afraid of?"

"Failing with the inn. Running out of money before the inn can support itself. I don't know. What I *do* know is that Louise and Alice have both put their hearts into making the inn work. Are either of your sisters wealthy women, Jane?"

"Hardly. Louise teaches music and plays for occasional events. She was married to a professor who made some money in the stock market but was hardly 'wealthy.' And

Alice, who knows? It seems to me that she's giving her money away every chance she gets—to teen groups, starving children, pet rescue centers. It would surprise me if she had ever kept more for herself than she needed to get by."

"And now, here they are, coming to the end of their working years, trying to create a business that they can also call home. You and I are several years younger than they. What will it be like for us then?"

"I hadn't really thought of it that way. Maybe it *was* fear speaking." Sadly, Jane realized that it made sense. Louise, feeling backed into a wall, had lashed out. As Jane took it in, her chest tightened. Is that what she had done to Louise? But why hadn't her sister spoken sooner?

Chapter Seven

The inn was silent when Jane returned. Only crumbs of cake were left under the glass dome on the sideboard, and the thermos of lemonade was empty. The guests were likely taking naps. A day or two in Acorn Hill affected people that way. The quiet, easy pace put the brakes on the hectic lifestyles their guests came to escape. Napping was a logical thing to do in Acorn Hill. She felt a bit weary herself. Perhaps if she were to slip upstairs for an hour or two, no one would notice.

As she mounted the stairs, it occurred to her that Alice had put some lace tablecloths into the second floor linen closet. Jane needed a table cover or two. She rarely stopped on the second floor since the guest rooms were Alice and Louise's domain. Each time she did, however, she was struck by how lovely it was. The wide hallway was elegant with original wood moldings. The glossy wooden floor set off the beauty of the long wool runner that had been purchased by her grandmother on a trip to New York City. The stylistic pattern of birds and vines was as beautiful today as it had been eighty-plus years ago.

The linen closet was overflowing with sweet smelling sheets and pillowcases, duvets, comforters and towels. She had to dig a bit to come up with the items she was seeking. Her arms full, she bumped the door closed with her hip and started back down the hall. A slight sound stopped her.

It was a mew, like that of a young kitten, so faint that had the house not been perfectly still, it might have gone completely unnoticed. It couldn't be Wendell, who was sleeping downstairs in a pool of light in the front hall. What is more, when Wendell made a noise it was loud, usually a belligerent complaint rather than a mew. She followed the sound to the door of Naomi's room.

There it was again, tiny, weak and strangely pathetic. Odd. Naomi wasn't likely to have smuggled a pet into her room. If it wasn't a kitten, what was it?

Jane tapped on the door. No response. She tapped again. Getting no answer, she tried the doorknob. The door swung open. The sight on the other side of the door froze her to the spot. That was no kitten crying. It was Naomi herself.

She had fallen to the floor at the edge of the bed and lay on her side, one leg bent, the other stretched out over it. One arm was extended and Jane could see the rug bunched beneath her hand as if she had been trying to drag herself toward the door. The other arm lay limply at Naomi's side.

Jane reached her in four strides and knelt beside her.

The mewing sound from Naomi's lips continued. Jane gently pushed the hair back from Naomi's forehead. "I'm here. I'm going to help you. Can you talk?"

Her mouth worked but nothing came out. Jane whipped the extra blanket from the foot of the bed and spread it over Naomi's body. "I'm going to call an ambulance. It will only take a second." On her return to the bedroom, she knocked heavily on Tim and Theresa's door. Not waiting for a response, she hurried to where Naomi lay.

"They're on their way, Naomi. It won't be long. I'm not supposed to move you," Jane said, "but I'm right here."

Naomi stared at her with wide, pained eyes and didn't speak.

"What's going on?" Tim and Theresa appeared in the doorway, blinking against the light. Tim rubbed his eye with the back of his hand.

"I heard an odd noise in here and found Naomi this way."

Tim dropped to his knees and put a finger to her pulse. "Weak and erratic. She's clammy, too." He looked up at Jane. "I've worked as a nurse's aide in a senior citizen's center and as a volunteer fireman. Learned a few skills." Then he bent over Naomi again and began talking to her in a soft, soothing voice.

Theresa's hair was tousled from sleep, and there were pillow creases on her cheek. She nervously shifted her weight from one foot to the other looking utterly helpless. "Does the ambulance come from Potterston?" Theresa glanced at the woman on the floor. "Won't that take a long time?"

"The ambulance service is part of our fire department," Jane said. The sound of tires screeching up to the front door of the inn made Theresa jump. "I hear it already. I'll be back."

Three paramedics were already scrambling toward the house with a collapsible rolling stretcher and an oxygen tank. Jane held open the screen door and as they passed said, "Second floor. Second room on the left."

Quickly, she told her story—the odd sounds that had drawn her to the guest room, the fact that Naomi had tried to crawl for help but could not and her wordlessness except for that disturbing mew.

By the time Jane reached the second floor, Tim and Theresa were standing in the hall. The others hovered over Naomi taking vitals and softly asking questions that she could not answer.

"How long did she lie there?" Theresa was flushed and looked as though she might cry.

"Awhile, I think. Did you all go upstairs together?"

"Naomi and I sat in the sun room for a while, visiting. After a while, I told her I planned to take a nap. She thought that sounded like a good idea and that she would take one too. She admitted she had not been feeling herself, that she had been dizzy and lightheaded.

When I suggested that she might have an inner-ear infection, she said she would have it checked. I left her then and didn't hear her come up the stairs."

Clipped voices and the thunks and thumps of the gurney coming out of the room signaled that the patient was being moved. As Jane and her guests watched, a very pale and silent Naomi was carried down the stairs and onto the porch.

Jane followed to the ambulance, its red light still flashing. "My sister Alice works at the hospital in Potterston. I'll call her so that she can meet you there in case there are other questions we might be able to answer." To Naomi, she said, "Don't worry. Alice will be waiting for you. We'll make sure everything is taken care of."

She, Tim and Theresa sat helplessly in the living room waiting for Alice to call. They had given up on small talk, all beginning to realize that the only people Naomi had to depend on right now were those at the inn. Jane didn't even know the name of the ex-husband, not that he would care, if what Naomi had said was true.

"I feel so helpless," Theresa blurted. "What can we do? I don't believe the hands on that clock have moved since we sat down."

Jane looked at the worried newlyweds and her heart went out to them. "Would you pray with me? It's about all we can do right now." She took their silence as an assent.

"Father, we come to You with prayers for Naomi. We don't know much about her, Lord, other than she's been having a difficult time lately, but we do know that she is Yours. We ask that You be with her at this moment and in the hours and days ahead. Overcome her fear and make her strong in both body and spirit. And let us know what part we are to play. Guide us to do all we can for her. Amen."

Jane lifted her head as Theresa wiped a tear from her cheek with the back of her hand. "I remember my grandmother praying like that. Grandma said prayer was the 'telephone line to God.' I'd forgotten how beautiful prayer is."

"And effective." Jane had lost that for a while, but it had come back to her in recent days. There was no explaining it, really, but it was the effect living here was having on her. She could pray again, feel it in her core and know that God was listening. She also knew what the power of prayer could do. More and more these days she felt that ground beneath her feet was solid. *On the rock of Christ I stand, all other ground is sinking sand.*

Her father had told the story of the child who came running to his mother with a weed, a big clump of earth still hanging to its roots. "Look, Mommy," he said. "I pulled this myself." "That's very good," his mother responded. "You must be very strong." The child nodded. "I must be, 'cause the whole earth was pulling against me."

People could have the whole earth pulling against them and still triumph.

After Tim and Theresa had gone for a walk, as a way of dealing with the wait for news, Jane called the hospital to inquire about Naomi. The nurse said Alice was still with her and would contact her as soon as she could. Jane felt as though she had electricity running through her veins. Worry and anxiety didn't suit her, so Jane did the only therapeutic thing she could think to do.

She opened Madeleine's recipe book, and her eye fell on a recipe that Madeleine had made often, if the food stains on the page were any hint. "Porcupines." Now there was a dish she had not heard of in years. The meatballs, barbed with rice and covered with a sauce, were one of the things she remembered her father cooking for her when she was a small girl. When she read the notation Madeleine had made at the bottom of the page, her chest tightened.

My little girls love these. They'd eat them every day if they could.

Her little girls. Louise and Alice.

Jane wasn't sure she could pour oil on the troubled

waters between her and her sister, but at least she could make a stab at a peace offering. She pulled a pound of hamburger out of the refrigerator, a box of rice out of the cupboard, and started mixing.

Porcupines

SERVES FOUR ADULTS OR SIX CHILDREN

- 1 pound hamburger
- ½ cup uncooked rice
- ½ cup water
- 1 teaspoon salt
- ½ teaspoon celery salt
- ⅛ teaspoon garlic powder
- ⅛ teaspoon pepper
- 1 can tomato soup
- 1 cup water
- 2 tablespoons Worcestershire sauce

Mix meat, rice, water, salts, garlic powder and pepper. Shape into two-inch balls. Place in an eight-by-eight-inch baking dish. Combine remaining ingredients and pour over meatballs. Cover with foil. Bake forty-five minutes at 350 degrees. Uncover and bake fifteen minutes longer.

She had just put the meatballs in the oven when she heard a tiny tap on the back door.

"Come in!"

No one came.

"Door's open."

Silence.

Curious, Jane walked to the back door. Tiny and big-eyed, Josie stood at the door. Her hands were stuffed into her pockets and Jane could see she had been crying by the streaks on her dirty face.

"Hi, honey, come in. What's wrong?"

Josie didn't answer.

Jane eyed the tear-streaked face. "Do you want something to eat?"

"Do you have cookies?"

Jane loaded a plate with chocolate chip cookies and poured two glasses of milk before sitting down across from the child. Josie devoured nearly half the cookies and drank all of her milk. Finally, she leaned back in her seat and sighed.

"Feeling better?"

"A little." The tears, which had been at bay while she was eating, welled up again.

"Want to talk about it?"

Josie's eyes narrowed. "Megan is mean."

One of Josie's classmates, no doubt. "Why do you say that?"

"She bosses me around. She tells me what to do. And if I don't do it, she calls me names." A tear spilled onto Josie's cheek. "I try to do it right. Why doesn't she like me?"

"Just because she bosses you around doesn't necessarily mean she doesn't like you, does it?"

Josie considered the idea. "Then why does she hurt my feelings?"

"I don't know. You tell me."

"We were making mud pies." That explained the dirty face. "I started using mud Megan said was hers. She said I was wasting her mud and that I'd use it all up before she got her mud pies done." Josie brightened momentarily. "We're going to sell them at the lemonade stand Megan's mother said we could have."

Aspiring chefs everywhere, Jane thought.

"She said she knew how to make them better than me 'cause she's older."

"How much older?"

"Two months."

Time to gather volumes of wisdom.

"She yelled at me and told me I was dumb and couldn't make mud pies unless I did it her way. She said that I was going to ruin our lemonade stand if I kept hogging the mud and that she shouldn't have let me make any mud pies 'cause she knows how to do it better." Josie looked indignant. "I can make them too, you know."

"So she wants them pretty for the lemonade stand?"

"I guess." Josie swung her legs as she sat in the chair.

"Do you want the lemonade stand to be nice too?"

Josie's head jerked up. "Yes! 'Cause Pastor Thompson told us he'd buy lemonade and a mud pie too. So did that man with the big stomach."

The mayor.

"We could get rich."

Josie had not been in the food business long enough to know that it was long, hard path to riches, Jane thought, amused. "So what do you want to do?"

Josie put her elbows on the table and rested her chin in her hands. "I want to tell Megan that she's mean and I don't like her."

"What will you do?"

Josie's face wrinkled with concentration, weighing the pros and cons. Finally she sighed. "I want to play lemonade stand more than I want to be mad." She made a face that made her look like she had been eating sour pickles. "So she can make those dumb old mud pies . . . and I'll make mud cookies." She brightened. "*That's* what I'll do!

"A fair compromise," Jane observed.

"Cookies will be more fun anyway. And I can make lots of them." Josie slid off the chair and came around the table to give Jane a hug. "Thanks for the milk and cookies." And she was out the back door before Jane could even say good-bye.

"Kids." Jane wiped the counters and returned utensils to their proper homes. "What silly things they argue about." She caught her reflection in the microwave door and might as well have been looking at Josie's freckled face as her own. Her argument with Louise was little different from Josie's with Megan. Like the two girls and their lemonade stand, she and her sister both wanted the inn to succeed. They both wanted this to work. So why were they at odds?

Was it, as Sylvia had suggested, plain, unadulterated fear of failure? Or, Jane wondered, was it her own hypersensitive feelings? It certainly was not because they disagreed on the outcome.

Jane waited up for Alice to come home from the hospital with news about Naomi. She dished up the meatballs that she had made, added thick slices of buttered bread and slid the plate in front of Alice.

Her sister stared at the plate for a moment. "Is this what I think it is?"

"Depends on what you're thinking."

"The last time I had these was nearly fifty years ago." Some of Alice's exhaustion seemed to lift. "Thank you, Jane."

"You're welcome. Now let's get back to how Naomi is doing."

"Well, as I said, she's resting quietly. I stayed with her and held her hand until she fell asleep."

Jane slid into the chair across from her sister. "Is she going to be okay?"

"It was a stroke. Her blood pressure was off the charts." Alice's brown eyes filled with compassion. "She's not in a good spot, that's for sure."

"She couldn't speak when I found her. Can she . . . ? "

"Her speech is a problem, and there's some paralysis on her left side. The doctors have said there's a good chance that it will be temporary. I've been praying all day that's true."

"We'll have to help her," Jane said. "She can stay here until we find her family or friends."

"Of course." Alice patted Jane's hand. "Now go to bed." She glanced around and saw stacks of containers filled with Jane's latest efforts, knowing full well what Jane did when she was distressed. "I can tell you've been upset. Look at all the food."

"We can't have another crisis unless someone brings me another load of plastic containers and a deep freeze."

"Man, oh man, it smells good in here!" Lloyd's wide face peered through the screen door.

How far away had he smelled the food? Jane wondered. The man could moonlight as a human bloodhound. "Come in, Lloyd. What's up? Where's Ethel?"

"Oh, she's on the telephone, talking up a storm to one of her kids. While she was chatting, I thought I'd come over and take a walk around your house to look at the foundation." His nose twitched. "Do I smell lemon cake?"

"Would you like a piece? It's not frosted yet."

Dashed, his shoulder drooped. "Well, if it's not frosted . . ."

"It's up to you. I was planning to bring it over to Ethel's later. I promised her I'd bake you a cake to make up for causing you to fall into that bush the other day."

His eyes darted from side to side as he considered how he should respond—angry about the skating incident or grateful for the cake. The cake won. "I don't need frosting. Why, that smell makes my mouth water so that I'm apt to drool on your nice clean floor."

Eager to prevent that possibility, Jane cut a large piece of cake and set it in front of Lloyd with a cup of coffee. He ate his peace offering with gusto.

"Would you mind?" He held out his plate for another go-around.

Nearly half the cake had disappeared before he got down to the business about which he had come; the result of his investigation was not positive.

"You can get by with that foundation of yours if you do some maintenance patching. It's not so bad as I expected." He sounded disappointed. Then he cheered up enough to add, "Still, it's an old house. There'll always be cracks and holes to fill. A few probably opened this spring. You haven't had snakes down there, have you? Once they find a way in, you've got trouble."

Shuddering, Jane slid into the chair across from him. "I've been down there a few times, and I haven't seen anything."

"They probably won't go looking for someplace warm to hide until fall. You'll want any openings patched up by then."

As if they all didn't already have enough to do.

"Fred Humbert can steer you toward the right product," Lloyd said confidently. "But it's going to take some work. Offhand, I can't think of anyone free to do it. Most every carpenter, mason and handyman in the county is busy during the summer months." He shook his head dolefully. "I'd hate to have you wait till after freeze up. If those snakes have little ones . . . why, I remember the day my father and I came across a nest of snakes at an abandoned farmhouse. I couldn't have been more than twelve. Anyway, they were so snarled up together that my dad picked a whole bunch up with his shovel and they just kept squirming around, tangled like cheap jewelry in a dime-store box. Ugliest thing I ever saw. Had dreams about that for months after."

Jane held up a hand. Her stomach was doing odd things. "You don't need to go on. I understand that this is important." But once Lloyd was on a roll with one of his stories, he was as hard to stop as an express train.

"You got that right! Ho! Man, a nice warm basement like yours to sleep in over winter . . . you could have batches of those things next summer. The Piersons over by Potterston had to burn their house down. Couldn't get rid of the snakes. One day his missus was cooking soup and a snake fell off the top of the cupboard right into the broth. Terrible kind of mess that was—stewing snake, Mrs. Pierson hysterical, supper ruined. Why I could tell you stories. . . ."

"Lloyd, I get it! I just want to know what to *do* about it."

"Maybe Fred has an idea who might be free for a little job. If not . . ." he looked her over. "You're pretty skinny to take on one more job. Looks like you need a rest."

She was not only too skinny but too sane to do it. She could handle one snake if she came upon it in the grass. What Lloyd had described made her blood run cold. "How much would it cost?" she asked.

"Depends on who you hire. Some people charge more for little jobs like these 'cause they're such a headache for what they earn. Could cost you upward of . . ." he threw out a sum that made Jane wince. *And Louise thought artichokes were overpriced.*

When she ushered Lloyd to the door he was carrying the rest of his cake and still telling snake stories. Jane was relieved to shut the door behind him. She leaned against the wall and closed her eyes. "Okay, God. You are a partner in this venture of ours too. You made the snakes. Can You show us how to keep them out of the basement?"

To get her mind off Lloyd's graphic description of potential infestation, Jane called the hospital to inquire about Naomi, but there was nothing new. Then she ran a grooming brush over Wendell, who howled as if he were being eviscerated, and sat down at the dining room table with a pad of paper and colored pencils.

Mentally switching gears, she recalled the astonishing clothing at Sylvia's shop. Picking up a pencil, Jane drew what was forming in her mind's eye. Dresses—costumes, really—vintage thirties and forties with a twenty-first-century twist. A pocket for a cell phone here, a place to slip one's credit card there. Instead of a full-skirted cotton dress swimming with sequined fish, she created a similar one marked with city skylines, racing taxis and silhouetted businesswomen carrying briefcases.

She was sketching a body-hugging, pinched waist suit with feathers decorating the collar when an idea struck her. It was so simple and so brilliant she wondered why she had not thought of it before now: If the basement of this house was filled to the brim with history, imagine what the attic might hold. She knew there were some of her grandmother's clothes up there. Perhaps she could find more inspiration for her sketches.

Feeling glad to be as far away as she could be from the basement, Jane jogged up the stairs to the attic. She needed a break from the kitchen and that vision Lloyd had etched into her mind of wriggling, writhing snakes filling her basement.

The attic was hot and dry. It was also in a state of complete and utter chaos. When the inn's roof was replaced, the carpenters had moved furniture, boxes and bookcases to the center of the room and covered the collection with huge sheets of plastic. Finding her grandmother's dresses would be like looking for a needle in a haystack.

Jane decided to work counterclockwise around the room. When she peeked under the first drape of plastic, something peeked back at her. After a squeal that she was glad no one else had heard, Jane looked again, this time knowing full well who was staring back.

"Hi, Gwendolyn. I had no idea you were still around." She folded back the plastic to view a large stuffed owl encased in glass. Gwendolyn had been around as long as Jane could remember. For a time Gwendolyn had sat in the library gravely staring down at the desk as if to say, "Get to work, Daniel." Her father said it made him nervous to have someone glaring at him from above like an irate member of his congregation, so he had moved the stuffed owl to the attic.

He and Madeleine had "inherited" Gwendolyn from Madeleine's father, who had purchased it from a neighbor with money troubles nearly a hundred years before. Apparently Jane's grandfather was the only one who would give the gentleman more than a dime for the owl. Daniel had never had the heart to dispose of the noble bird. It pained him to think of such a lovely creature being hunted. As girls, Louise and Alice had been chary of the stuffed creature, but Jane identified with her father. "We are stewards of the earth, Jane. God created this place for us. We must take care of the beauty around us, not destroy it." She had never forgotten.

Bookcases filled with books, and boxes of her old toys blocked her path. "Antiques, by now," she muttered. It had been a real shock to visit the Smithsonian and see a display of old toys that included several she had played with as a child.

She picked up a Slinky. Now *this* was a real toy. And her dolls. Unclothed, of course, and shorn of hair. She had never been able to resist undressing the dolls and swapping outfits among them. And, when she was particularly bored, she would play "beauty parlor" with them. Blunt school scissors had not made very good barber's shears.

What Daniel had not stored in the basement, he had wrestled up here. School papers, mismatched chairs, the studio couch that had once sat in his office, an old Motorola radio on four legs and as large as a chest of drawers, and even an old saddle brought back a rush of memories. Organizing this was going to be even more work than she had faced in the basement. She lifted another piece of plastic sheeting to find storage trunks of every description piled high and enticingly unmarked.

Her hand shook slightly as she opened the nearest trunk. The faint smells of lavender and dust wafted upward as the lid dropped back to reveal bedding, pillowcases and sheets tatted with the most delicate lace borders Jane had ever seen. There were small needlepoint pillows with intricate designs, including the bold letter *H* for the Howard family name. Crocheted dishcloths, doilies and a huge round tablecloth that must have taken months to complete were buried beneath the bedding, tea and finger towels and delicate aprons. She lifted out the contents layer by layer. Tantalized now, she packed the cottony fabrics back into the chest and sealed it again, eager to see what else might be in store for her.

The next two chests, filled with old magazines and newspaper clippings, were relatively disappointing. But there were a few interesting books, including one called *The White House Cookbook* with a rendering of that famous building on the cover. She would have fun with that one.

Each of those trunks would take a month of Sundays to sort through, she decided. She moved on to a small, detailed chest with a domed top and elaborate latches. She almost overlooked the name written in small letters on a leather luggage tag. *Alice*.

Heart pounding, she lifted the lid. There, on top of a pile of small white blankets and tiny dresses, was a pair of soft, worn baby shoes. Beside it was a well-loved rag doll with only one leg and a tear in the pocket of its jumper. Tucked into an envelope yellowed with age was a picture of a dimpled, smiling child. On the back, written in Madeleine's precise handwriting that Jane had grown to know so well through the recipe book were the words, *Baby Alice. How blessed we are.*

Louise's chest was similar to Alice's but slightly larger. The contents were much the same, except for the addition of a wooden string of ducks with wheels. Jane imagined Louise tugging on the pull toy as she walked across the room to her mother, and a rush of sadness swept over her.

Knowing that there was no tiny chest marked *Jane,* she turned to some of the other trunks. After unsuccessfully trying to open the latches of several of them, she came upon a dainty, feminine one with a rounded top and flowers pressed into the tin. The lid opened easily to show neatly folded satin, lace, taffeta and velvet creased and marked by time. She lifted a dress to the light. The waist was no more than nineteen or twenty inches around. These were not Madeleine *Howard's* dresses, but those of a much younger woman—Madeleine *Berry*. The young Madeleine had obviously liked ruffles, bows, pleats and petticoats—and little expense had been spared to provide them. Jane hugged the dress to her chest and buried her nose in the fabric, vainly hoping that her mother's essence could still be found in these old treasures. But there was nothing but aging material, the dry odor of old cloth and dust.

Feeling an emptiness that rivaled any she had ever experienced before, Jane gently folded the pale pink dress and returned it to the trunk. There were no clues here to the woman whom she sought. Was her recipe book the only place left for Jane to get a sense of her mother?

As she closed the trunk, she spotted a tiny chest, no bigger than a suitcase, on the floor. Inside, on a piece of lined paper, in Madeleine's hand were scrawled the words, *Our New Baby.*

Jane sank to the floor oblivious to the dust she stirred into the air. Her attention was fixed on the soft collection before her. Two white baby blankets had obviously been packed new. There was a rubber teething ring so old that the rubber was hard and cracked. Glass baby bottles. Pink diaper pins and blue ones. A rattle. A soft red and blue clown with features painted in a happy grin. Cloth diapers, sleep sacks and tiny white T-shirts. A note was pinned to one of the tiny blankets.

Madeleine,

Here is something for the new little one. I know you have hand-me-downs from the girls, but every baby needs something special of its own. You and Daniel are wonderful parents to my nieces. Love this baby just the same.

Ethel and Bob

And on a scrap page of an old calendar dated only days before Jane's birth was Madeleine's own, now-familiar handwriting:

Daniel—here are things for our new baby. Don't forget to unpack them before we come home from the hospital! Isn't this exciting? You are such a blessing to me. Yours always, Madeleine.

The room spun around her as light streamed through the window and dust motes danced in the beams. Jane closed her eyes and clutched the blanket to her chest as tears trickled down her cheeks. This was *her* baby trunk, lovingly packed by Madeleine herself, in anticipation of a new child. The threads of connection wove themselves tighter and tighter in her heart.

She did not hear Louise mount the attic stairs or realize that her sister was there until she had cleared her throat.

Jane scrambled to her feet. "You startled me." She held the blanket more tightly to her chest.

"I can see that." Louise looked strangely pale as she reset her glasses on her nose to get a better look. Fleetingly, Jane wondered what might be wrong.

"What have you found?"

Not yet ready to reveal what she was holding, Jane said, "Mother's dresses. The ones she must have worn as a teenager. Have you seen them?"

"Not for years. She showed them to Alice and me when we were small."

"She must have been tiny. She had the waist of a child."

"She was not much more than a child when she wore those." Louise's expression grew gentle. "Funny, we never think of our parents as ever having been young. And now, here we are, older than Mother when she . . ." Louise cleared her throat. "What is that?"

Jane offered it to her like a treasure. "She was waiting for me, Louise. *Waiting*. And I . . ." *Killed her*.

"Was born. Just as she had wanted," her sister finished the sentence for her. "And you were a blessing. Daddy told us how happy she was with you in the time before she died. She said you were 'A perfect little rose.'"

"Why haven't I seen this before?"

"I didn't know it was here." Louise studied the chest.

Jane laid the tiny blanket where she had found it, wiped at her cheek with the back of her hand and pointed at one of the larger trunks. "Sit down, Louise."

"I really don't have the time . . . I came looking for you because . . ."

"I have something I must say, and the longer I put it off, the more wretched I'll feel." Jane sat down across from her sister. "I can't let this fester any longer. I have to admit that I've envied you and Alice because you knew Mother and I didn't. It's senseless, I know, but emotions rarely make sense. I've never felt as close to you and Alice as I'd like because I didn't think you could ever forgive me for being the reason for Mother's death."

Louise opened her mouth to speak but Jane held up her hand to stop her. "But if we're to be in this business together, you'll have to begin to trust me, to believe that I'm not someone bent on ruining your world—again."

"You did not. . . ."

"I apologize for that grocery bill. I know you're concerned about going over budget, but I've been taking care of it. I've paid what we budgeted out of the inn's account and the difference from my personal account, but I didn't tell you and I'm sorry you got so upset. Now is simply not the time to scrimp on food or service. We're in a critical building stage for the inn. Rather than cutting things out that I know will be successful, I just decided to buy them for us."

She took a deep breath, and again Louise opened her mouth to speak, but Jane plunged in ahead of her.

"I'm happy to continue doing that until we can raise the kitchen budget. You can't tie my hands and tell me what to cook. I may know nothing else, but I do know food." She smiled ruefully. "I should have told you, Louise. I just didn't want to worry you."

Jane looked her startled older sister directly in the eye. "Instead, I believe I did something worse. We're partners. I'm sorry I made you think I was careless and insensitive to what we're trying to create. I thought I was doing something good for us, but now . . ."

"It is good, Jane, good and generous. If I had not been so . . ." Louise's lips trembled as if she were about to cry. "So *anxious* and fearful! I am not accustomed to the erratic nature of the hotel business. When I thought you were being reckless, not thinking about how we would manage," Louise sighed, "I am afraid I 'lost it,' as the young people say. I did not trust you, Jane. I treated you like a child. I am so sorry."

Sylvia had been right, Jane realized, and she herself had been so wrong. But there were things that she needed to say. "About that *child* thing . . ." She poked at the laugh lines near her eyes. "Do children have these?"

Louise smiled. "Not unless they're very unusual."

"Nor do they have ex-husbands, taxes to pay and their own color TV," she paused, "well, maybe their own TV. But I'm not a child anymore, you can treat me like an adult now."

"You will never know how many times I have regretted talking to you as I did when you were small. At the time, both Alice and I believed we had to take care of you. I suppose I thought I sounded maternal. Alice and I were trying to be children and little mothers at the same time. As it turns out, we were not very good at either."

"I wanted you to be my sisters, not my 'keepers.'"

"It was hard not to want to mother you, Jane. You were a beautiful child. Perfect. You slept all night and smiled all day. We all fell madly in love with you the moment Father brought you home from the hospital. You were the gift that made that awful time bearable."

The *gift*? Jane had always believed just the opposite.

"Father said it was important to make you feel loved," Louise continued, unaware of Jane's racing emotions, "that it was our job to help him make sure you did not miss having a mother too much. Alice and I were proud that he trusted us. We wanted to make you into our real live baby doll." She looked grieved. "I guess we got carried away. We became mothers and forgot to be sisters."

"Louie, does this mean that I can still buy artichokes if I promise to pay for them out of my own allowance?" Jane joked, to break the tension.

"You have no idea how much you remind me of Mother," Louise marveled. "She would tease us out of our 'spells,' too. We could never stay grumpy for very long."

They stood and Jane linked arms with her sister. "Will you tell me more about her? I want to hear every memory you have."

"I will. I would like that."

"And," Jane continued, as she pointed to yet another small trunk, "help me carry this down to my room. I want to see what's inside."

They carried the chest easily, working together to get it down the stairs without scratching the wall. As they did so, it occurred to Jane that Louise was willingly allowing her younger sister to carry her own part of the load.

Chapter Eight

"Hey, there, Jane." Fred Humbert greeted her cheerfully from behind the counter. For once, there was no one else in the store. Usually anyone who had a few spare minutes to chat ended up at Fred's. "I hear you've had some trouble at the inn. One of your guests . . ."

"Naomi had a stroke. Fortunately, Alice is working seven days in a row. She checks on her often, so the poor woman knows she's not alone. According to the doctors, she's doing remarkably well. They don't expect much permanent damage. She's already in physical therapy."

"What's she going to do next?"

"She can stay with us till she's strong enough to travel. Her niece said that she would come to get her when Naomi's ready."

"So you're an inn and a convalescent home now." Fred leaned back against the wall behind the cash register and crossed his arms. "Can you handle it?"

"We'll just have to manage the best we can. My father talked about the parable of the Good Samaritan too many times for us to do otherwise."

"You're good people," Fred concluded as he pushed himself off the wall and put his hands on the counter. "What do you need today?"

He laughed out loud at Jane's rendition of Lloyd's prediction about snakes coming through the foundation. "That Lloyd can sure get a twist in his shorts. Old houses do need constant upkeep, but you aren't going to have anything crawling into your basement for a good long time." He pulled a caulking gun from a nearby shelf. "Here's what you need. It's made especially for cracks and crevices. Go around the house with this and fill any cracks you might see. I'd probably take a look-see at it once a year."

"That's considerably easier than Lloyd made it seem, but still, I really don't have time to do that. Do you know someone who might want an odd job?"

"Wish I had someone who did. You can't imagine how many odd jobs people come in here wanting me to do. Tilling gardens, blowing snow, fixing bicycles—I just don't have enough hands to do it all, and not many fellas want such catch-as-catch-can work."

A glimmer of an idea formed in her head. "If I found someone to do my foundation and he wanted more work, would you consider hiring him?"

"You might as well pull a white rabbit out of your hat,

Jane, but good luck. Let me know when you find this miracle person."

Faith of our fathers, living still,
In spite of dungeon, fire and sword;
O how our hearts beat high with joy
Whenever we hear that glorious Word!

Third pew back on the pulpit side, old blue hymnal in hand, listening to the elderly voices behind her that could, with a touch more volume, break the glassware in the Assembly Room's kitchen, Jane realized that she felt more at home in Grace Chapel than at any other place in Acorn Hill.

Faith of our fathers, holy faith!
We will be true to thee till death.

Faith of our fathers, we will strive
To win all nations unto Thee:
And through the faith that comes from God,
We all shall then be truly free.

Growing up, she had believed this hymn had been written solely for the Father's Day program at Grace Chapel. The entire Sunday school would troop to the front of the church and deliver with more volume than tune:

Faith of our fathers, we will love
Both friend and foe in all our strife:
And preach Thee, too, as love knows how
By kindly words and virtuous life.

They had had no idea what, exactly, the words meant, but the children believed if they sang with enough gusto, their fathers would surely get the message that they were loved.

Jane felt that these hymns were sensory stimuli of the most powerful sort. It only took a few warbling notes of "Be Present at Our Table, Lord" for her to imagine she could smell brewing coffee from the Assembly Room and taste open-faced sandwiches made with ham salad, or with Cheese Whiz and sliced olives. She also recalled the cakes that were always brought in nine-by-thirteen pans—one yellow cake, one white and one chocolate—unless someone got a little adventurous and made marble. When the church ladies were not looking, she and her father would surreptitiously stuff their cake into a glass, cover it with milk and eat it with a spoon.

"Grace to you and peace, from God the Father and from our Lord Jesus Christ."

Pastor Thompson's voice carried into the farthest corners of the church.

"Come to Me, all you who are heavy ladened and I will give you rest."

The lure of that invitation was particularly strong for so many. *Heavy ladened*—that was Jane, her sisters, Naomi, Joe and a list of people so long that it would take a lifetime to recite. The news on the television and in the newspapers was a constant barrage of tragedy, strife, war, corruption and pain. But she did not have to carry those burdens alone—no one did. God was ready, His hands outstretched, ready to lift the load. All she had to do was ask.

Almost as if he had read her mind, Pastor Thompson said it from the pulpit, "God is *able*. Able to do anything we ask or dream, able to love us as we are, able to save us from ourselves and offer us salvation through His son.

You are here for a reason, Jane.

The words were as clear in her mind as if the pastor had spoken them from the pulpit. It did not matter that money for the inn was scarce, that Justin had betrayed her, that she and her sisters were still finding their way together or that she was only now reclaiming the full blessing of her faith. She *was* here for a reason. She did not know what reason yet, but God did, and that was good enough for her.

"Go in peace. Serve the Lord! Thanks be to God."

As the postlude rang out, Jane felt at peace. She was where she was supposed to be. Here. In Acorn Hill. Cooking at the inn. Loving her sisters. Championing Naomi, Josie and Joe Morales. It did not always seem to really make sense, but it did not have to. God was in charge, and it made sense to Him.

The chapel ushers had tried for years to get the congregants of Grace Chapel to wait in their pews until they could dismiss them. And for years, the ushers coming up the aisle to do so nearly had been trampled by the worshipers heading toward the door. Pastor Thompson, seeing this was a battle not worth fighting, had decided that it should be every man, woman and child for himself. Now the entire congregation rose at once, greeted neighbors, shook hands and pressed toward the back en masse. It was like trying to send a river's worth of water through a culvert—a flood on one end and a trickle on the other. Jane found herself wedged between Florence Simpson and Ethel, who were debating whether or not it was time to bleach the altar cloths.

Trying to catch Sylvia's attention, Jane almost missed the small, dark-haired man who darted from the back pew and skittered out the door of the church before the crowd pressed down upon him.

"Hey, Joe!" Jane piped. Vera Humbert and Hope Collins turned to stare. Jane waved weakly in their direction. She was tired of seeing this fellow scoot around like a shadow on the fringes of her world. They needed to talk.

When together she and Sylvia popped like a cork from a

bottle through the doors of the church and into the sunlight, Jane found that Joe had vanished. She turned to her friend. "Did you see a Hispanic man at the back of the church?"

"I've seen him around a few times."

"Aren't you curious who he is?" Were she and Rev. Thompson the only ones so drawn to him?

"Should I be? People pass through here every day." Sylvia wore a rhinestone brooch on her full-skirted turquoise cotton dress. Jane recognized the dress from the vintage clothing Sylvia had purchased.

"Love the clothes," Jane murmured to her.

"I had to pull it apart and re-sew it. I'm having so much fun with those old things that I'm hardly able to keep up with my alterations," Sylvia admitted. "You'd better come and take some of the fabric off my hands."

"I'll be over later," Jane promised. "I found a few things of my own in the attic."

She maneuvered past the clusters of people visiting on the lawn and walked quickly from the church to the house. She stopped for a moment to view the garden. The weeds were looking incredibly hardy compared to the greenhouse plants, which were becoming rather spindly. The garden needed some attention right now.

Jane changed from her pencil slim navy dress and bright chunky jewelry into stonewashed jeans and a plaid shirt that couldn't be harmed by a little mud or grass. Then she loaded a leather backpack with a sketchbook, pens, pencils and a small camera, slid her feet into a pair of thick-soled boots and headed downstairs. After a stop in the kitchen to find a liter of mineral water and an apple, Jane headed out the door.

She walked north on Chapel Road, waving at every driver who passed. A half hour later, she turned off Chapel Road and disappeared beneath an arch of low-hanging trees covering a trail, grandly called Fairy Lane, and tramped down the rutted path.

Her eyes grew accustomed to the dimness created by the overhanging trees closing out all but slivers of sunlight, and she took in the multitudinous shades of green, from palest celadon to emerald to olive. Dark brown bark, pale tan twigs and a footpath of umber, slate and gray earth accentuated the palette. She felt as though she were walking through a cave of leaves to reach a bright, pure spot at the center of the earth.

And there it was. Fairy Pond, small but delightful, provided a home for lily pads, fat green frogs and memories.

She sat down on the first thick log she came across. She had come here so many times as a child and as a teenager that she couldn't even count them. Every time that life had held a seemingly insurmountable problem, she had retreated to Fairy Pond and had come away with peace enough to face the situation. As a youngster, Jane was convinced that God had created this place especially for her.

It had not, however, surprised her one day to find her father sitting on a log, looking into the green water of the pond and watching a frog unroll his tongue to snag passing insects.

It had been the day after Joe Skelly's death. Joe and Daniel had been the best of friends, allied by a love of nature and a faith in God.

She could recall curling up beside her father on the ground, and being serenaded by the buzzing of insects and rustle of leaves. When he spoke, Daniel's voice was a whisper.

"'He who dwells in the shelter of the Most High, who abides in the shadow of the Almighty, will say to the Lord, "My refuge and my fortress: my God in whom I trust.'"

"Remember that, Janie, Psalm 91 (RSV). Put God first, and everything else will fall into place." He had stared out across the little pond, and she had wondered what it was—really—that he was seeing. "I know this is your sanctuary, Janie, but there's another safe haven, the refuge of His presence. Sometimes we need to withdraw and close ourselves in with Him alone. It is with Him that we can be refilled, consoled and protected." He had glanced around, the sunlight reflecting from his wire-rimmed glasses. "You don't need to come here to find Him, you know."

"It just seems easier somehow."

"Each time you come to Him, wherever you are, makes it easier to return the next time."

"Really, Daddy? Even now, after Mr. Skelly's . . ."

"Death? Of course. Where else could I go but to God?" His voice had quavered as he spoke. "Mr. Skelly was a big man willing to go to his knees every morning and give his day to God. When we were young men, he told me to follow the advice of the Psalmist and my life would be richer than I'd ever thought possible."

Jane remembered how it had shocked her to think that her father did not know everything there was to know about Scripture.

"'O Lord, in the morning thou dost hear my voice; in the morning I prepare a sacrifice for thee and watch (Psalm 5:3, RSV).' Spend time with Him, Jane. Give Him the best part of your day, the best of you. Read His word, talk to Him, and get to know Him. That is all He wants of you, a relationship. He created us to be in a relationship with Him. And when that bond is made, that connection sealed, you will have a secret place to hide and to heal any time you want."

It was in that moment that she had decided that God *would* have the best part of her day, that He would come first, before her friends, her school, the boyfriend of the moment.

When, she wondered, had she stopped giving God the best of her day? It was not a conscious act, certainly, but a result of distractions, of her move to California and the newness of her life there. And here she was, full circle. Fairy Pond seemed smaller now, and the once small trees now hovered over it like giants. New growth had sprung up. Generations of frogs and lily pads had come and gone. But God was still here—in the beauty, in the peace, in her being.

She sighed as she took out her sketchbook and pencil. "Okay, Lord, the best part of every day is Yours again. I'm beginning to see what You want of me. I'm a morning person, so I hope you don't mind getting up at five o'clock to talk."

She had just emerged from Fairy Lane onto Chapel Road when Pastor Thompson drove up. He put on the brakes, pressed a button to roll down the passenger side window and asked, "Need a ride or are you out for the exercise?"

Jane shifted her backpack on her shoulder. It seemed heavier now than it had three hours before. She had lost track of time in her private glade, but she had an impressive array of sketches of lily pads, fallen trees and shafts of sunlight sifting through a dense overhang of trees to show for her efforts. Her fingers were itching to get home and create a palette of greens before she forgot what she had seen.

"I'd appreciate a ride, thank you." She reached for the door handle, opened the door and slipped inside.

"Sorry about the mess on the front seat," the pastor said. There were two Bibles, a stack of Sunday school fliers, a concordance, papers scribbled with sermon notes and a plate of oatmeal cookies dotted with butterscotch chips.

He followed her gaze to the cookies. "I've been visiting Martha Bevins. She's almost as good a cook as you. It's one of the perks of the job—and one of the hazards. He glanced down at his board-flat stomach. "There's an unwritten rule in some small churches. If you love the preacher, feed him. If you want to persuade the preacher to change, feed him. If in doubt about anything at all . . ."

"Feed him!" they chimed together.

"You're complaining to the wrong person about that. All I know how to do is feed people," Jane said with a laugh. "I suppose I can dig out a few low-calorie recipes, if need be."

"Please don't. Have you had any more teas at the inn?"

"Not yet. We've had some issues about the grocery budget, so I want to pencil things out to prove that we can actually *make* money on them before I go further."

He pulled in front of the inn and turned off the motor. "Is everything all right, Jane?"

"What are you, an X-ray machine?"

"I sense something weighing on you, that's all." He

leaned his back against the driver's side door and put his right arm on the back of his seat so he could look at her.

"Things are . . . coming back, that's all. At Fairy Pond it was as if my father were right there with me, reminding me with his presence of . . ." she paused, surprised at the emotion lodged in her throat, "of some of the things he taught me, things I vowed I'd never forget—and promptly did."

The pastor's presence was so nonthreatening, his attitude so nonjudgmental that Jane wanted to continue.

"When I left here at eighteen, I assumed my faith was part of me, like the color of my eyes, virtually fixed. I never quit assuming that until I returned to Acorn Hill and discovered that my faith wasn't like the color of my eyes. It's more like a seed in a garden or a newly planted tree. Without proper attention, it withers without anyone ever noticing—not even me.

"If you'd asked me two years ago if I was a Christian, I would have said, 'Yes, absolutely.' There's no doubt in my mind where my salvation comes from. But I'm a Christian who hasn't been living the faith one hundred percent. I put God on a shelf and left Him there for more years than I care to admit. As my father always said, 'When He comes knocking, let Him in.' I let Him in, all right, and then ignored Him."

"But He never left."

"I know that now." She leaned back in the seat and looked out at the sky. "He's been murmuring to me all this time, and I've been foolish enough to ignore it."

"Welcome home, Jane."

She put her hand over his and gave it a squeeze. "It's good to be back."

Intent in conversation, they did not notice the reconnaissance going on through the shrubbery around the carriage house where Ethel lived. If they had, Jane might have had some warning about what would come next.

"Thanks for the ride and the talk," Jane said as she opened the car door and put one foot on the ground.

"Thank *you*. I've enjoyed getting to know you. You've been a very pleasant . . ." he chose his word carefully, "change."

"From negotiating the pitfalls of spending the memorial money and keeping the entire church board speaking to one another?" Jane smiled when he flushed. "I grew up with a preacher, remember? Sometimes it's good to talk to someone with a fresh perspective."

"You *are* my fresh perspective, Jane."

"You have permission to call next time the board decides to volunteer the church facility for a weekend seminar on 'The Diligent Church Board Member' without checking to see if you had any weddings scheduled."

He winced. "So it's all over town then?"

"You did the right thing, rescheduling the seminar. Even my father would have picked hand-to-paw combat with a mountain lion rather than tussle it out with the mothers of the bride *and* groom."

Inside the calm embrace of the inn, Jane noticed Ethel's vase on the foyer table. Knowing how particular her aunt was about her property, she decided to return it before someone snagged a purse on it and toppled it to the floor. She set her own bag on the floor, picked up the vase, and made her way out of the inn and through the hedge to the carriage house, and was promptly attacked by the Decorum Police waiting on the other side.

Ethel and Florence were seated in two wooden rocking chairs on Ethel's narrow front porch. They were grimly rocking in tandem. If properly wired they could have generated enough energy to power the town itself.

Jane was accustomed to her aunt and Florence looking disapproving—they likely woke up that way—but they looked even more censorious than usual.

"Hi, ladies. It's a lovely day to be outside, isn't it? I sketched for a few hours by Fairy Pond, and it was glorious. Aunt Ethel, here's your vase. Thanks again for the flowers."

"So *that's* what they call it now—sketching." For a short woman, Ethel sat very tall in her chair.

Florence took in air and blew it our through her nose in a snort of disapproval that might have removed her sinuses. "*Sketching*. Creative, I'll give her that."

"All I can say, Jane, is that you'd better be careful who you're *sketching* with. If not for yourself, for him." Ethel looked indignant. Curious little points of heat rode high on her cheeks and her nose was pink.

"What on earth are you talking about?" Jane put the vase down out of the way of the fast clipping rockers.

"You don't have to play dumb with us," Florence said. "We aren't *blind*."

"I never thought you were." Jane felt just as she had the night Ethel had caught her past curfew, parked in her boyfriend's Impala. They actually *had* been only talking, but she had been tried, found guilty and condemned long before Ethel reached the car. Fortunately her father had intervened before Ethel could design an "appropriate" punishment for such an infraction. Daniel had given Jane a mild lecture, extracted a promise from her that she would be on time from then on and left it at that. Ethel, on the other hand, had glared at her every time she saw her for the next three months.

But that was then and this was now…or was it?

"Excuse me if I'm being a little dense, but why are you

so upset?" She had to ask even though the sinking feeling in her stomach indicated that she already knew.

"We saw you come home with Pastor Ken. The way you two were talking and laughing, we knew it wasn't about church work," Florence declared indignantly.

Jane quelled an urge to laugh. She *was* a teenager again. Would she be eighty and the last of the family before it was her turn to be the adult? Or were they fiercely protecting the hapless, helpless Pastor Thompson from a wanton woman? It was a question definitely worth exploring. "Am I to assume that no one laughs or smiles when they're talking about serious matters?"

"Well, I certainly don't," Ethel chimed in. "We saw him practically put his arm around you."

Jane did a double take. Put his arm around her? No wonder eyewitnesses were considered such unreliable sources.

"And the way you held his hand..."

"Wait a minute. I don't know what you ladies thought you saw, but whatever it was is completely *wrong*. Pastor Thompson graciously offered me a ride home, which I gratefully accepted. We visited until I said good-bye, and then I walked over here to be thoroughly insulted."

She turned to leave, but Ethel called out. "Well, even if nothing happened, it didn't look good."

Jane counted to ten, reminded herself that Ethel was her father's sister and invited God to design the next words to come out of her mouth.

"Thanks for your concern, ladies, but you are reading much more into this than there is." There. She had been as polite as she could be—divinely polite, in fact.

Though it was slowly dawning on the pair that their overactive imaginations may have taken them a little further than they had intended, neither was ready to concede defeat. "You should know better anyway," Ethel said cryptically.

Jane stared blankly at her.

"He's not age-appropriate for you."

"I'm fifty years old, Ethel."

"Exactly."

Things were growing surreal. "I'm not a child anymore, Aunt Ethel."

"That's precisely my point. You're much too old for him."

"He can't be a day over forty-five," Florence added.

"I'm cradle-robbing?" Jane choked back laughter.

"Don't be difficult, Jane. You should be befriending men your own age, Wilhelm Wood, for example. He's at least fifty-four or fifty-five."

"Wilhelm Wood didn't offer me a ride home, Aunt Ethel." Jane felt remarkably good-natured considering the circumstances. This was the funniest thing that had happened in days. No wonder her childhood was so vivid for her here. To most people in Acorn Hill, she had never left it.

She looked at Aunt Ethel, still rocking vigorously, grappling to keep her composure despite having called the game all wrong, and at Florence, Ethel's cohort in gossip but also her dear friend. Jane's heart warmed. With a quick step, she covered the territory between them and somehow managed to gather them both into her arms.

With Aunt Ethel's White Shoulders perfume thick in her nostrils, she gave the pair affectionate hugs. Then she stood back and watched them regroup, patting their hair and straightening the shoulder pads they had refused to cut out of their dresses in the nineties. "You two must be the cutest ladies on earth," Jane blurted. "Thanks for caring." As she said it, she realized that she meant it.

She practically felt the two pairs of eyes, filled with confusion, watching her go. From now on she was taking the best of Acorn Hill and leaving behind what no longer fit. God was tapping on her shoulder every day. From now on she would pay attention and rely on His guiding hand.

"You've got to be kidding me!" Sylvia hooted as Jane told her about the incident later that evening. "No way!"

"Truth!" Jane put her hand in the air. "And they were so cute."

"I'm glad you thought so." Sylvia pushed her glasses back up her nose with her index finger. "You've more patience than I. Sometimes small-town living grates on my nerves. By the way, I've got someone to repair the fence around my house. The fellow you pointed out at church came into the shop the other day. Poor guy had a pair of pants that were in shreds. He wanted them fixed but said he didn't have any money so we bartered for services. I'm going to sew him a few simple shirts and sweat pants, and patch up his other clothes while he's working on the fence."

"Joe Morales?" Jane's pulse quickened.

"That's him. What a sweet man. He even fixed a loose hinge on my shop door before he left. Do you need work done too?"

"More than a little."

"I'll send him over when he comes to repair the fence. By the look of his clothes he could use a job."

Chapter Nine

"I think we need help around here." Jane planted her feet firmly on the kitchen floor, ready to do battle if necessary. "Someone to patch the foundation and work on the garden."

Alice looked up from the inn's ledger with a furrowed brow. "We haven't the money to hire someone just now. Maybe in the fall . . ."

It would be too late in the fall. Joe needed a job now.

"If I can find a way to finance a handyman who will work for a reasonable price, would you consider it?"

"How do you plan to do this 'financing'?" Louise asked. At least since their confrontation she was willing to listen before flying to judgment. "It does not involve turning off the electricity or not paying the water bill, does it?"

"No, it doesn't, and I don't think you'll be sorry."

Jane waited impatiently on the front porch until she saw Joe walking up Chapel Road. Perfect. Sylvia had sent him just when she said she would.

She met Joe half way down the block, prudently out of sight of Ethel's front window. "Hello. Thanks for coming." She greeted him as if they were old friends. "Remember me? You stumbled into my hedges?"

"I am so sorry. I did not mean any harm."

"I know that." She accepted his apology. "In fact, I was wondering if you'd like to do some work for me. I hear you're working for Sylvia Songer and she's very pleased. Pastor Thompson is a friend of mine too. He told me about your job at the dairy."

Joe's shoulders dropped, and she saw the fatigue in his face. "It is work."

"Where are you living?" She was beginning to sound like Ethel, but at least it was for a good cause.

"Here and there," he answered vaguely.

"Churches and barns?"

His expression told her that he was shocked at having been found out.

"You've been having a very hard time," she said softly.

He spread his hands in a helpless, telling gesture.

"Why are you in Acorn Hill?" Jane asked.

"Why not?" He shrugged. "My parents were migrant workers. I was born in this country during beet season in Minnesota. All my life, we worked at the same sugar beet farm."

"Why haven't you gone back?"

Joe's eyes grew sad. "The farmer died and everything changed. The land was sold, and we were no longer wanted."

"Where's your family now?"

"Mexico."

"And you're trying to make money to send home?"

He turned his head away but Jane could see the pain in his expression. "My parents are old now. They need help. My nieces and nephews, too."

"Would you like more work? Maybe something not quite so difficult?"

"There is no such thing for me." He did not even look up. The defeated slump of his shoulders told Jane that he was close to giving up.

"I can't pay you much, and the jobs I have for you are limited, but, if you'd like to meet a friend of mine, he might be able to help you." Jane prayed she was telling the truth. Poor Fred had no idea what she had in mind.

He looked at her strangely, but he followed her as she turned off Chapel Road onto Hill Street and stopped in front of Fred's Hardware.

"Will you wait here for a moment?" Her mouth was dry, and her heart was beating double time. Now, too late, she was having second thoughts. But Fred had *said* . . . She took a deep breath and marched into the store.

Fred looked up from the inventory sheet he was reading and grinned. "Hey, Jane. To what do I owe this pleasure?"

"It may not be a pleasure, Fred. Just promise you won't kick me out before I'm done talking."

His open, friendly expression grew puzzled. "That would be pretty hard to do, Jane."

"But you don't know how much I've been meddling in your affairs—or at least how much I want to meddle. I found someone to run your tiller and your snowblower. He can pick up the slack in all those areas you said yourself that you're too busy to do. What do you think?"

"It might be good and it might not. Depends on who this fellow is and where you found him. Are you sure he can do it?"

"I want you to find out." She pointed out the window to where Joe was waiting. He was picking up scraps of litter on the street and shoving them into a plastic grocery sack he had found on the ground. The sun glinted off his straight black hair as he bent to pick up a soda can. "Pastor Thompson told me about him," Jane forged ahead with the story. "And," she concluded, "Sylvia Songer is having him repair a fence for her. If he can work at the dairy farm, I'm sure he'd have no trouble with anything you'd find for him to do."

"Can he run machinery? Communicate with my customers? Run the store if necessary?" Fred did not look happy. But, under the circumstances, Jane thought, he was responding fairly well.

"Will you at least talk to him?" Jane heard herself plead. What had possessed her to do this, anyway? She could not seem to stop herself. It was as if God had placed His hand in the small of her back and pushed at her to beg Fred to hire a complete stranger. And if God wanted this, then it was good. She didn't have to understand.

"Fred, I can't explain it, but I believe this is a God thing. That's all I can say. Will you at least talk to him?"

Fred sighed and furrowed his brow. "Only for you, Jane. Only for you."

Lemon Drops

1 cup butter

⅓ cup powdered sugar

1 teaspoon vanilla

⅔ cup cornstarch

1 cup flour

⅛ teaspoon salt

Cream butter, sugar and vanilla. Add dry ingredients. Roll in tiny balls. Bake at 350 degrees for fifteen minutes. Cool slightly before removing. Frost with lemon frosting.

Lemon Frosting

1½ cups powdered sugar
2 teaspoons lemon juice
¼ cup butter

Mix frosting ingredients until well blended and smooth. Will make one-and-a-half to two-and-a-half dozen, depending on size of balls made. Smaller are daintier.

A lot of busywork for cookies, but so cute.

Later Madeleine had added,

Maybe someday one of my daughters will open this book, try a recipe or two and think of me. It's odd, but I never think of myself as an old woman baking for my grandchildren. Is it because I will never have grandchildren, or is it because I will never be old?

Jane poured herself a cup of coffee and sat down at the kitchen table. Her mother had always been thinking of others. What would Madeleine have done for Naomi?

Alice had brought her home to the inn from the hospital while Jane was out. She had checked on her soundly sleeping patient a half dozen times since she returned from the hardware store. Naomi, a pale, fragile figure in the big bed, had not stirred. Naomi, even when she was well, had not been a strong presence. Still, Jane sensed, she had it within her to fight back, to regain what she had lost.

Here was another puzzle that God had delivered to her. First Joe. Now Naomi. What did He want of her? She had assumed the inn would be a haven for travelers and the weary, but she had never expected this.

The doorbell had rung several times before Jane reached it, still wiping her hands on a blue and white cotton dishcloth. She tucked the towel in the waistband of her jeans and opened the door.

"Vera! What a nice surprise. Come in."

Fred Humbert's wife stepped over the threshold and stared at the gleaming wood and ornate rugs. "It's prettier every time I come here, Jane. How can that be?"

"I keep moving things around." Jane whispered conspiratorially, not knowing if Louise had returned from a visit to church. "'Fluffing,' I call it. I move a lamp here, a photograph there to make things more cohesive. So far no one's said a thing."

"You are quite something," Vera said, smiling.

"Thank you." Jane waved a hand toward the kitchen. "Come and join me. I'm trying one of Mother's recipes."

"So you found a cookbook of your mother's and are making her favorite recipes." Vera sat at the kitchen table drinking coffee and looking right at home. "How nice."

"My mother was a fascinating woman." Jane pushed the recipe book toward Vera. "Look at that."

I must remember never to have another luncheon for the ladies of the church. They came and ate like a horde of locusts, talked both ears off the dog and left more dirty dishes behind than I'd taken out of the cupboard. Daniel says I'm being uncharitable. Maybe it will pass with time. Lest I forget and think of doing it again next year, this note should bring me to my senses.

Vera burst out laughing. "So the ladies haven't changed so very much after all these years. Your mother must have been quite a woman. My grandmother always said if everyone in the world were like Madeleine, it would be a better place.'"

Jane stopped beating the frosting to stare at Vera. "Your grandmother knew her?"

"Oh yes. They were in a social group together. As Grandma grew older, she often reminisced about it. Those were the dearest friends my grandmother ever had."

"And your grandmother? Is she?"

"Passed away two years ago at the nursing home in Potterston. Her short-term memory was gone, but she still mentioned 'the girls.'"

"Tell me more." Jane didn't want Vera to see her hand trembling so she began to frost the first of the lemon drops.

"I don't know much more, really. Just that it was a group of ladies who got together every month and did . . . whatever ladies did then. A book club? A garden society? I never really knew. She did say that they'd promised one another that as, one by one, they moved away that they would always keep in touch. As far as I know, they never abandoned that promise. I wrote a few letters myself to Grandma's friends. As she got older, her eyesight failed and I took over her correspondence."

Jane carefully put the frosted confection onto a dish. "Do you remember who any of those women were? Or if any are still alive?"

"Some might be, but I don't have any way to find out. We didn't save Grandma's letters."

So close and yet so far. The idea of talking with one of her mother's best friends was tantalizing. In the eighteen years she had lived with her father and sisters, they had always spoken of her in a misty, loving way but without the kind of detail Jane craved. Ethel occasionally had brought up Madeleine's name, and the ladies of the church often had assured her how much she was like her mother in personality and style. But she had been a child. It had not occurred to her to ask the questions that might help her to know the person her mother had been. Everyone assured her that her mother was "nice," "kind" and "generous." But who was she *really*? Who was Madeleine in the privacy of her own thoughts and the emotions of her heart? Those were the things true friends might know.

Automatically, because she was so accustomed to serving food, Jane filled a plate with the lemon cookies, set it in front of Vera and poured more coffee.

"Scrumptious." Vera licked the frosting from her fingers. "And it brings me to the subject of why I stopped by today. I've been hearing about the tea you gave . . . ."

Ethel and Lloyd.

"Maybe this is too much to ask, but I was wondering if you'd be willing to cater a tea here. The teachers at school have a birthday club. For years we've gone out for dinner or to a movie. Now we've started meeting in each other's homes because we've used up all the restaurants in a thirty-mile radius. The inn would be an absolutely perfect place for us to meet. And if you'd serve a real English tea, it would be our best party in years." Vera looked so hopeful that Jane laughed out loud.

"I can't think of anything I'd rather do. It's a . . . a . . . stupendous idea." Already she was running recipes from Madeleine's cookbook through her head.

Vera's pleasant features relaxed and her eyes began to twinkle. "They're going to love this. Perhaps we could provide a favor for each of them to take home, something at each place setting. I wonder what it might be . . . ."

"Vera, my dear, I'll take care of it." Visions of candies wrapped in beautiful foil and inscribed with . . . what? Something would come to her, Jane was sure. Her energy surged at the idea of a challenge. If she could make the inn's kitchen succeed like she had the Blue Fish Grille's, she could cook day and night. And that was her idea of bliss.

"Naomi? Are you awake?" Jane poked her head into the bedroom.

"Come in." Naomi spoke slowly. The slight slurring of her words was disappearing rapidly and her arm, thanks to Alice and a physical therapist, was getting stronger every day.

"Play any tennis lately?" Jane sat on the edge of the bed and smiled.

"Three sets today. Jumped over the net twice."

"Good. That's more than yesterday. What are you going to do tomorrow? Bowl? Water ski? Ride horseback? Sit in the sun room and read?" They'd been playing this game since Naomi arrived.

"Sun room, I think. I don't own a horse."

"You're doing great, you know. The doctor has been amazed."

"Wonder Woman, that's me." She sounded discouraged.

"Are you feeling down again?"

"I'm so tired all the time. A trip to the bathroom is like a trip to the equator."

"Let's add another walk to your schedule tomorrow. You just need your strength back. Doctor's orders."

"You all do too much already." Her voice quavered. "I can't ask any more."

"Sure you can." Jane put her hands over Naomi's. "Let us help you. Don't deprive us of that."

"Why are you doing this?" Naomi's face was gaunt against the pillow.

Jane took a moment to consider the question. "Because we want to, and because I'm convinced that God wants us to. You aren't the only one who came to Acorn Hill to heal. I came with plenty of wounds myself. Occasionally someone touches a sore spot in me, but very seldom now."

Naomi was silent for a moment, the expression on her face revealing that she was deep in thought. "You know, I believe I could be like you someday." She smiled faintly.

"Maybe soon. What have I got to lose by being brave and taking care of myself? Not much. Being passive and shy hasn't done anything for either my marriage or my health, has it?"

"That's the spirit!" Jane handed Naomi the rubber ball she had been given to squeeze to strengthen her hand. "Keep practicing, champ. You'll never be a big league pitcher if you don't keep working." The smile she received was reward enough.

"How is she?" Louise met Jane in the hall.

"Hanging in there. It feels like she's turning a corner." Jane looked at Louise with gratitude in her eyes. "You and Alice have been simply great about Naomi. I thought she would be my cause, but you've both been amazing. Thank you."

"*Harrumph*. If this inn cannot be a place where people can come and heal—physically or spiritually—then what is the point of having it? We are not simply a business. Alice and I have talked many times about the inn as a ministry. Naomi is simply providing the opportunity for it to be that."

Humming, Jane mounted the next flight of stairs to her room with her favorite reading material—cookbooks—tucked under her arm. Madeleine's, of course, was right on top. It was always a pleasure and even a relief to return to her room. The formality and antiquated beauty of the inn was perfect for guests, but she needed a space that was her own.

Alice and Louise had stopped coming in here weeks

ago, always unnerved by the contemporary look Jane had given her room. To counteract the formality of the first and second floors, Jane had decorated the room with a low-slung contemporary bed covered with a down comforter robed in a silky duvet and a small, armless couch filled with pillows. Her blond Danish furniture showed well against the reddish purple paint on the walls. She loved the feel of the smooth wooden floor beneath her feet and the way it showcased her vivid, geometric rug. But it was the walls that pleased her most. Covered with the paintings that she loved best from her collection, they allowed Jane to run her gaze over them and enjoy an avalanche of memories.

Each painting represented a season of her life, from the portrait of her childhood dog to dramatic slashes of primary colors that she had had hanging in her home in San Francisco. The artwork of friends and her own moody pencil sketches done after her separation were all there, the timeline of her life.

When she spied the small chest that she had carried down from the attic, Jane put down her books and busied herself with it. With a nail file wrapped in cloth to prevent scratching, she pried the chest open. Fortunately the lock had served as little more than ornamentation. When she lifted the lid, she was disappointed. Just more papers, clippings and a few old photos of people she didn't recognize.

On top was a black-and-white photo of a young couple holding fishing rods. Snow-capped mountains bordered the expanse of a lake at their backs. The woman was holding an impressive looking lake trout, while the man wore the sour expression of someone who had endured a no-catch day. Something about the shape of the man's face struck her as particularly familiar. She picked up the photo to study it closer. Could it be . . . was he ever that young? A twenty-something Daniel Howard stared back at her.

Jane took in a deep breath. If this was her father, then . . .

It was Madeleine Howard, all right, holding the immense fish. Daniel had his arm around her delicate waist. Her face was oval-shaped and flawless, the picture of beauty and love in bloom. A new door opened before her. Madeleine and Daniel as newlyweds.

The chest took on new importance and the recipe books lay untouched, as Jane sorted piece by piece through the remnants of her mother and father's life together.

Her mother had loved household hints, it appeared, for there were a number of brittle yellowed clippings: "For a toothache, apply a clove to affected area," "A slice of bread will keep the brown sugar in a canister soft," "Brown soap works wonders against poison ivy."

There were church bulletins on which she had taken

notes and had circled Daniel's name with flowing lines or tiny hearts.

It was near dusk by the time Jane got to the bottom of the chest. Her stomach was growling, and she knew there was hearty potato and bacon soup waiting in the refrigerator. The last layer of paper was different from the rest—envelopes, letters bound in silk ribbons tied with bows. The handwriting was curlicued and elaborate, done in a feminine hand. She would take time to open just one letter. The rest could be set aside for later.

The faded handwriting was embellished with scrolls and swirls. Pale blue splotches on the vellum revealed that the author had used a fine-tipped fountain pen.

Dear Maddie,

Just a quick note to say hello and tell you how we're doing here. The twins have had the croup for days. Finally they're sounding less like baby seals and more like baby humans. Dr. told me to use steam in their rooms. I did as he said and now the wallpaper is drooping off their walls. How are your girls? That little Alice is such a dumpling, so smiley and calm.

Is Louise still insisting on hammering on the piano every time you try to play? Maybe she'll grow up to be organist at Grace Chapel!

It makes me sad, sometimes, to think how little we see of each other now that we all have husbands and babies to care for.

How is Daniel? Still preaching up a storm? Curtis is teaching English, history, geography and art at the high school here in Potterston. Can you believe it? Art! From a man who can hardly draw his own breath!

I've been using your recipe for tapioca every week. The family loves it. Have you considered writing a cookbook? I'd give them for Christmas—especially to Curtis's sisters who need to learn their way around the kitchen.

Are you still hoping to put another "bun in the oven"?

Maybe you'll get twins like mine. I can guarantee more than your wallpaper will droop!

Next time Daniel has a ministerial meeting here, ride along and we'll visit. Sometimes it's not as much fun to grow up as we'd hoped, is it? I miss your sense of humor and your laughter.

Love and big hugs,

Gracie

She didn't know how long she sat, holding the letter in her

hand, but she was startled to hear doors opening and closing on the first and second floors and to realize that the sun had disappeared below the horizon. Reluctantly, she put the letter back into its envelope and into the trunk.

Maddie. Louise hammering on the piano. Another bun in the oven. A young mother with friends, toddlers, a loving husband and a desire to have another child—the picture it drew showed yet another side of Madeleine's life. Jane had been a planned baby, wanted long before she was conceived. Somehow that made a great deal of difference.

Alice was heating the soup and carving thick slices of bread from a loaf that Jane had baked earlier while Louise set the table. They both looked at Jane when she walked into the room.

"Since you weren't here, we started fixing supper—warming it, actually. We've been very spoiled by all the food that just seems to appear on our table . . . ." Alice paused. "Is something wrong? You look pale."

"Not wrong, exactly." She dropped into her chair at the table and twiddled with the silverware. "I opened that chest we carried down from the attic, Louise. It was full of mother's clippings, photos . . . and letters. Do either of you remember a friend of mother's named Gracie?"

"I wonder if it's the same Gracie Mother went to school with. She and several other friends used to get together with Mother and visit while we children played." Alice paused, knife in mid-air. "I remember how they laughed, those women, just like schoolgirls. I was actually jealous a time or two that they were having more fun visiting than we little ones."

"Mother had a lot of friends," Louise added.

"This woman lived in Potterston when the letter was written. I wonder if it's possible that she could still be there."

"She would have to be ninety-something by now. It is unlikely that she is still living. Why?" asked Louise.

Too late. That is how it always seemed to Jane in her quest to find her mother.

"I don't know, just wondering. It would be nice to meet someone who was young with Mother, don't you think?"

"Nice? Yes. But I would not get my hopes up," Louise said bluntly as she sat down to eat.

Louise and Alice were upstairs chatting with Naomi.

Jane slipped through the kitchen door and traipsed toward Sylvia's Buttons across the lawns and alleyways that paralleled Hill Street. She was making that trip so often now, that Sylvia usually left the back door open so she could slip in whenever she chose.

Sylvia was there, as always, this time with a large

unopened safety pin protruding from her lips. "Hullo," she mumbled. "Hep me w'd this coverlet."

Jane opened her hand and Sylvia let the pin fall into her palm. "Thanks. If you'd just help me turn this thing forty degrees or so, I can finish pinning it." She tossed red hair back from her eyes with a flip of her head. "This is so bulky. I remember now why I don't usually agree to sew bedding for anyone. What's up?"

When Jane finished telling her about the letter and the ones yet unread, Sylvia leaned back in her chair and screwed her face into a frown. "You've been working too hard for too long. And when you aren't working, you're thinking. You'll sprain your brain if you aren't careful. Let's go antiquing tomorrow. I'll drive"

"I live in an antique. I don't need more."

"Arting then."

"What, pray tell, is that?" Jane fell captive to Sylvia's cheerfulness. Sylvia was more jovial now than when Jane had first started coming to the shop. Jane liked to think that she had had something to do with it, but she suspected all those cartons of clothing and fabric had done as much as she.

"Looking for things to make art with, of course. And looking at art itself. We'll throw in a few antiques just for fun. I'd love to get my hands on a jar of old buttons and an antique pincushion. Maybe you can find some old jewelry to redesign. And there's always lunch. Don't you ever get tired of eating your own food?"

Jane laughed. "That's what keeps me on my toes. I refuse to eat food that bores me—including my own. Just keeping myself from being bored usually keeps me pretty far ahead of the pack cooking-wise."

"There's a great little pizza place in Potterston, the best in Pennsylvania, I think. Will that do?"

"Perfect. Pick me up at nine."

"And we'll start off at Acorn Hill Antiques. Rachel and Joseph find some lovely things for their shop. I have them looking for buttons and pincushions too."

Jane felt lighthearted as she walked home. She needed a day away. And, if she could find a last name on one of those envelopes she had not studied yet, maybe she would try to look up the mysterious Gracie.

Louise and Alice,

Going to Potterston with Sylvia. Egg bake in refrigerator. Don't overcook. I made fresh granola with honey and almonds yesterday. Delish.
You know the routine.

Back later.

Jane

She felt like a child playing hooky from school. It seemed a little naughty, this day all to herself. Determined to make the most of it, she headed for Sylvia's car, which was waiting in front of the inn.

"Let's go to Rachel and Joseph's first," Sylvia said as Jane slid into the passenger seat. Sylvia took off the enormous straw hat she was wearing and laid it on the seat between them.

"Where did you get that hat? It looks like a Frisbee on steroids."

"Don't make fun of my hat." Sylvia patted her cheeks. "Redheads don't do well in sun. Be glad I have it. Otherwise I'd turn into a single, giant human freckle—if I didn't get sunstroke first."

"You paint a pretty picture. Do you have sunblock?"

"SPF fifty." She turned to grin at Jane. "This is fun. I can't remember the last time I actually put a sign in my front window saying 'Closed. Back tomorrow.' How about you?"

"It's been awhile. I really don't look on the inn as burdensome work. Hard and long, yes, but cooking is my passion. How many people can say that they've made a living with their passion?"

"Me," Sylvia admitted happily. They exchanged a knowing glance. Shared experience was one of the reasons they had fallen into this comfortable friendship so quickly. "The Holzmanns are just opening the store. I've heard they've recently been on a few shopping expeditions. We can see what's new."

Acorn Hill Antiques was housed in a building that had once been an old creamery, where local farmers brought and sold milk and eggs. Jane wished she could get her hands on "real" eggs more often, the kind from free-range chickens, the yolks of which were a vibrant golden yellow and were far tastier to Jane's palate than the store-bought kind. She remembered trips to the creamery here as a child, to the front counter where they sold orange soda and milk in real glass bottles and had bins of candy from which to choose. She and her friends had sat on the high stools by the counter swinging their legs as they sucked orange sodas through straws and divvied up the penny candy they had purchased.

The Holzmanns had left the rough brick walls in their original state, so that the building truly appeared to be as much of an antique as the things it housed.

Joseph Holzmann, a short, thin fellow who wore scholarly looking wire-rims, greeted them. "You ladies are out early."

"We're on a mission," Sylvia said, her manner suggestive of a cloak-and-dagger assignment. "Buttons, pincushions, old jewelry and fabrics. Can you help us?"

Chapter Ten

By one o'clock, Jane and Sylvia had sifted through every bead, button and bauble in Potterston's antique shops. Jane rubbed her back with her free hand; the other was loaded with shopping bags. "I've got to sit down. My eyes are crossed, and my lower back is killing me."

"But you made out like a bandit," Sylvia pointed out cheerfully.

"You're right. Some of these things will make standout pieces of jewelry. Now all I have to do is figure out when I'll have time to work on them. Not until after Vera's tea, I'm sure." She eyed Sylvia's bags. "You didn't do too badly yourself. I had no idea you were such a shopper."

"Vintage buttons, three pincushions and a couple more classic outfits. I've started a collection." Sylvia lifted a finger to point toward a small brick building at the far end of the street. "See that little brick place? That's Bernardo's, the best pizza in Pennsylvania. Are you up for it?"

"Absolutely, bring it on."

The small building had an oddly shaped roof and a

neon sign in the window that flashed both "Open" and "Closed" as if it could not make up its mind which it was. "Unusual building, isn't it?" Jane commented.

"Originally it was a blacksmith shop."

"So even our lunch will be in an antique. That's fitting."

Ordering was simple because the choices were few. Jane liked that. She had never trusted a place that had too many items on the menu. It usually meant that a good share of them were heat and serve from the freezer. At the Blue Fish Grille she had insisted on having a limited menu but with the choices so appetizing that even finicky eaters could not resist.

While Sylvia picked up the pizza to take to the table, Jane studied notices on the cork bulletin board by the wall near the door. Business cards, kittens to give away, a dog—kennel and all—two thirteen-year-olds advertising for babysitting jobs, and a brightly colored flier. She took down the flier and, back at the table, placed it in front of Sylvia. "Look at this."

"Read it to me. I left my glasses in the car." Sylvia dropped a piece of pizza onto her plate and licked her fingers.

"'Potterston Art Festival. Features the area's finest local sculptors, painters and craftspersons. Buy your Christmas gifts now. One-of-a-kind items, gallery displays, tasting booths from the finest local restaurants. Music by several local bands, including MoJo, Mirror Image and Sticky Feet. If you love things of beauty, this is not to be missed.'

"Then it lists some of the participating artists and restaurants. Have you ever been to this, Sylvia?"

"Not since it's become such a big affair. I've meant to drive over for the last few summers but haven't made it yet. A lot of people from Acorn Hill attend. It's become quite a tourist attraction. Hot peppers?"

Jane declined the shaker of dried peppers that Sylvia offered and stared intently at the flier. Impulsively, Jane stood up and went to the counter. "Do you mind if I take this? Or could I get a copy?"

"Take that one. There's more in the office."

When she returned to the table, Sylvia was helping herself to another slice of sausage and mushroom. "Are you thinking of entering your paintings?"

"I don't know what I'm thinking yet," Jane said. "But something is brewing. I can feel it. Why don't you have a booth for *your* art?"

"Quilts and dresses? Who'd want to see that?" Sylvia leaned back in her chair and moaned. "I know what's brewing for me—another three pounds. Will you please eat some of this pizza before I burst?"

Halfway home, Jane groaned out loud. Sylvia asked, "Problem?"

"I'd meant to ask the people in the antique shops if they'd ever heard of my mother's friend Gracie. I know she was from Potterston at one time. Vera Humbert also told me her grandmother and my mother had a mutual friend there. I thought I'd ask around a bit, maybe."

"Your mother has been gone fifty years, Jane. Her friend would have to be ninety years old. Is it likely that she still lives in Potterston? You might be pinning your hopes on something that will disappoint you."

Was she clutching at straws, hoping to make some miraculous connection to one of her mother's old friends? *Still* . . . Jane had never been a quitter, and she was not about to start now.

"Maybe Aunt Ethel knows more than she's said, although I'm not sure how close they really were." Jane smiled. "Mother's recipe book did hint that Ethel could be difficult, even then."

"That's one smart cookbook," Sylvia said.

"Looks like our new guests have checked in," Jane commented as they pulled in front of the inn.

"Does it bother you to share your home with strangers? I think it could get to me after a while." Sylvia eyed the house with a little awe.

"I like it most of the time. Of course, I do retreat to my room occasionally."

"Do you paint there?"

"I've been sketching at Fairy Pond and experimenting with watercolors in my room. They're better to use than oils when we have a houseful of guests, so no one has to put up with the odor of turpentine seeping out from beneath my door. Would you like to see what I'm working on?"

The first-floor rooms were empty as the two friends mounted the steps to the floor the sisters called their own. As they passed the second floor, the reflection of the setting sun off the highly polished hardwood floors was nearly blinding. Sylvia shaded her eyes. "You could do surgery on any floor in this place. It's immaculate."

"Thanks to Alice. I've told her that people could tolerate a single speck of dust if need be, but she doesn't buy it." Jane paused at her door. "But being a nurse has its blessings. Alice has carried most of the load since Naomi came back from the hospital."

"How is she?"

"Better. She still occasionally searches for words, but that's improving every day. She's been overwhelmed by the outpouring of concern shown to her, considering she was a stranger just passing through Acorn Hill. She believes God directed her here for a reason. I don't know what might have happened to her if she had been alone in a hotel room when she fell ill. It could have been a long time before anyone found her."

"What happens next?"

"Her niece is coming to pick her up and take her home. Naomi is delighted. She'll be near her sister and family. And," Jane chuckled, "she's feeling very grateful for the memory loss she experienced."

"Really? Why?"

"She can hardly remember what her ex-husband looks like or how he behaved. Most of the time it's as if he didn't exist."

"God works in mysterious ways," Sylvia murmured.

"Naomi's stroke moved her onto a path toward emotional healing. It's odd, isn't it? We don't have to seek excitement at the inn. It comes to us. It could be Acorn Hill's motto, 'Miracles Happen Here.'"

"I had no idea how much emotional and physical work an inn like this could be," Sylvia observed.

"With three of us, it's not too bad. Besides, I'd rather cook than clean any day. And watch miracles happen." Jane let the door to her room swing open.

"I just stepped through a time warp." Sylvia announced as she slipped inside. The contemporary furniture, the unfinished watercolor on the easel and the table of paints and divided boxes filled with shimmering beads and burnished stones did make Jane's room look like a world different from the rest of the house.

"It's easy to forget what century you're in when you spend all your time around here. You should have been here for the decorating fuss when we were making decisions about the inn. I'd never . . ."

But Sylvia wasn't listening. She was standing transfixed in front of a large oil. "This is amazing."

"Thanks. I did that before I started working at the Blue Fish Grille. Back then I had more time and inclination. It's a color study I call *Paradigm*. I've had a couple of people offer to purchase it, but I wanted to keep it for myself."

"*You* did this?" Sylvia squinted at the signature in the color. "It says you did, but I had no idea—" She blushed. "I mean that I never dreamed—what I mean to say is, I guess I didn't know just how talented you are."

"Thanks." Jane pretended not to notice Sylvia's embarrassment. "That's nice, coming from you, knowing your eye for color." Then she grinned. "And I'm a better cook than I am painter."

"May I look?" Sylvia dropped to her knees in front of a stack of framed abstracts leaning against one wall.

"Help yourself." Jane was accustomed to people in

Acorn Hill being surprised at her talents. Her own family had been taken aback. Of course, when she left at eighteen, she had not yet reached artistic maturity.

"Here are some of my latest." Jane laid several pieces of jewelry on the table.

"This is remarkable," Sylvia lifted a long silver chain with a pendant of polished rock and crystals on hammered brass. "Unlike anything I've ever seen."

Sylvia held it to the light. "Would you mind if I sold a few of these in my shop? They'd make beautiful gifts."

"People don't shop for jewelry in the same store they go to for alterations and quilting fabrics, my dear. Trust me."

"Not in other towns maybe. But they might here."

"If you'd like to take four or five pieces, go ahead. Maybe you can drape them across your sewing machine and people will race to pick them off."

"You just wait," Sylvia said as she gently lifted a bold silver pin with inset stones of red and black. "Lady, I can make you famous."

Laughing, Jane flopped across her bed and sank into a sea of decorative pillows. "And I thought you were shy."

"I am, until I'm on to something special. Then nothing stops me. Right now, I'm so excited that I have to go home. I'm going to put a sign in the window that says, 'Designs by Jane—local artist debuts her latest jewelry collection here at Sylvia's Buttons. To meet Jane and receive her latest flier, come to the shop on—' "

"Wait a minute. I can't remember agreeing to be a merchandizing tool, even if it is for my own stuff. And I don't have a flier."

"I'll make you one." Sylvia eyed the box of finished jewelry before her. "May I take fifteen pieces? I know they will sell."

Jane picked up the limp, sleepy Wendell who had been sawing logs on the porch rocker and sat down in the chair with the cat in her lap. His warm body melted against her thighs, and his purr was deep and soothing. She closed her eyes and slipped into that state between dozing and wakefulness. She might have fallen soundly asleep if footsteps moving toward the porch had not disturbed her reverie. Jane opened one eyelid to see who it was.

There, holding a battered hat in his hands and smiling shyly, was Joe Morales.

She sat up so quickly that Wendell dug his claws into her thighs to hang on. Wincing, she pulled the pin-sharp nails from her pants and the skin beneath, gathered the indignant cat into her arms and stood up. "Hello."

His smile was glowing. The tension around his eyes was gone, and he looked ten years younger.

"I came to thank you." He spoke deliberately, as though he had memorized his words. "Because of you, I have a new job."

Good going, Fred!

"And I have a place to live."

That took her aback. "You do? Tell me more."

"Mr. Humbert hired me to till gardens. He says he has three jobs for me already. And he will rent out me and his snow blower this winter."

She had never seen someone quite so pleased at the idea of being *rented* as a bonus to go along with a piece of heavy equipment.

"And where will you live?"

"Above Mr. Humbert's store." His eyes danced with delight. "It is the nicest home I've ever had."

The joy and gratitude in this man's eyes over a place as basic as the attic of a hardware store were humbling to see. There was no doubt Fred Humbert had just hired his most loyal employee.

"What would you charge to do some garden work for me?"

He shook his head adamantly. "For you I will do it free. You were the one who told Mr. Humbert about me."

"I can't let you do that, Joe. You'll need paying jobs now that you have a home."

"Mr. Humbert says that I can stay there free as long as I

work for him." The wonder and awe of it made his voice quiver. "And I will keep it very clean for him. I'm going to build him some new cupboards." Jane could have hugged Fred.

"Will you have enough for food and clothing?" He was wearing the pants that Sylvia had patched for him. "Joe, will you work for me if I pay you in food?" Perplexed, he tilted his head to one side. "I'm a cook, Joe. I love to make meals. I'll make them for you, and you can take them home to your new apartment to eat them. Then, when you've saved some money, you can shop for your own groceries." She could see him rolling the possibility around in his mind. "You can think about it for a couple days," she offered casually, "but in the meantime, let me give you some pot roast and grilled vegetables. Do you like salad? How about blueberry pie?"

Lemon Curd

3–4 tablespoons lemon zest
½ cup fresh lemon juice (4–6 lemons)
1½ cups sugar
6 tablespoons butter
3 eggs, lightly beaten

In saucepan over high heat, combine lemon zest, lemon juice and sugar. Bring just to boil, reduce heat and simmer for five minutes. Add butter and stir until melted. Remove from heat and cool to room temperature. Beat eggs into cooled lemon mixture until blended. Cook over medium-low heat, stirring constantly for ten to fifteen minutes or until mixture thickens. Remove from heat. Store in refrigerator.

At the bottom of the recipe, Madeline had written,

Wonderful for popovers. (I told poor Daniel I needed lemon zest. When I sent him to the store for lemons, he looked all over for a bottle of zest! Finally, after twenty minutes of his wandering about, a clerk asked if he could help. Wasn't Daniel's face red when he discovered that one makes zest from the peel of the lemon! Good thing he's in the pulpit, and I'm in the kitchen.)

"What are you up to?" Alice shuffled into the kitchen in her robe and slippers. "Aren't you exhausted?"

"Actually, I'm exhilarated." Jane grated the lemon peel into a little mass of bright yellow crumbs. "I'm preparing a few more things in advance for Vera's upcoming tea."

"Did you and Sylvia have a nice trip to Potterston today?"

"Yes, we did. What do you know about the Potterston Art Festival?"

Alice poured a glass of milk and took a frosted molasses cookie from the cookie jar. "Many of the hospital staff go every year. I hear art collectors have started to attend, looking for good pieces by unknown artists. There's food and music and a section just for children to finger paint, work with clay and the like." She bit into the cookie. "*Ummm*, Jane, these are just like Mother's. They were my favorite cookies as a little girl."

Jane put the butter into the rest of the simmering mixture and waited for it to melt.

Alice cleared her throat and shifted around on her chair as if it were growing too warm to sit on. "Jane . . ."

Jane glanced at Alice, wondering what was so difficult to get out.

"I want you to know how I've appreciated all you've done here."

"I haven't worked any harder than you."

"Since you've come, you've brought the most wonderful memories of Mother back to life. The smells in this kitchen, the delicious food, the laughter . . . it all reminds me of my childhood." Alice looked shy. "Thank you."

Jane studied her sister. "I've been trying to put the

pieces together about Mother since I was very young. I wanted to know her, to be touched by her. This is the only way I know how."

"It's a happy circumstance for all of us." Alice drained the last of the milk from her glass. "And even if Louise is a bit edgy sometimes, she knows it too." She stood up. "Good night. Don't let the bedbugs bite."

"And if they do, I'll hit them with my shoe."

Smiling at the silly little singsong routine from their childhood, Alice left the kitchen.

Jane capped the jars of lemon curd and tucked them into the back of the refrigerator for the day of the tea, cleaned the counters and went to bed.

"Jane? I forgot to tell you . . ." Alice knocked on her door and walked in without waiting for an answer.

Jane laid her sketchbook face down on the bed before she looked up. "Yes?"

Alice stared at the necklaces, pendants, pins and earrings spread out on Jane's worktable. "You did these?" She picked up an antique metal brooch depicting a figure with hair made of wire curls, sitting on a swing, holding on to ropes that disappeared into thin air.

Jane was surprised when Alice said, "I'll bet Eleanor in medical records would enjoy this for her birthday. Do you sell them?"

When she finally got her mouth closed, Jane said, "I suppose, but not to my own sister. Help yourself."

"Oh no. We always take a collection and buy something as a group. We'll take it. Everyone will be delighted to give her something she doesn't already have."

"That was the easiest sale I've ever made." Marveling, she smiled at her older sister. "Is that what you came in for, shopping?"

Alice appeared flustered. "I have a conflict the day of Vera's party. I know I promised I'd help you, but today the nursing administrator asked if I would do her a personal favor and stand in for her while she travels to see her new grandchild. If it were anyone else, I'd have said no, but she works so hard and asks favors so seldom."

Jane bit her lip to remain quiet. It would hurt not to have Alice on hand to help out. "That's okay. I'll figure something out." *I hope.*

"I'll do all the cleaning and setting up. You make a list of things that can be done the night before, and I'll take care of them." Alice backed toward the door enumerating all the chores she would handle.

Still, there was the problem of serving. These ladies were coming to be pampered and petted for an afternoon, not to carry their own plates. But Jane did have an idea—maybe a brilliant one.

Chapter Eleven 

"Joe, you look absolutely fabulous." Jane turned to Louise, who was flushed and refilling platters as fast as she could. "Doesn't he, Louise?"

Joe was dressed in crisp black pants and a white, long-sleeved shirt, good buys at a Potterston thrift shop. He had been to the barber shop and had had his hair cut. Alice had dug out one of their father's old black belts and a black bow tie. With a crisp white linen towel draped over his arm and his posture ruler straight, he made a remarkable butler. "You look like you have been a professional waiter for years," Louise acknowledged. "Very nice."

Joe stood even straighter. Then Louise thrust the refilled tray into his hands. "Do not forget to serve these with tongs," she reminded him. "And smile!"

He was barely out the kitchen door when Josie's mother, Justine, entered. It had taken all of a second for her to agree to help with the tea when Jane called. Josie apparently had filled in her mother on Jane and the inn.

"Those little cream puff swans are a big hit." She held up

an empty tray. "And the ladies ate their truffles first and are raving about those." In her outfit of a black skirt, white blouse and black bow tie, she looked every bit as impressive as Joe. Her hair, blond and curly as Josie's, was pulled into a twist at the back of her head. The style emphasized her bright blue eyes. She, too, could have been nicknamed Cornflower.

Jane, who had been filling the cream puff swans with vanilla cream, exchanged plates with her. "How are the sandwiches holding out?"

"Cucumber and watercress are good, salmon is going fast, the rest are steady sellers. And I'm going to cut into another cake right now. The ladies are just crazy about the decorations. I don't think one has ever before had a cake decorated with real flowers that they can eat." She shook her head. "Who'd have thought it?"

When Justine returned to the other room, Louise turned toward Jane, who had begun putting chocolate leaves on tiny wedges of flourless chocolate cake. "You came up with a delightful serving staff, Jane. It was a stroke of pure genius."

"They're great, aren't they? The best part is that they'll all have a little extra money in their pockets—which we know they can use—and the inn will make a nice income from the tea as well." She finished what she was doing and began putting sugar cubes decorated with tiny frosting flowers onto a tiny tray. Josie's job was to carry the sugar, lemon and creamer behind the tea server. She was on her very best behavior today, proud to have been invited to help her mother. After all, most of the teachers from school, including her own, were among the guests.

"Louise, I'll take over here. It's time for you to soothe them with music. And they'll want to sing 'Happy Birthday' too."

She nodded and started for the living room but turned to look back at her younger sister. "Jane, this is a remarkable party. Everyone is having a wonderful time. The food is," she searched for the right word, "superb. This is how this house is meant to be used. I remember it being this way when Mother was alive. She had the same knack for entertaining that you do. It's as if, when you came home, you brought Mother with you."

Jane stared dumbfounded at the doorway through which Louise disappeared. Jane had come home to Acorn Hill to find and learn to know her mother. And now Louise was saying that she had brought her mother with her when she came. What a radical shift in perspective that was.

Sometimes when she was poring over the recipe book that Madeleine had left, it was as though she was reading thoughts she might have had herself. Madeleine's sense of humor and turn of a phrase were much like her own, as well as their love of cooking. Maybe Louise's off-hand comment had a whisper of truth in it.

Jane was still standing in the kitchen when Joe returned with more empty trays. "Miss Jane?" he said shyly.

She had to shake herself free from her amazing thoughts to answer him. "Yes, Joe?"

"I want to say thank you."

"I should be thanking you, Joe. The ladies love you. I'm guessing you'll be getting plenty of calls about work after this."

"That's what I want to say thank you for. You changed my life. Two weeks ago I was homeless. Now . . ." he swept his arm in front of him. "I have a home, I have food, and I have a job, because of you."

She felt tears forming.

"Sometimes I wonder why," he went on. "Why do you help me?"

Why had she helped Joe? What put her on his trail and forced her to stay there until he was helped? Or Who? "You stumbled into my rose hedge, and I couldn't forget about you."

He tipped his head inquiringly.

"Joe, I think God *sent* you to my roses that night. You kept coming to mind as if I wasn't supposed to rest until your circumstances had improved. I can't say why you're here, but I believe with all my heart that God has plans for you in Acorn Hill. If that's the case, Joe, then I'm just an instrument He used to make that happen."

She had not realized until just then that tears were streaming down his cheeks. "You make me sound . . . important."

"You *are* important. God counts the hairs on our heads and the sparrows in the sky. If you'd been the only person on the planet, He still would have gone to the Cross for you. You can't get any more important than that."

He bobbed his head, and when he lifted it to look into her face, his eyes were shining. "I don't want to let God think He wasted His time on me. But what do I do?"

"Ask Him." Jane said.

Just then Justine burst through the kitchen door. "Maybe you'd better go talk to them. Everybody wants your recipes." She narrowed her eyes, "But shouldn't you keep them secret or something? Then they'd *have* to come here to get them."

"You, my dear woman, have great marketing sense. You're right. It's time for me to go and visit with our guests." She and Joe exchanged smiles as they followed Justine into the gathering.

The room was ablaze with color. The celebrants had decked themselves out in pastels and brights, florals and stripes. Several, at Vera's encouragement, had worn hats.

Everyone was laughing and talking, but when Jane stepped out of the kitchen, the entire assemblage erupted in applause.

The unexpectedness of it took Jane utterly off guard. Of all the accolades she had received for her cooking over the years, none had felt quite so satisfying as this.

Vera came over to her, her eyes twinkling with happiness. "My friends think I'm brilliant because of you. Oh, Jane, this is so much more than I expected. I knew you must be good, but this is incredible. We've already discussed it. We meet several times a year, and we want to book all our parties here." For a moment she looked concerned. "You don't mind, do you?"

Mind? This was music to Jane's ears. "I'm thrilled, Vera."

"Word of this place is bound to spread." She cast her gaze over the room. "There's not a woman here who isn't going to tell everyone she knows. I'll call you tomorrow with the dates, okay?"

Jane saw Alice slip through the front door in her nurse's uniform and stare at the festive disarray.

"Looks like everything worked out," she murmured to Jane. "I heard rave reviews on the way through the foyer. And who's this beautiful little server?"

Josie smiled at Alice, and then turned to Jane. "Can I do this again?" she asked. "It's fun."

"Josie, don't be begging." Her mother held a handful

of empty trays. "It was nice of the ladies to ask us just this once."

"If you'd like to do it more often," Jane offered, "it sounds as though we have a few more large teas coming up."

"Really? No kidding?"

"No kidding."

Justine's face lit with pleasure. "I'm going to buy Josie some new clothes with what I earned today. Maybe next time, I'll get some for me." As she walked off, Josie followed, skipping as she went.

Amazing, Jane thought. *God even organizes tea parties to serve His purposes.*

The next day Jane and Louise were moving slowly. "Even my toenails hurt," Louise groaned. "I had no idea how much work that would be."

"Welcome to the restaurant business." Jane yawned. "Fun, though, isn't it."

"I counted up the checks from yesterday," Louise said. "After paying for all the food and supplies as well as for Joe, Justine and Josie, we have enough left to give a tithe to the church, pay the bill at the hardware store, buy the new towels we need and give us each a little spending money besides."

"Shouldn't we be putting it all toward bills?" Alice

asked. She was in charge of breakfast today. Since Naomi was their only guest and had become like family, Alice was giving Jane a much-needed rest.

"Jane took reservations for several more teas this morning," Louise replied. "Vera called with her birthday club's dates, and two others have also been scheduled—one for a baby shower, the second for a bridal shower." Louise was obviously delighted with this turn of events. Jane knew that it had chipped away at some of the fear that her sister had been harboring. For that alone, all the work was worth it.

Naomi came slowly down the stairs to join them. She was still pale and had not regained the pounds that she had lost in the hospital. Jane was attempting to rectify that with daily chocolate malts and midday snacks. Still, Naomi was holding herself straighter and had almost a jaunty set to her shoulders. "Your party must have been wonderful. It sounded as though I was living above a chicken coop yesterday."

"I wish you'd come down," Jane said. "You could have at least sat in the kitchen and been our taste-tester."

"You are the dearest women I know. You've made me so happy." Naomi said slowly, still not quite sure of her command of her own speech. Tears filled her eyes.

"Happy, Naomi?" Alice, ever compassionate, looked anxious. "Then what's wrong?"

"I talked to my niece last night. She and her husband are coming to pick me up this evening. If you have room for them, they'll stay here tonight and we'll leave in the morning. Her husband will drive my car back to their home. Otherwise we'll probably start out and find a hotel somewhere along the road." She wiped away the tear that had slid onto her cheek. "I'm going to miss you all so much. You've all been role models for me. Do you know that?"

"Oh dear. What did we teach you?" Alice asked, surprised.

"Toughness. Bravery. Humor."

"All of that? Us?"

"Quit sounding so modest, Alice," Jane said teasingly. "You know we're terrific."

"I'm going to live my life differently now, more boldly. I'm tired of being a doormat. If someone tries to step on me now, I won't allow it." Color appeared in her cheeks as she spoke, and Jane knew she meant what she said.

"There is plenty of room for your family if they want to stay." Louise appeared genuinely grieved at the idea of having Naomi leave. "I hate to see you go."

"Something happened to me here," Naomi said as they settled at the table for breakfast. Alice had fried eggs and made toast. "And I don't just mean the stroke. Odd as it is to say, I *healed* here in spite of it."

"It doesn't hurt that your memory bank closed down where your ex-husband is concerned." Jane tried to keep the moment light even though she, too, felt like crying.

"Nor did it hurt to be in the company of three women of faith who shared their hearts and home with a complete stranger. You'll never know how much this place has meant to me."

But Jane *did* know. She, too, had been fed by the miracles happening around her—Joe, Josie and her mother, the recipe book, and the gradual thawing of her sisters until not only did she love them, she actually *liked* them.

The phone rang and Alice jumped to get it. When she returned, she was wearing a frown. "That was one of Vera's teacher friends. She was wondering if she and the others could have your recipes, Jane." Jane felt a flip in her stomach. She had hoped the women would not pursue that any further.

"You can't do that." Naomi looked alarmed. "It needs to be out of the ordinary here. What's the fun of coming here if you can make the same food at home?"

Of course it was flattering to be asked for one's recipes, but at the Blue Fish Grille everything that she did she had kept under wraps. Trent had wanted *nothing* to get out. He had a corner on the market and would not give it up, as he put it, "by giving away the store." And Madeleine's recipes, they were like private letters from her mother. She didn't feel ready to share them with anyone. Was that so terribly selfish?

Louise, noticing Jane's silence, spoke. "I don't think it is fair of them to ask. This is our livelihood. Musicians don't give away pieces of the music they compose to just anyone."

"Thanks to both of you. I agree. And yet, it seems so stingy to say no."

"It would be different if you were getting paid for it," Louise said. She paused and said it again. "*Paid*. People could *buy* your recipes."

"I couldn't do that," Jane protested. "Ask the people of Acorn Hill to buy my recipes?"

Naomi looked at her with a smile. "Isn't that what recipe books are all about?"

Jane chewed at her lower lip for a moment. "It would be different if the money went to pay bills at the inn, or for scholarships for vacation Bible school, or . . ."

"It would be easy to tell people to wait for the book," Alice said, looking more hopeful. "Everyone would understand."

"And I could choose those recipes I want to share." Jane felt the tightness in her stomach relax. It was Madeleine she was clinging to, not the recipes. She had hundreds of fabulous ideas, not just those in Madeleine's book. For now, she could hold them back. Besides, recipe books didn't just happen. They took years.

"Well, it *would* be great advertising," Naomi said. "I know your guests would love them as souvenirs. You could tell the story of Grace Chapel Inn, the church, the history of Acorn Hill . . . ."

"I'll bet Viola would sell them," Louise added quickly.

Jane stared at her sister. Louise never got terribly excited about anything.

"And we should sell them here," Alice said. "It wouldn't hurt to have a small display somewhere, if it was done well."

Her sisters were beginning to sound like true businesswomen. Suddenly a whole new world was opening up, right at the table of Grace Chapel Inn.

I am so sick of pickles! Daniel calls it a "plentiful harvest." I call it "too much work." Sweet pickles, dill pickles, garlic pickles, watermelon pickles, beet pickles, pickle relish, pickled onions, pickled pickles. When I say pickles over and over, my tongue grows numb. Must have the little girls try it—it will make them laugh.

Every time Jane read something her mother had written, Madeleine's personality flowed off the page. What followed were recipes and directions for every pickle Jane had ever heard of and then some. Her mother had even drawn pickles with large eyes in the margins.

"*Yoo-hoo!* It's me." She heard Ethel's footsteps. Her aunt had not yet given up trying to convince Jane that the picture of a mermaid in the powder room was inappropriate and was coming over frequently to give what she termed "helpful" suggestions for a replacement. So far it had taken everything in Jane's power to refrain from "helping" Ethel right back out the door. There was a doggedness about Ethel that was both admirable and frustrating.

She had come up with a plan for diverting Ethel from her single-minded devotion to censoring the bathroom artwork, however, for Ethel was, after all, one of the foremost living authorities on Madeleine. Sometimes Ethel was too annoying to be sought out, but today Jane was ready for her.

"*Yoo-hoo!*"

"Hello, Aunt Ethel." Jane emerged from the kitchen just in time to catch her aunt peeking at the newly delivered mail lying on the table in the foyer. "It's mostly bills."

"Well, I didn't mean, ah—" Ethel stammered, not liking to be caught spying. She liked spying well enough; it was being *caught* that she did not enjoy. "How are you, dear?"

"Well. We're all a little sad that Naomi's leaving today, but otherwise fine. Would you like some coffee? Tea?"

"Have you been baking?" Ethel's nose twitched like a mouse's catching the scent of cheese.

"I promised a pan of cookie bars for a meeting at the chapel and decided to bake another to give to Joe. Come, have one."

"I don't see why you take such good care of that fellow. He's not family. Why, you don't even know him. A stranger like that, from a foreign country . . ."

"He was born in the United States, Aunt Ethel, during beet-picking season. And he spent every summer here for years as a migrant worker."

"'Migrant'? Isn't that like 'drifter'? Don't you ever listen to the news, dear? The police are always looking for drifters."

"We don't have much time for the news here, Ethel. Now I have—"

"What *do* you do?" Ethel and Lloyd were great television watchers, and they both loved game shows. If someone came to the house when one of Ethel's programs was on, he or she might as well leave and come back later—unless talking to someone whose gaze never left the television screen seemed like a good idea.

"Well," Jane said, with mock seriousness, "when we're not lounging about, I paint or work on jewelry, Louise sits down at the piano, and Alice spends her free time with the youth group from church."

"I've been meaning to talk to you about that," Ethel announced, missing Jane's irony. "About your hobbies . . ."

Oh oh, here it comes.

"You know, dear, this isn't California. I should think you'd find something more productive to do than twist wires into trinkets and hang beads on string. Who would want them anyway? A good set of pearls is all one really needs. Pearls . . . oh that reminds me. Florence and I are talking about starting a bridge club. We're looking for people to play. Now that would be a productive evening, getting out, seeing people."

Learning every bit of gossip in a thirty-mile radius. No thanks.

"It's nice of you to ask, Aunt Ethel, but I think I'll stick with making 'trinkets.' By the way, I have some questions for you about my mother."

Ethel eyed the bars and took the largest from the plate. "What is it you want to know about Madeleine?"

"What was she like? What was her favorite color, her favorite flower? What made her laugh . . . and cry?"

Ethel put down the cookie and sat back in her chair, lost for a moment in thought. "Her favorite color was lavender, that blue-gray-purple of lilacs in the spring. She was giddy as a child when the lilacs bloomed. She put vases of them everywhere in the house, and when she passed by, she would always bury her nose deep into them and inhale. Why, I can almost smell those lilacs myself when I think of Madeleine."

Jane waited.

"In the winter, she would touch a little lavender oil to the lamps and it would fill the house with the fragrance. You know, I gave your mother lavender soap for her birthday every year. I couldn't find it in Acorn Hill, of course, so I ordered it from a catalog. She told me once, 'Ethel, don't you dare stop giving me that soap. It's the thing I most look forward to on my birthday.'" The mention of lavender had sparked a wealth of memories. "She also loved to wear lilac, too. I don't believe she had many party dresses in any other color."

"Tell me more about her, Aunt Ethel."

"She loved to laugh. Things that would have made me furious, she laughed about. Once the dog broke through the screen door and dragged her entire roast off the counter and ate it under the table while Madeleine was talking to her guests. Imagine! I would have cried, but not Madeleine. She hauled us all into the kitchen to see what had happened to our dinner and promptly started to make creamed tuna and peas on toast. And every time she repeated the story it got funnier in the telling."

"What else made her laugh?"

"Fireflies, children, silly jokes, riddles, ridiculous hats

and pompous, self-important people. And how your mother loved animals! She would always be rescuing something out of a tree or nursing it back to health. She fed a kitten with an eyedropper for three weeks once."

"Who were her friends? Other than you, I mean."

"There aren't many of us left anymore. Madeleine's friends were slightly older than she. Some of them have died, others gone to their children in other states. Madeleine and Vera Humbert's grandmother were close friends, but she's gone too."

"Can't you think of anyone else?"

"There was Adele Waring. She used to live in Potterston. So did Goldie Case and Grace Andresen, last I heard of, but that was several years ago. I have no idea if they're living anymore." She plucked two more sweets off the tray and wrapped them in a paper napkin. "I'd best go now. I have company coming soon." She hesitated a moment and looked at Jane, who saw the sadness in her aunt's eyes. "It was nice to talk with you about the old times. No one else seems to want to hear about them. Now you be sure to think about that bridge club."

And quit making those baubles you call jewelry. That, Jane knew, Ethel had left unsaid.

"Come again, Aunt Ethel," then, to her own amazement, Jane heard herself add, "soon."

"They've decided to start back tonight," Naomi said. Her niece and husband were standing in the doorway of the inn. "They couldn't find a babysitter for tomorrow evening and need to get back. I'd better gather my things."

When Naomi had gone upstairs with Alice, her niece reached to touch Jane's hand. "Thank you for what you've done. Even ill, my aunt looks happier than she has in years." Her expression clouded. "My uncle was a difficult, demanding man. He simply sucked happiness and life out of her. She loved him and didn't believe in divorce, so even though it shouldn't have surprised her when he left, it did. She was devastated, and I wasn't sure that she'd recover, but she has." The young woman shook her head in amazement. "Thank you all so much."

At that moment Naomi descended the stairs holding the package Jane had given her. "I can't thank you enough for this—one of your beautiful paintings."

"A sketch of Grace Chapel Inn, that's all. Something to remind you of us." Jane remembered the day a haunted looking Naomi Hopper had checked into the inn. So much had happened in so little time, but the Naomi who was leaving was very different from the one who had arrived.

"There's no way to completely show you my appreciation for what you've done for me."

"Just be happy. That's enough for us. And keep in touch and visit often."

Naomi couldn't speak. Instead she threw her arms around Jane and hugged her.

"We wanted to stay," Naomi's niece was saying to Louise as they walked out to the car, "but maybe another time."

"Bring her back, won't you?" Alice draped her arm around Naomi's shoulders. "We miss her already."

After Naomi's departure, the sisters gathered in the kitchen in silence. It was Jane who spoke first. "I think we need to pray.

"Heavenly Father, thank You for giving us this home. I sense You have plans for this place that we can't even imagine. Are we to be a haven? A place of healing? A respite from a difficult world? Whatever it is, Lord, make us good stewards for You." Jane could feel the warmth of her sisters' hands on her own and marveled at how far she—and they—had come.

"Got a minute?" Sylvia peered out of her store as Jane strode by Sylvia's Buttons with her dry cleaning.

"Always for you. What's up?"

"Nellie was in here yesterday. She saw your jewelry and went wild for it. She bought three pieces. When I told her who'd made it, her eyes nearly fell out of her head. She wants to sell it in her clothing store, too." Sylvia's eyes sparkled. "What do you think of that?"

"Everywhere I turn there's a new surprise," Jane said with a laugh. "Do you want to get rid of my business?"

"We can both have displays, can't we? We have different clientele. You'd sell twice as much."

"You're certainly enthusiastic. How many pieces do you have left? I can change them out for something new."

"None. They flew out of here like they had wings. Will you bring me whatever you have and go talk to Nellie too?"

"None? Nada? Zip?"

"You've got it."

"Will wonders never cease? I'll bring something over tomorrow."

"And bring a few of those miniature oils I saw in your room if you're willing to sell them. I think my customers would like them." She pointed at the only wall in the place that was not filled with fabric, quilts or sewing equipment displays. "I'll hang them right there." She gave Jane a quick hug. "And I'll tell Nellie that you'll call."

By nightfall, Jane had struck a deal with Nellie and had supplied both her and Sylvia with what jewelry she had on hand. After dinner she would spread her supplies out on the kitchen table and see what else she could create.

Louise served the roast chicken and glazed carrots while Alice delivered the mashed potatoes to the table.

"I'm beginning to like this taking turns cooking," Jane commented. "It's not often in my profession that I get served like this."

"Louise and I decided, after seeing what kind of effort you put into that tea, that we needed to give you a rest in the kitchen. Do you want dark or white meat?"

"Some of each." She reached for the rolls. "I loved doing the tea and using Mother's recipes. It felt right to be having a party in her house, don't you think?"

"Yes, I do. And speaking of recipes," Alice said, "have you thought any more about that cookbook?"

"It would be fun, but we'd need a 'hook,' something to make it different from the rest."

"We could talk about the inn," Alice suggested. "And have a photo of the kitchen."

"It should be more than that," Louise interjected. "We could incorporate the entire history of the house. About how our parents inherited it from Mother's parents, something about the architecture . . ."

"And some of Father's old stories. Maybe even a few photos of us as children," Alice suggested.

"That is a good idea. We could make it a history of the inn and our family, a recipe book and souvenir."

Jane listened to the exchange between her sisters in astonishment. Another transformation had taken place. For once, she was the one holding back.

"I don't want to commercialize Mother or the rest of the family," Jane began.

"But think how much our guests would enjoy such a book. What a great boost for the inn." Alice glowed with anticipation.

"You mean it would be an *advertisement*? That awful concept that always makes Lloyd think we're going to lose our quality of life if we let others know we exist?"

"Oh, that is just Lloyd," Louise promptly dismissed him. "Besides, we could use a few more guests. We have none tonight or tomorrow."

Jane hardly knew what to think. Her sisters were taking hold of a progressive idea even more quickly than she. *Maybe I'll wake up soon,* Jane thought. *Surely this is all a dream.*

Chapter Twelve

"*Yoo-hoo! Yoo-hoo!* It's just me."

Alice and Jane exchanged a glance. "Isn't she coming over more than she used to?" Alice asked. "I wonder why."

Jane did not dare tell her that the open invitation she had offered to their aunt had generated this attention. "It's a test," she said, "and we're going to pass it with flying colors." *Even if it kills us.* She took a deep breath and went to meet Ethel.

"Oh, there you are, Jane. I just had to come over and show you—what on earth are you wearing?" She pushed up her glasses that had slipped down on her nose to study her niece. "You look like a . . . ballerina in combat."

She would have enjoyed disagreeing, but Jane realized that Ethel might be right. Jane had exercised this morning in a black, long-sleeved leotard. Then, because she was going into the attic to look for old photos for the recipe book, she had slipped into a pair of camouflage pants and thick black shoes that actually did resemble combat boots. With her hair in a ponytail and with these clothes, she undoubtedly looked like GI Jane.

"Hi, Ethel." There was no point putting up a defense. Even in combat boots she would not win.

"I've been meaning to talk to you about this, Jane. You wear the oddest clothing. Leggings, tunics, leather pants and those loose jackets with the odd scribbling on them."

Hand-painted silk jackets—to-die-for accessories in my crowd.

"The only other place I see people wearing clothes like yours are on those entertainment channels where they show emaciated young women strutting like peacocks down a ramp."

Designer fashion shows.

Quickly deciding to take Ethel's outraged comments as roundabout compliments, Jane smiled and ushered her to the kitchen, where she ensconced her aunt in a chair with a cup of jasmine tea.

Before Ethel could start in again on her clothes, Jane asked, "What was it you were going to show me?"

Ethel lifted her large purse and clutched at it. "I wanted to show you the gift Lloyd just gave me, but now, seeing you like this, I'm sure you wouldn't be interested. It's not nearly odd enough to go with what you wear."

"Show me anyway." Perversely, Jane had begun to enjoy Ethel's tactless behavior. She was, at least, one person you could count on to speak her mind.

Gently, Ethel lifted a small box from her purse. With

great care, she lifted the cover from the box and showed Jane what was inside. It was a necklace, a silver dove with wings spread wide, hung on a fine silver chain. The olive branch it carried in its beak was made of tiny bits of emerald.

"Isn't it beautiful? It reminds me of Noah in Genesis 8:11 (RSV)."

"'And the dove came back to him in the evening, and lo in her mouth was a freshly plucked olive leaf; so Noah knew that the waters had subsided from the earth.'"

"Yes, that's it, a symbol of hope and of God's faithfulness. It is so lovely."

"Why, thank you, Ethel," Jane said quietly, watching her aunt's face for her response.

"You're welco—,"she broke off. "What do you mean?"

"That's one of my pieces. I'm delighted that you like it."

"You made this?" Ethel stared from the delicate bit of art to Jane's camouflage pants and spurt of ponytail. "You?"

Jane laughed and leaned over to give her flabbergasted aunt a hug. "Don't judge an artist by the clothes she wears, Aunt Ethel. That would be a good thing for you to remember, especially around me. Now, do you want more tea?"

"Good news. We have a guest coming tonight after all. His name is Ned Arnold, and he will be here off and on." Louise looked like a cat that had just lapped a bowl of cream. There was nothing she liked better than regular customers. "He is going to be filling in for Chuck Parker at the pharmacy. Chuck wants to ease into retirement, so he is planning to have Ned come once a month and give him a few days off."

"That's nice." Jane yawned. She had been staying up late working on projects for Sylvia and Nellie—and on another project about which she was not yet ready to talk. She had been so busy that if she was to be honest, she would be just as happy not to have to get up in the morning to fix breakfast. "When's he coming?"

"Any time now. He is only going to stay a couple of days this trip, but he will be back. Chuck and Betty are thinking of visiting their children in Oklahoma.

Jane excused herself and left her sister in the kitchen. She walked to the front porch where she loved to sit and watch the world go by. From there she had seen Josie barreling down the street on her bike. Joe had fixed the bike up with a new coat of paint and a new chain. Josie was wearing the clothes that her mother had bought for her with the money earned at the tea.

Joe often stopped by, and each time they laughed about her hedge's grabbing his shoe and how it had changed his life.

Occasionally, Craig Tracy dropped in to deliver the edible flowers for the cakes Jane was now being asked to bake. He even stayed to see how she worked them into the rest of what he called "Jane's frosting art."

Things had picked up speed lately, and Jane did not exactly like it. She had spent a good deal of her free time on the phone making fruitless calls to names gleaned from Madeleine's old letters and clippings. So far it appeared that none of the "girls," Madeleine's old friends, was anywhere to be found. The best lead that she had was for "Gracie," who had been living in Potterston in the 1990s, but even that seemed to have run into a dead end. Surely someone, somewhere, was familiar with this Gracie. Jane had just asked the wrong people so far—she hoped.

A sleek, silver foreign-made car glided up the drive and pulled into a parking spot. The man who emerged looked as elegant as the car. Silver-haired and immaculately dressed in a casual suit worn over a pale gray knit shirt, he was not the usual visitor to the inn. Jane was more accustomed to young lovers and sightseers.

"Hi, is that the right place to park?"

"Just right." She extended her hand. "Hi, I'm Jane, one of the innkeepers. Welcome."

He shook her hand and smiled a smile that would have

melted ice. "Ned Arnold, nice to meet you. I'll grab my bag and be right in."

His bag was actually a handsome leather duffle that he swung onto his shoulder as he returned to the steps.

"So you're filling in for our pharmacist for a couple days." Jane had a hunch business would increase at the prescription counter once some of the single women got a look at him.

"Yes. I think I'll enjoy coming out here once a month. It's really beautiful."

At that moment, Louise and Alice descended on them, and Jane stepped aside to let them help Mr. Arnold check in and show him to the Sunset Room. He looked like the kind who would enjoy the Impressionist works that hung there. He walked up the stairs, flanked by her sisters, but at the top of the stairs he stopped and turned. And, to Jane's amazement, he winked at her.

Madeleine's notation identified another favored breakfast recipe.

Daniel's current favorite. He wants them stuffed with berries and topped with whipped cream. A boiled overshoe would taste good that way!

Swedish Pancakes

MAKES FOUR SERVINGS

- 1½ cups flour
- 1 tablespoon sugar
- ½ teaspoon baking powder
- ½ teaspoon salt
- 2 cups milk
- 2 tablespoons melted butter
- ½ teaspoon vanilla
- 2 large eggs

Mix first four ingredients. Stir in the other ingredients. Mix with hand beater until smooth. Lightly butter griddle and heat. Pour a quarter cup batter for each pancake onto griddle. When bubbles form and undersides of pancakes are light brown, loosen pancakes with spatula, turn and cook. Continue same steps with remaining batter. Delicious served with maple syrup or powdered sugar.

(Lots and lots of powdered sugar!)

Jane barely had the coffee pot on and the pancake batter mixed when she heard Ned come down the stairs. She hurried from the kitchen to greet him. "I'm sorry, I haven't set the table yet. I'll do it right now."

"Is it just for me?"

"You're the only guest. Usually my sisters eat in the kitchen."

"Then may I eat in the kitchen too? Seems a shame to muss things up in here just for me."

"Well . . . I suppose. It will be easier anyway since I'm making pancakes. Tomorrow I'll be ready to serve you in the dining room."

"Great. Now how about some of that coffee I smell?"

He looked right at home in the middle of their big kitchen drinking coffee from a fat mug and watching her cook. She grilled the bacon to a perfect crispness, squeezed him a glass of orange juice and filled his plate three times with pancakes.

"These are the best I've ever eaten."

"Swedish pancakes. I like them too." He had questioned her all through breakfast about the inn, her cooking, her experiences in California and even her childhood in Acorn Hill.

Now it was time to turn the spotlight on him. "Tell me about yourself." Jane sat down with a mug of coffee.

"Pretty straightforward. I owned a small chain of pharmacies in Maine. My wife and I were divorced three years ago. She said she was sick and tired of a man who did nothing but work. It was ironic." He looked at Jane with eyes that were a mixture of gray and blue so that even they looked silver. "My wife left me. *Then* I figured out she was probably right, so I sold my stores and started to do fill-in work for lone pharmacists in small towns. They need to get away and rarely get a chance. I don't want anyone else to lose a wife because he never took her on vacation or spent an evening with her because he was doing paperwork. That means I can take jobs anywhere I want, visit for a while and then move on. Actually, while I'm filling in here, I've also been offered a part-time job at the hospital in Potterston to relieve their pharmacist. Looks like I'll be around awhile. Once Mr. Parker gets a taste of freedom, he'll be wanting me to come more often."

"A roving pharmacist."

"Works for me." He glanced at his watch. "I'd best get going. Is the pharmacy far?"

"Just down Chapel Road on Hill Street."

"Within walking distance?"

"Oh yes. I have to pass it on my way to the General Store to pick up some special chocolate they ordered for me. I'll walk with you and show you the way."

"Perfect. Let's go."

They strolled leisurely down Chapel Road, past Fred's Hardware and on to the pharmacy. "This is a great little town. So picturesque. It's a little pocket of calm tucked away in the trees," observed Ned.

"Our mayor is determined not to let that change either," Jane said. She was enjoying the fresh air and the sunshine on her upturned face. "He practices crowd control already. He doesn't want to let too many tourists in at once."

"That doesn't sound good for a business like yours." Ned carried a white jacket over one shoulder. Jane wondered how he managed to keep it completely unwrinkled in his travels.

"We don't have enough rooms to really scare him. Besides, he's seeing my aunt who lives next door. Lloyd knows enough to tread lightly where my aunt Ethel is concerned." She paused and pointed at a building to their right. "Here you are."

"Thanks for the walk. I'll see you tonight." As Ned sauntered to work, Jane headed for the General Store. Little did she know that several residents of Acorn Hill were across the street in the Coffee Shop having their breakfast and staring with avid interest at Jane and the good-looking stranger.

Louise and Alice were both gone for the day. She did not want to work on the recipe book again until she had asked her sisters for their input, and she had stayed up late to work on jewelry for Nellie's and Sylvia's stores. She had sketched some exciting new designs and ordered more materials. All bases were covered. It was time to start her experiment.

"Semisweet chocolate, heavy cream, finely chopped nuts. Almond, orange or raspberry flavorings. Confectioner's sugar, unsweetened cocoa powder . . . *hmmm.*"

She settled down to work making truffles that even Madeleine could never have imagined.

"Craig, do you know anything about entering the Potterston Art Festival?" Jane was sitting on a stool in the back of Wild Things near his working counter, surrounded by ribbon, florist's wire and greenery.

"A little. Hand me that gold ribbon over there, will you?" He was putting together a bouquet to be delivered to Pastor and Mrs. Ley, who were celebrating a wedding anniversary. "It's grown in popularity and has a reputation as a spot where buyers can find quality pieces of art at reasonable prices. The food booths are out of this world. I've considered having a booth there myself to show people my work. I'd have to do them in silks, of course, because fresh would wilt. Why do you ask?"

"Would you consider sharing a booth with me? I've got

several pieces of art to show and new jewelry designs too." *And a surprise up my sleeve.*

Craig tucked the congratulatory card on a plastic stake into the bouquet and took the other stool. "It's not a bad idea. You can put out fliers or advertisements in the booth. We could work it into an artistic and romantic theme—flowers, jewelry, art and a romantic bed-and-breakfast getaway—a little candy and we'd have the whole romance subject covered. It could be beautiful." He grabbed a pad and started to sketch. "I'll tell you what, Jane. I'll check into the booths and see what I can find. If I can get one and they approve our idea, are you in?"

"I'm in. And don't worry about the candy, Craig. I'll work something out."

Entering the Nine Lives Bookstore was always an adventure. Jane marveled at the care Viola took to display the books on her "approved" reading list and to hide those best-sellers that Hope had blackmailed her into carrying. There was a gigantic display of non-fiction at the front door, including *Making Your Own Garden Pond, Bird Watching in Depth, The Philatelist's Guide to Stamp Collecting* and Jane's favorite, *Building Dogsleds, The Alaskan Adventure*. She thought that the demand for that one must have been overwhelming. Someday, perhaps, there would be a few copies of the new recipe book in Viola's display.

In the rear of the store, she found the thrillers, beach reads and romances on the bottom shelves in the fiction section. Hope was going to have to do a little more threatening and cajoling to move the new titles to a higher place in the stacks. One practically had to lie down to pick out a book.

"Well, well."

She looked up from where she had hunkered down by the shelf to see Viola looming over her. "Hi, Viola, what's new?" Jane unfolded from the floor, the books she had been seeking in her hand.

"It seems that I should be asking what's new with you," Viola said, smiling slyly.

"Cooking, mostly, which isn't a complaint with me. I'd probably sleep in the kitchen if I had a chance."

"All right, don't tell me," Viola said, then turned and busied herself behind the counter.

Jane stared at her, dumbfounded. What was that supposed to mean?

The bell on the door rang and Hope came sailing in. She was still wearing her Coffee Shop apron. "Viola, did you get those books we ordered—oh, hi, Jane." Her eyes twinkled. "I see you've been having a little fun."

What was wrong with everyone? It was not until Lloyd Tynan walked through the door and spied her that things came into focus. "I see you've got a new gentleman friend,

Jane. Pretty good-looking, I might add. Now you don't mind your aunt Ethel. I know she's in a snit 'cause she didn't know about it until we saw you walking down the street together, but she'll get over it. You know how she loves to be up on the latest news. Say, Viola, did my book on furniture building come in yet? Ethel needs a bookcase and I thought I'd try to make one."

"So that's what this is about." Jane turned to Hope. "Did everyone in town see me walking the inn's guest to the pharmacy?"

"He's at the inn? He's not here to visit you?" Hope sounded disappointed.

"Of course not. He's the fill-in pharmacist for Chuck Parker."

"Oh." Then Hope whistled. "The Coffee Shop was plumb full of customers this morning, Jane. If I were you, I'd expect to field a lot of questions in the next couple days."

"Close your eyes. No peeking, Alice. Louie, keep them closed."

"Goodness, Jane, I am going to trip on something and fall flat on my face." Louise shuffled along clinging to Jane's arm.

"Don't run me into the doorjamb," Alice warned. "I can't go to work with a black eye."

"You two aren't being any fun. I have a *surprise* for you."

"Jane, you're always a surprise. Nellie told me yesterday that one of the best-selling things in her shop is your jewelry. Did you know that?" Alice asked.

"That's nice," Jane said vaguely. She had something far more interesting on her mind. "Careful, Alice, here's a chair. Sit down but don't open your eyes."

When she had them both sitting at the table, Jane went to the counter and picked up a large silver tray that she had polished especially for the occasion. She set it on the table in front of her sisters. "Okay. *Now* you can open your eyes."

They did so and both stared at the platter in bewilderment. "Yes, so? It is a tray of lovely candy, Jane, but what's so special about it?"

"I do not see what all the fuss is about," Louise said. "You took me away from the piano for this?"

"Look closer." She waited as her sisters studied the candies displayed in tiny, silver fluted paper cups and silver boxes. Several of the candies were wrapped in silver papers and tied with a sliver of a black and white striped bow.

"It is a brand I've never even heard of," Louise observed. "What is this Madeleine and Daughters?" She appeared thunderstruck. "*Madeleine! Daughters!* Where did these come from?"

"Is this *our* Madeleine?" Alice gasped. "That would mean the daughters are us."

"Have one. The truffles are in the silver boxes. There are several flavors. My favorite is the one that's pure, unadulterated chocolate, and there are plenty more where that came from."

"You made these?" Louise asked. Then she bit into the morsel and her eyes fluttered closed in pleasure. "Delicious!"

"Tell me how—who—" Alice stammered.

"Do you want some coffee with those sweets? I brewed a fresh pot."

"Please." Alice scanned the plate. "How do I pick?"

"Have one of each."

"Whatever made you think of doing this?" Louise asked. She had a speck of chocolate on the corner of her lip that she nonchalantly licked off with the tip of her tongue.

"Mother's recipes."

"These all came from the recipe book?" Louise sounded surprised.

"Let's say they were all inspired by the cookbook. This one," Jane pointed to a chocolate truffle rolled in pecans, "is Mother's recipe. I've been experimenting, trying some new things until I found what I wanted." She grimaced. "And put on four pounds taste-testing."

Madeleine's Truffles

MAKES ABOUT EIGHTEEN BALLS

12 ounces (2 cups) semisweet chocolate chips

3 tablespoons butter

¼ cup heavy (whipping) cream

1½ tablespoons orange flavoring

Finely chopped pecans

Line cookie sheet with aluminum foil. Melt one cup of chocolate chips in a heavy saucepan over low heat. Stir constantly. Remove from heat and stir in two tablespoons butter. Stir in whipping cream and orange flavoring. Refrigerate twenty minutes or until thick enough to make into a ball. Drop by teaspoonfuls onto cookie sheet and shape into balls. (If it's still sticky, refrigerate until firm.) Freeze balls for thirty minutes. Heat remaining tablespoon butter and one cup chocolate chips until chocolate is melted and mixture is smooth. Remove from heat. Dip truffles one at a time into melted chocolate and return to cookie sheet. Sprinkle truffle with nuts and refrigerate until set.

"But these foils! And the beautiful boxes with Madeleine and Daughters inscribed on them . . ."

"My old boss, Trent, has connections to a chocolatier who has been working with me on this, negotiating with Trent to make our chocolates his 'signature' at the Blue Fish Grille. We'll supply Trent and see if it works out. It could be a nice little bonus for all of us."

"And you kept it a secret from us. You must have spent every minute we weren't in the house working on this."

"And loving it." Jane said. "For the first time in my life, I feel I'm beginning to understand who my mother was. She was whimsical, kind, compassionate, playful, zany, loving, loyal and a million other things. Working with that recipe book and living in this house have made her real to me, something I've longed for all my life." She picked up one of the candies. "And this is a celebration of her—and of us. How He did it, I'll never know, but God turned an ugly separation from my husband, a town in which I'd never felt at home, and a cookbook into experiences and people who've helped me to heal and get on with my life. I feel at peace with my circumstances and who I am. Do you know how wonderful a gift that is? Even my artwork is better, more creative. Amazing, isn't it?"

"All things are possible with God," Alice said. "*All* things."

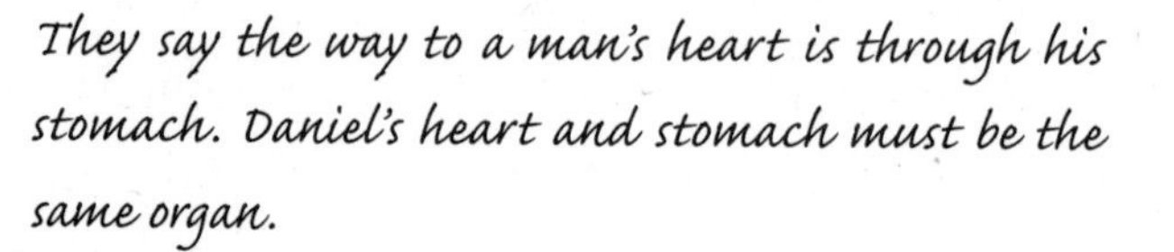

Chapter Thirteen

They say the way to a man's heart is through his stomach. Daniel's heart and stomach must be the same organ.

"What are you laughing about?" Craig Tracy asked as he arranged the vases of roses he had brought from his shop to the open-air revelry of the Potterston Art Festival.

"My mother." Jane replenished the tiered silver trays displaying her Madeleine and Daughters collection of chocolates that had been selling by the dozens. "I was thinking how clever and funny she was, the upbeat way she approached life—and how much she would have loved it here today."

"It is pretty remarkable. This was a great idea you had." Craig studied their booth—a small, roofed tent. It had been turned into a Victorian hideaway with flowers, antique furniture and murals depicting the inn's Garden Room that Jane had painted on canvas sheets that covered three sides of the booth. Craig's over-the-top floral arrangements and

Jane's clever display of jewelry and paintings had been a big hit with festival goers.

In the neighboring tent Sylvia puttered with a rack of vintage clothing. Her booth, too, was a reproduction of one of the inn's rooms. The Sunrise Room in blue, yellow and white showcased the best of Sylvia's work. Intricate quilts were spread across a makeshift bed of cardboard boxes. Clothing was artfully strewn about as if the owner of the room had just rushed out for an appointment. Sylvia wore a sleeveless plum sundress from the forties and a matching wide-brimmed portrait hat to keep the sun off her face and neck. The entire display was an explosion of color that few festival attendees had been able to resist. The two booths had enticed a steady stream of visitors.

"How's business?" Pastor Thompson paused in front of Jane, looking very much like the sightseer he was. He was holding a chocolate dipped banana on a stick and grinning like a schoolboy. "This looks fantastic."

"Business is good. Sylvia has had offers on several quilts and orders to make others. Her dresses are a big hit with young girls who think secondhand clothes are the best things ever. Craig's been handing out business cards and selling arrangements like crazy. He stayed up until three A.M. preparing his supply."

"And you?"

"Good. My jewelry and watercolors both have had a great response. Two significant collectors are planning to call me. People love our romantic theme—flowers, jewelry, chocolates and a cozy bed and breakfast. All in all, I think it has been a successful experiment."

"A 'successful experiment'? Is that it? Where's your enthusiasm? I've heard people happier over a root canal. What's going on?"

She sighed and sat down on one of the Eastlake chairs she had brought from the inn. "Aunt Ethel's been in a snit ever since I told her that we were going to be displaying here. She thinks I'm 'betraying' Lloyd and his dream for Acorn Hill."

"That can't be all. You're accustomed to Ethel's ways. Even if you were a serious threat to Acorn Hill's serenity—which you're not—it wouldn't shake you like this."

"'Water off a duck's back,' that's what my mother wrote about handling Ethel. I guess I should take her advice. Want to take a walk?" Jane stepped out of the booth and called back to Craig. "I'll be gone ten or fifteen minutes."

They fell into a comfortable pace as they meandered through the sea of pristine white tents that lined the entire Potterston Park. Beautiful Pennsylvania pottery was everywhere, as were stained-glass displays, statuary, carvings and paintings.

"Well?"

"It's ridiculous and I know better, but I've harbored a fantasy that someone would notice our tent and connect Grace Chapel Inn or Acorn Hill with my mother and father. I strike up conversations with everyone seventy and older who comes by, hoping that *someone* will recognize the name 'Grace Andresen' when I mention it. It's a faint hope, I know, but surely someone somewhere in this town has heard of my mother's friend."

"So this big effort isn't actually about the artwork? Or letting people know about the inn?"

"It is. I'd just hoped for something more."

"Maybe it's time to let it go, Jane. You've already learned a great deal about her."

"It's difficult."

"You've moved on in your life, Jane. What more do you want? Where's God in this?"

"You're right." Jane breathed a deep sigh. "Let it go. Move on." She rubbed her forehead with her hand. "You could buy me a disgustingly greasy hot dog with chili and pickles to make me feel better."

"Done. But don't blame me when you wake up tonight with indigestion."

"Hey, Ms. Howard!" Josie came skipping out of the crowd just as Jane took a huge bite of her hot dog. Her mother, Joe and Louise materialized behind her. "Mrs. Smith asked us if we'd like to come." Josie danced around Jane like a wood sprite. "And we're havin' fun."

"Hi, Jane, Pastor Thompson. I would trade my piano for some of this child's energy," Louise said, wiping her brow with her ever-present white hankie.

"Come on, Mom, let's go to the little kids' painting booth again. I want to make a picture for Ms. Howard too." Josie tugged on her mother's hand. "You come too, Joe. You can watch me paint."

Louise waved them off. "I'll meet you by the entrance in twenty minutes."

"Motherrrrr . . . come on!"

"It was awfully nice of you to bring them," Jane told her sister. Then she grinned. "But I see you have your hands full."

"Full to overflowing. But it is all worth it to see the looks on their faces." Louise mopped her brow again. "I want to stop at the booth that displays those lovely handmade clocks. I'd better hurry or Josie will have my head." Without even a backward wave, she trotted off.

"And I'd better go too. We're going to have another go at distributing the memorial monies tonight. I have to get to the church early." Pastor Thompson looked at her with gentle compassion in his eyes. "If you're meant to learn more about your mother, Jane, you will."

She nodded and waved as he walked away. When she

got back to the tent, she offered to take over so that Craig could look at some of the other tents.

He had not been gone ten minutes when Ethel arrived at the booth.

"You came despite what I said. What are you thinking, Jane? And dragging Sylvia and Craig into this too. Craig's a newcomer, of course, and may not know any better, but Sylvia." Ethel had bought Lloyd's philosophy hook, line and sinker. "Don't you have any respect for Lloyd? You know what he wants for our community, and it isn't tourists."

"This little festival isn't going to cause us to be overrun with tour buses. If we get five new guests and I sell some jewelry and chocolates, I'll consider it a success."

"What about *her*?" Ethel pointed an accusing finger at Sylvia, who had peeked around the corner of her own tent to see what was going on. "Now they'll be driving from everywhere to buy her quilts and look at those old dresses."

"I wish," Sylvia muttered and ducked her head out of sight to listen to this ridiculous conversation from a safe distance. Jane longed to do the same.

"You'll break Lloyd's heart," Ethel intoned dramatically.

"Did he tell you that?"

"Of course not, but no one knows Lloyd like I do."

"Really."

Her niece's tone of voice made Ethel turn to see what Jane was staring at.

Lloyd rambled down the walkway toward them eating a blob of cotton candy from a stick and nodding at everyone he passed. In his free hand he carried an overstuffed shopping bag of giveaways and advertisements. What appeared to be the tail of an animal protruded from the bag.

"There you are. Thought I'd never find you. Wait until you see what I bought for the top of my television—it's a ceramic squirrel. Cutest little critter you ever did see. This is quite a place. I could spend all day here—Oh, hi, Jane, Sylvia."

"Having fun?" Sylvia, who had ventured out of hiding, asked.

"More fun than a mouse in a cheese factory. Nice rig here, Jane. Got any candy giveaways?"

For the first time in ages, Ethel was mute.

"Only for you." She picked up a display plate and offered it to him.

"But, but, but . . ." Ethel spluttered like a go-cart engine. "Aren't you angry?"

"About what?" Lloyd unwrapped a chocolate and popped it into his mouth.

"These . . . traitors."

"They aren't traitors, Ethel, they're business people.

Besides, I don't think any of them will attract a shopping mall to Acorn Hill or ruin the traffic patterns. Why, I've talked to a dozen people who've said that Acorn Hill had the finest representation here." His chest expanded. "I'm mighty proud. Mighty proud."

Ethel was stunned. In fact, when Lloyd beckoned her away from Jane's booth to see if a fresh batch of spareribs at the Barbeque Shack was done yet, she hurried after him, a bewildered look still on her face.

"Who would have predicted *that*?" Sylvia blurted. "Will wonders never cease?"

"'Blessed is he who expects nothing for he shall never be disappointed,'" Jane quoted Benjamin Franklin. "That is my new motto for handling Aunt Ethel and Lloyd. I certainly wasted a lot of energy worrying about them."

"Worrying about who?" Neither Sylvia nor Jane had noticed Alice approaching the booth.

"Aunt Ethel and Lloyd. Who else?"

"They'd be a full-time hobby if you'd let them," Alice said cheerfully. "How are things going?"

"Great!" Sylvia answered. "I must have collected fifty business cards and addresses so far. Now I have to develop the brochure I promised to send out."

"Speaking of the mail . . ." Alice dug into her purse, "I left these in my car last night and forgot to give them to you." She handed Jane a letter and a brightly colored postcard. "The Fairchilds send us greetings from Hawaii. George says that when we've got the teas mastered, we should consider a luau."

"I think I'll pass on that," Jane said with a chuckle. "Digging a pit and roasting a pig in Aunt Ethel's backyard is a little over the top, even for me."

"The letter is from Naomi," Alice went on. "She's doing well, better than well, in fact. She's moved into an apartment in the same building as her sister and has found a part-time job in the local library. She says it's just enough to keep her occupied without wearing her out. Her employers have said that as she improves, she can work into a full-time job. God answers prayer."

Alice glanced at her watch. "I'd better run. We're having an ANGELs meeting tonight."

"The crowd's thinning," Sylvia observed. "I think I'll look through the names and addresses I've collected."

"May I glance through them too? Next time I'm going to do the same. Developing a mailing list is a great idea."

"Here. Take these." Sylvia thrust a stack of cards in Jane's hand. "Pick out the ones who've indicated they're interested in the clothing, will you?"

Jane mindlessly scanned each card and placed it in the appropriate pile. She was almost done when one snagged her attention.

"Betty and Jim Andresen, 13055 Carver Road, Pittsburgh, Pennsylvania . . ." Jane gasped. "Sylvia! Look at this." She thrust the card in front of her friend.

"Oh, I remember them. Nice couple. They were interested in having a quilt made for their master bedroom. In pastels, I think . . . or was it golds?"

"Look at the name!"

"Andresen. Yes. So what—Grace *Andresen*! Do you think they might be related to your mother's friend?"

Jane willed herself to stay calm. It was a long shot. There were no Andresens listed in the Potterston phone books, but . . .

"Oh my . . . they're leaving on vacation this week," Sylvia added. "I remember now. They were taking a 'road trip' to visit their children."

"They're already gone?"

"Yes. Potterston's festival was their first stop."

So close and yet so far.

But, to her surprise, Jane felt no disappointment. It did not matter, not really, not anymore. Pastor Thompson was right. She had already found more than she had been seeking. Madeleine's recipe book had seen to that. Her mother was real to her now. And her relationship with her sisters continued to develop in positive ways. The inn had provided common ground, and they were learning to know each other again. Life in Acorn Hill was filled with friends like Sylvia and Pastor Thompson, Craig and Joe, Fred and Vera, Josie and her mother.

It was time to "Let go and let God." A cliché? Not for her, not now. He had brought her back to the place that she had never wanted to revisit and gifted her with all that she had desired. God had provided for, healed and blessed her here.

Jane leaned back in the little Eastlake chair and grinned. Anything more right now would be gravy, frosting on the cake, the cherry on the sundae, and—as usual for her—food metaphors said it all.

Tales from Grace Chapel Inn®

Back Home Again
by Melody Carlson

Recipes & Wooden Spoons
by Judy Baer

Once you visit the charming village of Acorn Hill, you'll never want to leave. Here, the three Howard sisters reunite after their father's death and turn the family home into a bed and breakfast. They rekindle old memories, rediscover the bonds of sisterhood, revel in the blessings of friendship, and meet many fascinating guests along the way.

The author of over sixty-five books, Judy Baer has won numerous awards for her writing. She lives near Minneapolis, Minnesota, and feels especially blessed by her wonderful children and a patient husband.